SMITH

A Sylvan Interlude

SMITH

A Sylvan Interlude

BY BRANCH CABELL

*"To look at the man is but to court deception
. . . for no man lives in the external truth,
among salts and acids, but in the warm, phan-
tasmagoric chamber of his brain, with the
painted windows and the storied walls."*

WILDSIDE PRESS: MMIII

Published by
Wildside Press
P.O. Box 301
Holicong, PA 18928-0301 U.S.A.
www.wildsidepress.com

For

JOHN LOTTIER CABELL

Jauntily as Mr. Smith
Ordains that Branlon be a jumble,
Heaven makes each man a myth—
Narrow-minded, ardent, humble,
Loosely-living, love-led, mean,
Opinionated, greedy, grieving,
Timid, noble, gay, obscene,
Trustless; and in self-deceiving
Illimitably past believing.

Equably as Mr. Smith
Regards his children's odd appearance,
Canny persons traffic with
All their kindred's incoherence.

Brethren need not criticize
Each the other's variant metal
Loudly—nor in any wise
Let *x* the pot flout *y* the kettle.

CONTENTS

*   *

*

PART ONE: THE BOOK OF BRANLON

    I. How Charlemagne Came, 3
   II. Thus Roland Reported, 9
  III. The Tale of Turpin, 17
  IV. Eyes of a God, 23
   V. A Pedlar Reflects, 27
  VI. What Urc Tabaron Thought, 31
 VII. Mr. Smith Upon Fatherhood, 41

PART TWO: THE BOOK OF VOLMAR

  VIII. How They Bragged, 49
    IX. Doom of a Liar, 54
     X. The Brown Priest, 62
   XI. Grief of the South Wind, 70
  XII. Mr. Smith As to Keys, 78
 XIII. The King Without Stain, 83
 XIV. Observations in Osnia, 89
  XV. Remarks on the Frontier, 94
 XVI. The Queen's Progress, 99
XVII. Parting in Anger, 105
XVIII. The Truth of It, 109

CONTENTS

PART THREE: THE BOOK OF ELAIR

    XIX. How They Quested, 117

    XX. Lands Beyond Common-Sense, 120

    XXI. Women by the Way, 126

    XXII. Talk with a Tippler, 136

    XXIII. The Gray House, 142

    XXIV. In Regard to Oina, 147

    XXV. Mr. Smith Upon Modesty, 150

    XXVI. The Water of Airdra, 157

    XXVII. A Wizard's One Oversight, 161

    XXVIII. The Great Burning, 169

    XXIX. How a While Passed, 177

    XXX. Trouble at Supper Time, 181

    XXXI. The Eternal Husband, 190

PART FOUR: THE BOOK OF CLITANDRE

    XXXII. Highway Robbery, 195

    XXXIII. Mr. Smith Plays Chess, 207

    XXXIV. In Nicole's Room, 214

    XXXV. Maids of Honor, 220

    XXXVI. Regarding a Window, 225

    XXXVII. The Compassion of Women, 236

PART FIVE: THE BOOK OF LITTLE SMIRT

    XXXVIII. Marriage of Bel-Imperia, 243

CONTENTS

XXXIX. Conclusions of Madam Tana, 249

XL. The Dead Hand, 253

XLI. Chastity of a Scholar, 257

XLII. The Inglorious Journey, 266

XLIII. On a Lost Garment, 271

XLIV. Prosperity of a Fraud, 276

XLV. The Frog That Talked, 280

XLVI. Relative to Two Women; 286

XLVII. The Judgment of Mr. Smith, 291

XLVIII. In Black and Silver, 295

PART SIX: THE BOOK OF TANA

XLIX. Deals with Contentment—, 301

L. —Which a Clock Qualifies, 307

PART ONE

THE BOOK OF BRANLON

*   *

*

"*The present value of standing timber in the forest of Branlon is estimated at $480,000,000. Of the forest lands some 65% are owned by professional wizards and companies having saw mills, pulp mills, paper mills, etc. About 90% of the sawn and planed wood is exported, 70% of the wood pulp, and 60% of the paper as it is specially prepared for romance writing. Pine, ebony, fir, redwood, maple, mahogany and other valuable cabinet woods are produced here, in addition to magic and much cedar for the manufacture of cigar boxes.*"

*   *

ONE

HOW CHARLEMAGNE CAME

*

They recount how Charlemagne, the Franks' Emperor, combined religion with his family squabbles by setting forth to relieve the Pope at Rome. That holy city was then being besieged by the Emperor's father-in-law, Desiderius, King of the Lombards, whom Charlemagne proposed to destroy piously. They relate how, upon the primitive road between the kingdoms of Rorn and Ecben, the great army of Charlemagne came to the forest of Branlon. And they tell how a pedlar (who had just put aside a cigarette) stood in the Emperor's way, barring the all-conqueror's armed advance with a wooden staff, and crying out that upon this forest had been laid an enchantment.

"Expound," said the Emperor.

"Highness," replied the pedlar, "the nature of this magic is not comprehended any longer. But in the old time, and in the days which have gone out of man's memory, Mr. Smith was Lord of this forest."

"Now, of Mr. Smith," the Emperor declared, with

3

his hands and his voice, all three, uplifted by his deep
wonder, "I have never heard in any myth or legend.
Yet Mr. Smith is a most marvelous divine name. It
is strange and terrible. It appals. It is ruthless. It is
a name which in every respect befits a divine being."

"Well," the pedlar explained, "and hereabouts a
not very important sort of divine being did wear
this name—but not ruthlessly—a long while before
any Pharaoh had reigned or bright Babylon became
mighty. Wolves hunted where your fine city of
Aachen now stands, highness; seven fishermen held
Tyre; nor had Troy arisen in that quiet day when
Mr. Smith was a little god ruling over this forest, a
god friendly to all mankind, and to the light-haired
daughters of mankind in particular."

"It is known," said the Emperor, with that harsh
curtness which befitted a good Christian, "that the
lewd gods of the heathen are to-day changed into
demons."

"That is known everywhere, highness. But Mr.
Smith was not any longer a god when the Crucifixion
was accomplished, for the eternal redemption of
mankind, and was properly entered in the police
records of Judea. It was then a great while since Mr.
Smith had been famous in all prayer-books as a
divine being and as the leader of the Seven Stewards
of Heaven, ruling over them in his own paradise,
in high Åmit, under another name than the name of
Smith."

4

"But what was that name?"

The pedlar replied, reverently, "He was then called SMIRT."

"And that superb monosyllable," declared Charlemagne, "is a large miracle which I have encountered before to-day, although I do not recollect in what place it was."

"That is likely, highness: for sublime SMIRT was once known in every place. But he relinquished heaven, on account of a woman. He descended into the estate of a local deity; and his epithet became Smith, a name so narrowly famous that not even the most learned Romans in the days of Augustus have dared hazard a conjecture as to the nature of his cult."

"Yes, yes!" said the Emperor.

"For I, highness, I do not agree with Herbastein, that Varro cites an inscription in which Smith is joined with Pomona."

"Spare me," the Emperor commanded, "all this misplaced erudition."

"I obey, highness, remarking only that the passage occurs nowhere in the treatise called *De lingua Latina*. So Mr. Smith became less known, and even yet less widely known, as the loud centuries marched by, without any deliberation of Mr. Smith; and one after another, a host of spruce parvenu gods ruled over the planet which All-Highest & Company had first given to sublime SMIRT."

5

"In this world," the Emperor philosophized, "all greatness must have its tumble."

"Yet the truly great," said the pedlar, "will tumble gracefully. They remain always urbane. At all events, Mr. Smith had kept only this forest when the Olympians flourished. He was not known in any heaven; he was honored at utmost, here and there, by peasants and by pessimists and by poets. Strong Jahveh, when he smote down the Olympians, had not any cause to distrust Mr. Smith, the local deity of Branlon, or to covet his lean sacrifices of salt and of fruit, of hexameters and of slim maidens with pale-colored hair. For this reason, Mr. Smith was not changed, nor was his domain altered. He still kept that very little kingdom which he had chosen here in this forest after Arachne betrayed him—in his own shop, highness,—and after the shock of her blood-thirst had awakened him from his long dream of being SMIRT."

"I have it now!" said the Emperor. "I remember that superb and quite indescribable being, because" —here Charlemagne inclined his head reverently— "because SMIRT once came to my court, in a jiffy. His wit, his fancy, and the vast stores of his erudition, were limitless. Indeed, he himself told me so. And he was then looking, I can recall, for a girl named Arachne."

"That is probable, highness. They record that, in his long dream about his own omnipotence, SMIRT was much pestered by women. And upon four of

6

them he begot children, who were born of a dreaming god and of a woman who existed, it may be, only in the dreams of that god."

Charlemagne said, pondering, "But all this appears to me to be nonsense."

"It is quite plainly nonsense," agreed the pedlar. "Nevertheless, it was a fact; and all facts are of considerable interest to a sound logician. So this fact forever afterward troubled Mr. Smith. It troubled him because, to a sound logician, the deduction was far too obvious, that for children, and quadruply for four children, born of such most irregular parentage, there could be no place in any world known to us."

"Still—" said the Emperor.

"No, highness, but I can assure you that inference was a mere matter of logic. Not even Aristotle, in his *Constitution of Athens* and his *History of Animals*, has disputed this point."

"Pedlar, I would not question the correctness of Aristotle's remarks in his *Constitution of Athens*, or in his *History of Animals*, either. Yet does Aristotle really matter at this special moment?" asked Charlemagne.

"He does not matter in the least, highness. What truly matters is that this discrepancy very often troubled Mr. Smith, long after he had awakened from this superb dream of being SMIRT, and of being made unconquerable by the keen wit and the sparkling fancy and the unlimited erudition of SMIRT—to which you but now referred, highness, as having impressed you so favorably,—and had found that SMIRT was but a misreading of Smith, a mere local deity."

"You appear to be somewhat over-deep in the confidence of Mr. Smith," observed Charlemagne, drily. "Were his eyes changed, do you think?"

To this, the pedlar replied, smilingly, "My eyes have not ever rested upon the eyes of Mr. Smith."

"That," said Charlemagne, "I concede to be likely. At all events, it is none of my concern."

Then the Emperor meditated; and, with that tinge of self-centeredness which is sometimes encountered in business-like persons, the imperial thoughts appeared to stray back toward Charlemagne's own affairs. To march forward through this forest, without any delay perilous to all Christendom, was the counsel both of religion and of common-sense, because a devout son of the Church upon his way to defend the head of the Church must necessarily be defended by Heaven against any possible assaults of magic, over and above the fact that Charlemagne had always felt wholly capable of defending himself.

Nevertheless, he looked yet again at the eyes of this pedlar. After that, Charlemagne gave orders.

*   *

TWO

THUS ROLAND REPORTED

*

Duke Roland, that flaxen-haired fine fighting-man, returned to Charlemagne the great Emperor. The young eyes of Roland were blue and shining like the flame of a candle; and bright armor was upon him. This Roland said:

In the forest of Branlon I rode but a short way. I rode among oak-trees and ash-trees and thorn-trees. I came to a lordly house builded of copper. The draw-bridge was down. The figured copper gate stood open.

I entered the courtyard very warily. I found there no living creature. The stables were empty of grooms. The stables were full of echoes. The name of each horse was painted above its stall, in a blue lettering. The stalls were empty.

Yet in the stables I perceived corn and hay. With this I fed my own horse. I tethered him, in the court-yard, with a copper chain. It was fastened to a pillar of copper.

In the main hall of the house a fire burned cheerily. This hall was hung with bright-colored tapestries.

They depicted the intimacy of Dame Venus with the Chevalier Adonis. I ascended the daïs. It was covered with a blue cloth. I sat in a tall chair of estate. There were two such chairs. They were placed side by side. The arms of these chairs each ended with the head of a lion very handsomely carved.

I waited.

A dwarf came. His face was white as marble. He had copper-colored hair. All his clothing was of a blue color. His clothing was trimmed with white fur. The toes of his shoes curved upward. They were fastened about his ankles with a thin chain of copper. I observed him with an uneasy attentiveness.

Me this dwarf did not heed. Silently he spread the long table before me with a white cloth. He brought loaves of white bread, sprinkled with caraway seeds. He set forth crystal flagons containing white wine. He lighted torches. He disposed them about the walls of the place, in brackets of copper. He made all things ready for supper.

And I waited. I did not move at all.

Now into the bright hall came noiselessly a young girl. She was attended by twelve serving women. These women were dressed alike, in white and in blue. Between the breasts of each woman hung a disk of engraved copper. I did not look very closely at these women. The young girl whom they attended was well known to me. So likewise was the fact known that she had been dead for a long while.

Roland, the brave warrior, was silent. He made a little swallowing motion, saying:

"I have striven to forget that dark quiet girl in many bedchambers, and to shut out the sound of her voice with much laughter. I have not succeeded."

Charlemagne nodded. He said:

"That girl is known to each one of us, Roland of my heart. The grave hides her body; the rose-colored flesh which delighted us now delights gray worms: or it may be that some ageing and tousled-haired woman yet waddles about earth bearing the name of that all-wonderful girl libelously. In either case, we strive to forget. In either case, we do not forget. Proceed, Roland my son."

No one of these women looked at me (Roland continued). I did not move. They washed their hands, with old formal gestures. I could not understand these gestures. So did each one of them wash her hands, in a large embossed bowl of copper.

Then they approached the table. Gerda sat down in the empty chair of estate. Six waiting maids sat to the right of her. Six sat to the left. At her side was the other tall chair carved with lions' heads. In this chair I remained motionless.

So did I sup with my betrayed dead love. The dwarf served to us white bread and white wine. We partook of both reverently. There was no sound anywhere.

Nobody regarded me save only Dame Venus and the slim Assyrian knight Adonis.

The dwarf brought toward us a harp. Then Gerda arose. She looked down at me. She smiled, with that divine mingling of tenderness and of comprehension which Gerda, which Gerda alone has revealed, oh, Gerda alone, in all my lifetime. She did not again look toward me after that one brief glancing. Instead, she made on her harp a music. This music was dim and perplexed. This music was exceedingly proud. This music spoke of much sorrow. Yet this music remained proud. So was it that I heard, as I now think, the dirge of my youth and of all that world which youth contrives out of youth's ignorance, and makes lovely with callow fancies, and colors everywhere with the impossibly fine notions of youth.

I would not dispraise our human life here nor the brave earth which is its theatre. I have found life very good. I praise life. It is only that a boy creates in his day-dreams a life which is better. Yes, for young people build up more aspiringly, in their valiant and absurd day-dreams, than the Eternal Father, through His wisdom, has seen fit to build anywhere in reality. A boy's fancy creates more nobly than God creates. That is all. We foreplan in our youth a life which we do not live in our maturity, if only because every young person must design, with a high heart, the impossible.

That, I repeat, is all. That is a truism. Ah, but that

is likewise a tragedy, as we come by-and-by to acknowledge, in a strange and perturbed loneliness, when we
lie awake at night, and when the slow moments of
night pass by, very heavily, like dark mourners who
commemorate the burial of those dead, and foolish,
and frail, and most lovely notions of our youth—and
yet, too, the moments pass then like dark weary-
hearted fiends who are jeering at these notions.

Now Gerda sounded the proud dirge of these same
notions, so I believe; and her music troubled me. I
had got much of life. It seemed not rational to lament
that I had never got of life a splendor to which no
man anywhere attains, except only in the day-dreams
of his youthfulness. I, at least, I disliked and I loved
this music which troubled me beyond reason, oh, very
far beyond reason.

I thought about my wealth. I thought about my
famousness. I had served the great Emperor Charlemagne not unworthily. Some glory was behind me.
Yes, and new times which had not yet come would
remember to applaud Roland, telling how he did not
go into battle without fetching a victory out of it;
and how he never took his leisure in any king's house
but some woman of beauty, and it might be the king's
daughter or the queen's self, fixed her love on Duke
Roland.

These things were true. These things did not satisfy
me. For beside me stood Gerda. In my first youth, in
my boyhood, I had loved Gerda as I have loved no

other human being. And with Gerda I had broken faith. I saw the fine curve of her throat. I had forgotten how lovely was the white throat of Gerda.

I knew that this girl was dead. She was lost to me. I had only much wealth and honor and my famousness. I had only a great name which would be applauded after I was past hearing what men said about it. A skull has no ears. Yes, I had bargained with my one life upon earth unthriftily. I saw now how very poorly I had bargained, and a large weariness possessed me. I slept, because a dim and proud music lulled me. I slept, because nothing mattered any more.

When I awoke, it was morning. I lay among dead leaves, under a thorn-tree. Beside me stood my bay horse. It was tethered to an ash-tree. There was no copper house anywhere. I had but dreamed about much unhappy and faded and quite inconclusive nonsense, I reflected.

Charlemagne said: "These dreams about dead women have no profit in them. They trouble contentment. Such dreams are known to me. Such dreams make only a wasting, yes, and they make an unhappiness also, in the life of their dreamer."

"Not so, my uncle," replied Roland the fine fighting-man: "inasmuch as my horse was tethered to the ash-tree with this same chain of copper which you behold now about my neck. My dream does not any longer make an unhappiness now that it has made also a chain of copper, a chain of Dame Venus' true metal, to be a bright and assured token that Gerda has forgiven my unfaith. She awaits my return, in high paradise, I deduce from this chain of copper; and so, by this chain of copper, am I led to believe that the magic of Branlon is kindly."

Then said the pedlar: "Let the young poets come to Branlon. Let the gray poets whose hearts yet keep their youth seek Branlon for their hearts' comfort. So will Branlon delude all these into such contentment as now has helped Duke Roland, for the magic of Branlon is compassionate and above reason. For absurd loyalties this forest has made a haven; this forest feeds magnanimity; this forest revives the hurt daydreams of youth. Let all the young in heart repair to the country home of Mr. Smith, the retired poet, because in this way, for so long a while as the slender, blended, tender magic of Branlon endures, may they believe that all life may be made noble and highhearted."

The Emperor cleared his throat, in a thoroughgoing fashion which shook his white beard.

"Your remarks," observed Charlemagne— "coming, as they do, in the form of an addition to my dear nephew's moonstruck story—have set me to thinking about more women than I need name. Hah, and by Holy Magdalene! I cannot see that their forgiveness of our shared doings is called for. I cannot see that such

15

forgiveness is either an assured or a very important matter. These poets! I reflect: and my opinion of most verse-makers takes form as a shrug. Moreover, I do not think that a copper chain, howsoever unaccountably acquired, and no matter how shiny, establishes beyond moral doubt a fixed assignation in paradise, or anywhere else."

Afterward he dismissed Roland indulgently, because the Emperor loved this young man as dearly as if the flaxen-haired champion were his own son. And indeed it was generally whispered, among his detractors, that he had reason to love Roland in this way.

"Now then," said Charlemagne, "now that the most brave has spoken, let the most shrewd continue. Let us hear what Archbishop Turpin reports."

*　　*

THREE

THE TALE OF TURPIN

*

Turpin, the bland Archbishop, ruling over Rheims, was a quiet-spoken clergyman, with a serene, thin and very noble face, having gray hair. On his steel helmet was the head of a cherub moulded in silver; and his close-fitting shirt of mail was of pale gold woven out of little chains as pliant as silk. This Turpin said:

I rode into the forest of Branlon but a short way before I came to a house builded of silver. In the courtyard I found a woman whose face was not strange to me. There is no living woman more beautiful, nor more prodigally tricked out with those demure, those soft, those glowing, and those most damnable snares such as betray men's flesh, than this girl whom I had known in my ruinous youth. It was troubling to reflect that she had died a great while ago, for this woman was no phantom. The hand which I kissed— with that civility which befits a prince of the Church in dealing with all living creatures—was so warm and tender that in touching it my own hand trembled.

Her robe might have been a cloud, so soft and

white it was. About her wrists were broad bands of silver. At her girdle hung a net very finely woven of silver threads. In her face stayed that tenderness which I had not merited, so the obtuse said, when my better nature and all the orderings of common-sense led me to abandon a woman so godless that but a little while afterward she committed the dreadful crime of *felo-de-se* . . . I wept for her misdemeanor, I remember. I was very young then . . . Well, and now the appearance of this same woman stood beside a bright shallow pool in which were swimming small fish of twelve colors.

"My dearest," she said, "the gray years of our separation have been long, but they have gone by now, as a smoke vanishes; and only the love which was once between us endures."

"It endures," I replied, "variously. Love departs from us forever. Only the ghost of love may return, oh, even from out of the deep grave may that bright and bitter ghost return, bringing strange and terrible gifts and unfed desires."

She said, "You speak of gifts."

"In addressing gentlewomen, Mathilde, I have found that to be the opening most generally looked for in a prince of the Church, who cannot well speak of marriage."

"It is a long journey, Turpin, from the grave to the arms of my lover. Because of that journey I must have my bride-gift."

My voice answered, hollowly: "A gift for a gift, Mathilde; for I likewise have fared a long way, even from out of our shared iniquity to the dear portals of heaven; and you bid me retrace that journeying."

She smiled; and in heaven, as I well knew, there could not be anything more dangerous, or more beautiful, than Mathilde.

"Give me," she said, "the archbishop's ring from that hand which has so often caressed me amorously."

"Give me," I replied, "the net from your girdle which I have so very often unloosed before to-day."

So did we exchange gifts, rejecting alike the service of good and of evil because of that love which endured between a great prince of Holy Church and a dead harlot. Mathilde smiled up at me happily. She was frightened, I thought, now that I held the silver net; and yet she was proud of my shrewdness also. I had half forgotten how lovely she was, how brave where I was not over-brave. I looked at her for a while, so that I might remember always how dear to me was the lewdness and the folly of my youth.

Let none misunderstand me. I believe that for the lewdness and the folly of his youth a good Christian ought to repent with his entire heart. Yes, and he ought to repent not over-belatedly, but at the very first moment that age has made of such carnal matters a temptation feeble enough to be resisted with convenience. There is much comfort in repentance, a virtue which in many cases leads directly to the endowment of cathedrals and convents and to other pious offerings. Yet is charity also a virtue, that all-embracing charity which applies to all persons, including oneself.

As a prince of the Church, I know that every man is bidden to forgive in his neighbor—according to the mathematics of the most holy Matthew—seventy times seven sins. Likewise, upon the authority of the same Apostle, and of two other Apostles, is every person commanded to love his neighbor and himself equally, without any least difference. Logic infers, I submit, that on account of this equal affection a good Christian must necessarily overlook his own errancy into an equal number of criminal offences.

Yes, such is every man's divinely allotted allowance of misdemeanors, even unto seventy times seven. It is an affair in which I would counsel no excess. I say only that not prior to the commission of some four hundred and ninety-first crime may the remorse of a good Christian awaken, or any reprobation of his own conduct be justified, if he has considered our sacred Scriptures with the carefulness proper to a prince of the Church.

Secured by this course of reasoning, and by my tight hold on the silver net, I made bold, in the time that I looked fondly upon the eternally damned, the very lovely, and the most dear love of my youth, to recall with indulgence the more intimate frolics of our carnal offences. I forgave, with a clear conscience,

my part in all these enormities, which by my arithmetic
could not well have exceeded four hundred at utmost.
Perhaps I ought to explain that necessarily, after this
long lapse of time, I figured the sins of each separate
evening as a single unit.

I groaned then. I cast the net so that it fell about
her golden fair head; and so, for one heart-beat, she
yet smiled at me through the silver meshes.

What happened after that was dreadful, for the
flesh of Mathilde blackened, then it became gray, and
it crumbled into foul dust. I stooped, weeping; and
from among these ashes I took up again the ring which
declared me the faithful servant of all-seeing Heaven.
My hands were damp with sweat, so that a gray pow-
dering of these ashes clung to my finger-tips. And for
another odd thing, I noted that the fish of twelve
colors had become little creatures having the shape
of small frightened men, differently dressed. They
were climbing out of the shallow pool, running away
in all directions. I was left alone in the forest.

Then Archbishop Turpin sighed. He spread out his
plump, well-shaped and very carefully washed hands,
so that his happily preserved episcopal ring gleamed
handsomely, in the while the Archbishop was saying:

"That is all, highness. I returned unmolested. There
is in this forest a disrespectfulness, which does not
honor the dignity of a prince of the Church."

Now said the pedlar: "Let the kings and the high priests and the judges of this earth, and let all other persons that have overwisely compounded with prudence, avoid the home of a god who fell very long ago from his godhead. For these also are fallen gods who have lost the divine unreason of youth. And in quiet Branlon they perceive this, with sullen and hungry eyes."

FOUR

*   *

EYES OF A GOD

*

So," said the Emperor, "so—since we speak of kings —it appears that this forest, with its house builded of silver and its house builded of copper, is subject to the old laws of faëry. Now, by these known laws, any third adventurer, even though he be a king, must come, of necessity, to a house of gold."

"That is known everywhere, highness," the pedlar returned.

"And in this house," Charlemagne went on, "he likewise would encounter a woman. Yes; for the legislators of faëry, and of its many provinces, abhor novelty. They are a most conservative people."

With that, the Emperor became silent; and the pedlar regarded him silently.

Charlemagne to-day wore his accustomed simple dress. A long blue cloak hung over his shoulders, closed as far as the loins, where this cloak divided into two parts, of which the shorter part fell before him to his knees, and the longer part hung down behind him to his ankles. His legs were clothed in rather short blue trousers, laced at the outer sides with a silver cord, and he likewise wore blue silk stockings. His legs were regrettably skinny. He wore beneath his cloak a white tunic; and a belt of silver encircled his waist, from which hung, in an ornamented sheath of blue leather, the world-famous sword Flamberge.

But in his wise, wrinkled, white-bearded face great Charlemagne wore only an air of serene meditation. He said now,—

"Well, and what long-lost paramour would I, who am a king, tall pedlar, be finding in that same house of gold?"

The pedlar replied: "No one of your four wives, highness, nor yet any one of those five acknowledged mistresses who have borne your acknowledged children. You would find instead, in that golden house, the appearance of Madame Gilles."

"Hah!" said Charlemagne.

"I mean, highness, your dead sister, the Lord Roland's mother."

Now Charlemagne sat absolutely still, seeming for that instant, inside his somehow collapsed blue mantle, a gray and stricken old dotard. He laughed then. He said, with unshaken lordliness:

"My Roland was born, even as you tell me the four children of sublime SMIRT were born, of a dream which has forsaken its dreamer, long and very long ago. Dreams are not durable, not steadfast . . . Yet the eyes of a god remain always steadfast. They are

24

like the eyes of a serpent. The eyes of a god do not twitch or blink or shift restlessly, as do the eyes of mankind. So may one recognize a god, tall pedlar, whatsoever be his disguise."

Then the pedlar answered, yet again, with not-ever-failing urbanity,—

"That is known, highness."

"Now the eyes of a god," said Charlemagne, "see clearly. It is permitted them to perceive far-off matters from which my own eyes turn away resolutely. I have sinned against nature, and beyond pardon, it may be. At all events, I am no poet to rhapsodize in picked words, no priest to repent smugly, over the doings of my boyhood. Instead, I must be about my kingly work in this world, laboring to let my good deeds outbalance my ill deeds, in the while that I rule over my people as best I may, without sparing time to consider that which is by-gone and disastrous and dead."

His wrinkled, brown-blotched old hands gripped each other, in a sudden wild gesture.

"Oh, and more dear to me than is my wide kingdom," he said, "even now! There was love. There was death. To-day there is only much power. And it does not matter. The great power of Charlemagne and all the world-famous doings of Charlemagne are derided by those two commonplaces which we call love and death!"

"Nevertheless, highness," said the pedlar, slowly, "that power remains supreme in all earthly matters.

So does it not follow that you should invade Branlon without any superstitious backwardness?"

"To the contrary," replied Charlemagne, smiling rather sadly, "I was about to say that for the sake of my supreme power, and for my sanity's sake likewise, I, who have conquered all the world, do not dare enter this forest. For in Branlon it is just possible, one may come to consider gravely—as my Roland has done, and as shrewd Turpin has not done—the two supreme commonplaces which we term love and death."

He gave orders. Then the great army turned northward, skirting the forest of Branlon, as they went out of Rorn into Ecben, all marching with their backs turned toward Rome. By hundreds and by scores of hundreds they went northward, leaving the Holy Father as yet entrapped by Desiderius, that Lombard infidel, toward whom Charlemagne entertained all the dislike suitable to a relative-in-law, and leaving likewise a planet's doom undecided, rather than that Charlemagne the all-conqueror should again face the woman whom alone he had loved with his whole heart.

*   *

FIVE

A PEDLAR REFLECTS

*

That crowned tired man has wisdom," declared the pedlar. "Yes, as kings go, he has done well enough in capping an infamy with a cowardice. For they who have mastered this daylit world through their common-sense, and who fare unperturbed about its high places, may find in Branlon no comfort. But to the conquered and outworn this forest ministers with fair dreams; to the young it brings a surety of all conquests. And I whom the Olympians conquered, I have outlived all the Olympians nowadays, and as yet I remain young."

Thereafter the Lord of the Forest laughed, and his appearance became a bright shining. Very white birds wheeled circle-wise about the dark ringlets of his divine head, and then flew away in every direction, singing with light sweet voices. His staff gleamed like bright silver; at the top of it showed a blazing fir-cone.

So was it that Mr. Smith strode back into the unviolated woods which were his home.

And yet, as he now reflected, it sometimes appeared to Mr. Smith that this Branlon was only his temporary home, a mere resting place upon that not ever ending journey which Mr. Smith had begun—so it seemed to him—in his fine dream about being a master of all gods.

Ah, but then (replied reason) there had been that yet earlier dream, about your being a gifted literary genius, in an era so remote from the present as the twentieth century, pursued everywhither by the public at large. It is not possible that your past life should have been spent thus gloriously so far in the future.

"I admit that," said Mr. Smith, "as a sound logician. Yet it was a fine dream while it lasted."

Moreover (reason continued) there was that dream about your being a blue-bottle fly which was dreaming itself to be a man of letters who was dreaming that he was a master of gods ruling over a planet presented by the All-Highest—

"And that too," Mr. Smith interrupted the promptings of reason, "was a fine dream, even though it may have been a bit too subtle for all persons quite to understand it."

Well, then (reason summed up), from each one of these dreams, and from a great many other dreams, in turn, Mr. Smith had awakened, quietly and naturally. Mr. Smith knew now that Mr. Smith was no one of these things—not an all-powerful god, nor a writer who would not be born for ever so many centuries, nor a rather large blue-bottle fly descended from the great race of Diptera—but a mere local deity, the bucolic Lord of the Forest of Branlon. Mr. Smith thus remained neither more nor less than the sole survivor anywhere of an immemorial mythology so very ancient that it had nowadays been forgotten by everybody, including himself.

"Yes, that is logic," Mr. Smith assented.

And in a way, as you got on in life (his thinking continued), it was an actual relief to have done with all such magnificent fancies. You regarded them, however, with a bias of indulgence. You even admired them, a bit wistfully. You now and then missed their high-pitched irrationality. Yes, that was true; and, as he lighted one of those Virginian cigarettes with which a charmed pocket piece continued to supply him, this truth wrung from the Lord of the Forest a resigned sigh.

None the less was there a sober consolation to be got out of the knowledge that, at a last howsoever long, you were facing the plain facts about yourself. These facts were not veiled nowadays by the perhaps too complex fantasies of your imagination. You had awakened from all such unprofitable dreaming. You now— at length wide awake, and with the fond nonsense of your dreamland forever put by—you perceived that in point of fact you were no more than a majestic mythical figure living in a charmed forest between two semi-fabulous kingdoms; and to know this beyond any doubt—to have touched actuality at last—was a sound comfort, Mr. Smith reflected, with yet another profound sigh. He sighed because, as a poet, he could not but deplore, in defiance of all logic, his lost faculty for dreaming about the improbable.

*　　*

SIX

WHAT URC TABARON THOUGHT

*

Now by the wayside sat Urc Tabaron, who was the most famous of wizards in those parts, and, as some said, the greatest of all living wizards in the lands beyond common-sense. He offered to Mr. Smith a gray bowl, crying,—

"Hail, Lord of the Forest!"

Mr. Smith saw then that this bowl contained mangled flesh and blood. And so Mr. Smith at once waved aside the abhorrent tribute, saying,—

"This is not my required offering in Branlon."

"Nevertheless," said Urc Tabaron, "it is your need, if only you knew what is good for you."

"To the contrary," Mr. Smith replied, "this mixture is my special abhorrence. For not long ago—oh, but only in a dream, a mere nightmare—I once visited a country in which the inhabitants were made of this dreadful stuff. And my traffic with these luckless persons was unhappy. They lent to my dream a sorrow. It seemed to me that I lived imprisoned, in a horrible and a very noisy place, among a perplexed and frightened little people who knew not what next to do, and whose fears begot frenzies."

"Great virtues have worn flesh and blood, O too hasty Lord of the Forest. Great thoughts have quickened in it. Yes, and the great faith of flesh and blood has builded fine great mansions beyond the tomb."

"I admit that flesh and blood has its merits in the way of imaginings and of aspirations and of all anodynes which help flesh and blood to forget the true nature of flesh and blood. The sad part of it is that in practical fields the achievements of flesh and blood should be second rate. Though why, indeed, do I say second rate?"

"Why you say anything," Urc Tabaron returned, "remains always to me a mystery, because there is not ever much sense in it."

"The prosperity of a sublime saying, my dear fellow, depends upon the agility of its hearer's wit. I say, then, that this is the true tragedy of flesh and blood, that its best products are perceived to be tenth rate the very instant that one has compared them with the best products of the lands beyond commonsense. For I have but now returned from a brief interview with Charlemagne: and I shall remark only concerning this superb overlord of mankind that very especially he did not remind me of any known President of the United States. Then yet again, last week I was visited by Achilles, who of course brought with him his two wives, Medea and

Helen, and his exceedingly pretty minion Patroclus, all three of whom he maintains in Leukê."

"Well, and what of it, Lord of the Forest? and why do you always pick out these lecherous items to dwell upon?"

"But I do not do anything of the sort. I observe merely that this is a ménage which, in itself, would disqualify Achilles from holding any military command in a God-fearing democracy; yet did I find swift-footed Achilles, with his lax lovely entourage, to be rather more splendid than is the average brigadier general, with his liver complaint. Yes, and in the same way, Urc Tabaron, have I compared your fellow wizard Merlin, who continues to advise King Arthur in Avalon, with the financial wizards who advise the White House. I have compared Icarus with the best advertised aviators, and Simple Simon with pre-eminent statesmen. I have compared the Supreme Court with Minos, Æacus and Rhadamanthus. I have compared the Senate with the Seven Sleepers of Ephesus, and Congress with the charmed lovers of Circe, those passionate full-voiced pigs at their feeding-trough. Well, and in every case was my verdict the same: I have cried out, 'Alas for flesh and blood!'"

"You would," said Urc Tabaron, darkly.

"In brief," Mr. Smith continued, "the country of flesh and blood is, relatively speaking, a land of drab pygmies. There have been many great persons in flesh-and-blood countries. But no one of them would have risen beyond the lower reaches of mediocrity in a more exigent realm such as any poet can create out-of-hand."

Urc Tabaron replied, "Bah!"

"Yet I speak from experience," Mr. Smith reminded him, "because I, who am a demi-god, once dreamed I was flesh and blood. I do not know why. I can imagine no crime, nor any excessive supper, which deserved to be requited with any such nightmare. The cheapness, the dishonesty, the hypocrisy, and the staid feeble-mindedness which need blending in order to produce a well-thought-of flesh-and-blood leader in any practical field are beyond a mere demi-god's belief. And for another matter, the quite sincere reverence which, in that nightmare country, is accorded to a neat union of these vices establishes beyond any doubt the future of flesh and blood. No, no, Urc Tabaron: a race which accepts such befogged charlatans as statesmen and patriots, as rulers and lawmakers and executives, or even as dependable dog-catchers, is irretrievably damned, because that race is not any longer able to distinguish between the fine and the abominable."

"Pah!" said Urc Tabaron.

"In brief," Mr. Smith summed up, "it is the misfortune of flesh and blood that in all practical fields it admires the tenth rate sincerely. Yet I do not say this in blame. I commend, rather, the fact that, in these not unimportant fields, flesh and blood should admire, for its own comfort's sake, the best which it has produced. Yes, for all facts are of considerable interest to a sound logician. In short, a logician considers facts; he does not lament them. So in plain logic I may not now lament that, by the standards of our more favored lands beyond common-sense, the best products of flesh and blood should be tenth rate."

"Yah!" said Urc Tabaron, "and you think yourself so much better than anybody else!"

"Ah, but, my dear fellow, does that follow quite inevitably? It appears to me at least possible to point out the obscurity of an Ethiopian's complexion without asserting oneself to be a blond. Nor do I believe that Jeremiah meant to deny having any freckles when, in the same passage, he went on to refer to the spots of a leopard. Still, your reply is as logical, and as familiar, as could be expected. Yes, your reply is common—in both senses, I regret to remark."

With that, Mr. Smith lighted yet another one of his endless cigarettes; he exhaled then a perfect smoke wreath, observing tranquilly:

"At all events, I have now awakened from that perplexed dream in which I ascended from being a flesh-and-blood person to become a supreme god. I have now returned to my own home in Branlon, wherein harbor more temperate diversions. And I am well content."

"You are not content," said Urc Tabaron, "nor have you awakened, as yet, from your dreaming."

"What does that mean?"

The urbane Lord of the Forest had spoken almost sharply; and in the clear radiance of his face you saw hope blend with anxiety.

"Unhappy Lord of the Forest," replied Urc Tabaron, "you. have confused dreams and realities until it is in your own far-fetched and gaudy imaginings alone that you put any faith. In that land of flesh and blood which you revile, with a bad mixing of tediousness and of envy, you none the less remain, at this very instant, locked up, like a prisoner, in the time-impaired body of a middle-aged mammal, which is asleep and dreaming and—as I will not conceal from you— is snoring also."

Now was Mr. Smith an embodiment of every sort of dignified divine joy; and he said, happily:

"So I am not here at all! I am sound asleep in some other place. Ah, but, my dear fellow, but you bring me most excellent news, because in that event, I still dream; and to do that is my true métier, Urc Tabaron, as I was reflecting not ten minutes ago."

"You were not ever SMIRT," said the gray wizard, gravely bowing his wise head as he spoke the sublime name; "nor did SMIRT ever exist except in your dreams."

"At all times, Urc Tabaron, I knew this, at the bottom of my heart. None the less was SMIRT a fine dream."

"That," said Urc Tabaron, "is a question of taste,

especially of bad taste. For myself, I say only, *De gustibus*— Moreover, I say to you that you have now passed into yet another dream, in which you are Mr. Smith, a deposed god, the bucolic Lord of the Forest of Branlon: but no one of these fancies is true, either."

"I can but ask, then, after a venerable example, what is truth?" declared the Lord of the Forest; "and who am I, if I be neither Smith nor SMIRT? and, lastly, how did you, Urc Tabaron, come to find out about these things?"

"But I do not know the answer to any one of these questions," replied Urc Tabaron, with unconcealed patience, "nor would any rational dreamer be putting any such very silly questions to me. For with truth I have no concern; I am but a thin prattling patch-work of your fancies and of your desultory reading in folk-lore; nor have I any existence except in your dream."

"Yes, that, that at least, is true, according to your most interesting hypothesis," said the Lord of the Forest. "For, by this hypothesis, all Branlon and all the contents of Branlon and I too—all these superb matters are but the products of my wit and my fancy and my erudition,—such, I append modestly, as these little talents may be."

Mr. Smith considered for some while the perplexed and imperilled nature of his present existence. Then Mr. Smith smiled benignantly.

"Well, but," said Mr. Smith, "but, to the other

side, all Branlon and all the contents of Branlon—including you, my dear Urc Tabaron," Mr. Smith added, with his not-ever-failing politeness—"are quite to my taste. Besides that, I entirely enjoy being Lord of the Forest. So I do not complain. If I indeed move in the affairs of a dream, I can but accept this fact. All facts are of considerable interest to a sound logician."

Mr. Smith paused; and he raised his divine shoulders, self-deprecatingly, in the mere sketch of a shrug, saying:

"Moreover, upon every æsthetic ground, I cannot but notice that this dream reflects some little credit upon its dreamer. That I admit to be an ingratiating circumstance which prompts me—we artists being what we most notoriously have always been—to accept, if but out of auctorial vanity, your odd notion that you do not exist in reality but only in my imagination. Toward you, my dear fellow, in this uncertain condition, which you must necessarily find harrowing, I extend, of course, all appropriate sympathy; but as concerns me, I perforce stay content."

Now the wizard stroked his majestic white beard; and from under his shaggy eyebrows he regarded the Lord of the Forest almost compassionately.

"You are not content," said Urc Tabaron. "You never will be, I imagine, no matter how much you may chatter and try to cheat yourself. Such is your nature. And because of that nature—as I well know—

you will by-and-by be asking of me an odd number of
magics to revive, and to draw back to you, some portion of your lost dreams about being SMIRT."

"Ah, but come now," said Mr. Smith, indulgently,
"you are now aping Roland and Turpin and Charlemagne, in this talk about 'lost dreams.' 'Lost dreams'
are quite out of date: they are an anachronism; they
are as completely Victorian as the religious doubts of
Mrs. Humphry Ward or the economics of Karl Marx
or a painting of dead ducks in the dining room. Let
us keep clear of the obsolete, even in a nightmare. Let
us intrepidly meet our dreams as they come. Let us
not lose but cherish them with the respect they deserve; and acclaim without any faltering their complete handsomeness. For I, I have dreams which are
upon a scale commensurate to my talents. And I accept the inevitable, in an awed silence, because after
all it was divine Providence, rather than my personal
endeavors, that got for me my unusual talents. So let
us avoid *hubris*."

"And what manner of strange monster may that
be?" Urc Tabaron interrupted.

"*Hubris,* my dear fellow, was the name given to
that over-weening pride which destroyed Œdipus,
and Prometheus, and so many other protagonists of
Greek drama. *Hubris* is an injudicious amount of
self-conceit and self-complacency. *Hubris,* in brief, is
my *bête noire*, which I avoid zealously, just as I would
avoid too much talking, or too much smoking, or any

39

other indulgence which I knew to be ill-advised. I distrust *hubris*. That is why I am now ready very humbly to accept the inevitable, my dear Urc Tabaron, without criticizing unfavorably its entirely pleasant aspect, inasmuch as my life here as a local deity leaves nothing whatever to be desired, by me."

*   *

SEVEN

MR. SMITH UPON FATHERHOOD

*

Then Mr. Smith went away jauntily, toward his home in the midst of the forest. He said, with contentment:

"Though Branlon be but a dream, yet Branlon is wonderful. It abounds in the superb improbabilities of myth, and at will I create to inhabit Branlon new myths also. These attend me, who am Lord of the Forest, and we make sport together in this wood. The entire effect is baroque and rococo, of course; my bucolics incline to the school of Chinese Chippendale. Yet this Branlon contents me. I would not willingly be leaving Branlon."

No, for he had always admired, and he had liked most cordially, this forest of Branlon during the time when he had thought it merely his native home, in which he had awakened from his dream about being a master of gods. Now the surprising discovery that all Branlon was but a part of another dream, and that his own abilities had created all the wonder and the beauty of Branlon, rather troubled Mr. Smith, on account of his remarkable modesty. It was a discovery which could not but tempt any person, he felt, in the direction of pride and vainglory.

It accounted, too, for a certain vagueness about the trees and the vegetation in general, because he had never known much about botany. Moreover, he could now see that, in this charmed forest, the flora of the north-temperate and of the sub-tropical zones were mixed a bit indiscriminately. Yet if his inattentive recollection of mere trees and bushes had furnished Branlon without any scientific and slavish adherence to veracity, with what lavishness had Branlon been peopled by his erudition!

There was hardly any mythology, he reflected, which had not helped to colonise Branlon. Not only had Branlon its fauns and satyrs and nymphs of the eight classes, its fays and its gnomes and its wood spirits, such as you found in all forests of the lands beyond common-sense: Branlon displayed a population very much more varied. In Branlon, for example, were to be met the Kogaras, and the Vilas, and the Gübiches. The Metsik went about Branlon, mounted on a wild boar with golden bristles; and in the tree-tops of Branlon could be seen now and then the tiny red caps of the Nïagriusar as they peeped down at you.

Moreover, the Wild Huntsman, green clad and wearing upon his head the horns of a stag, rode impressively about Branlon, side by side with the Tutosel, who dressed as a nun, and who hooted, very delightfully, like an owl. The Kirnis guarded the cherry-trees of Branlon; in the hollow tree-stumps of Branlon lived the Norg; and the Vargamor had charge of the wolves of Branlon. And there were hundreds of yet other quaint woodland creatures come out of the folk-lore of all nations to live happily together in Branlon.

Yes, Branlon reflected some little credit upon its compiler, Mr. Smith admitted, even in the teeth of his never-failing modesty. It was exceedingly good to be Lord of the Forest.

After that, Mr. Smith said: "Yet it does trouble me, that when I was not merely a local deity, but a supreme god, I begot children. My wives in that very lofty dream were Tana, who served darkly the sinister white rabbit which lives in the moon, under a cassia-tree; and Airel of the Brown Hair, a conversation woman dwelling upon a glass mountain; and Rani, the South Wind's third daughter, an erratic queen of philosophers, in her fine paper palace erected upon a weather vane. Moreover, I imprudently married Arachne, the Spider Woman, who lives everywhere, and who devours her mate. I do not count Oriana, the Dwarf King's widow, for even though I did marry Oriana also, yet I was prevented from the discharge of my marital duties. I regret the omission, which circumstances made unavoidable: but above all do I regret Tana, whose deformed hands brought peace to my thinking."

That was it, he reflected. From many women he had

43

got pleasure: but the strange hands of Tana (upon neither of which was there a little finger) had brought him peace. He remembered always the charming, the unexplained, tranquillity of that moment when he had sat at the feet of Tana, and she had caressed the dark curls of his hair, and had spoken magic words, —those incomprehensible and humming and droning words which were like the sound of a spinning-wheel. That moment, in all his long dream about being a master of gods, and throughout so much of applause and glory, and among all the prodigies and the love-making and the adulation which delighted him everywhere in his proud dream—that moment had been his one moment of contentment. There was in this fact no apparent sense; and perceiving this, he sighed, as became a sound logician who is confronted by the inexplicable.

"However, upon four of these women I begot children. That memory troubles me. It may be that these hapless children of mine are yet astray in that uncomfortably exalted dream from which I have been released to become well-satisfied and bucolic Mr. Smith in, as I now learn, a quite different sort of dream."

It was a situation which brought out his charmed pocket piece, because the affair called, rather clamantly, for some cigarettes and some matches to facilitate clear thinking.

"Now this Charlemagne yet keeps with him fine flaxen-haired Roland, the fair son of a dream which has forsaken its dreamer. It is true that about the historic figure of Charlemagne have grown up so many romantic accretions as to render all his doings open to doubt. I considered it suspicious, for example, that this eighth-century emperor should be followed by an armed company of musketeers in costumes of the seventeenth century; nor were the four elephants with gilded tusks, which transported his luggage, un-flavored with anachronism."

Mr. Smith weighed for some while these mysteries; and he decided that, while such mixtures were fre-quent enough in the lands beyond common-sense, yet he could not make anything out of them by any rule of sound logic.

In consequence, Mr. Smith said: "Yes, it may well be that this Charlemagne is but a king of romance who exists only in, and by virtue of, my rich-colored superb dreaming about him. Yet in my present dream, if I still move in the affairs of a dream, I permit Charle-magne to keep his Roland, the one being whom Charlemagne yet loves; but I deny myself the dear company of my own sons. To do that, is to carry phil-anthropy and self-sacrifice too far. For I also am a king of romance, ruling over Branlon; and in Branlon that which I desire must happen. So I will, yes, after all, I will humor Urc Tabaron by accepting from him four magics, because kings ought to be gracious to everybody. And with these magics I will draw vari-ously out of my ancient dreaming the four children whom I begot as SMIRT. I will draw them to Branlon, so that at worst, like the great Emperor Charlemagne, I shall not be bereft of my children."

Then the tale tells that he went back to Urc Tabaron. And the tale declares that the gray wizard answered the Lord of the Forest sternly, saying:

"No, Lord of the Forest, because I prophesied that you would ask of me an odd number of magics. You cannot expect me to soil my good name as a sooth-sayer by pretending that four is an odd number."

"Yet four is an excellent number, my dear fellow, as the Four Evangelists and the main points of the compass and every bridge-table will testify—"

"Nevertheless, Lord of the Forest, that which you ask is quite out of reason. To regain your content-ment you will need by-and-by five magics to draw out of an old dream, not four, but five, of your gaudy human-shaped illusions. And even then—I imagine—your nature being what it is, your contentment will hardly outlive one clock-tick."

"Well," Mr. Smith replied, graciously, "I shall not haggle with a friend whom I esteem beyond vocal expression. So in place of the four magics which I con-sented to accept from you, I will now accept five. But let us not talk any nonsense about clock-ticks: there is no clock in this forest."

PART TWO

THE BOOK OF VOLMAR

*　　*

*

"Throughout Osnia farming is unusually highly developed. In 1934 the yield of grains, wheat, wild oats, rye, scotch, bourbon, barley and maize was 7,104,578 metric tons from 8,727,251 acres. Sugar beet production was 3,961,428 metric tons from 322,807 acres. The mineral wealth of this kingdom likewise is considerable, coal, iron, graphite, blarney stones, copper and garnets being abundant. The revenues of Osnia during 1934, as figured in lakhs of rupees, showed a deficit of 47.01."

*   *

EIGHT

HOW THEY BRAGGED

*

Now the tale speaks of the first magic of Urc Tabaron which Mr. Smith used in Branlon; and the tale
tells about how, in far-away Osnia, this magic began
its working when it loosened the loud tongue of Count
Gaubert.

"At the siege of Moscow," declared this Count
Gaubert, "I unhorsed the proud Tzar Alexis, rolling
him over in a ditch publicly, while five armies applauded."

"Hah, but with only a handful of men," cried out
Andrew of Lower Chamgui, "I captured and I burned
the two-score-and-two extremely strong and compact
towers of El Gazib. For that reason do the Turks still
shudder at a mention of my name."

"All this is nothing," replied Jocelyn of Brienne,
"inasmuch as it was I who killed the Sultan of Babylon, and cut him into halves, and tore the black
wicked heart out of his pagan body. Now he, I would
have you know, was called Saleh Nagim Addim Aijub;
and that is a name before which everyone shudders."

49

Thus they boasted: for to-day the King of Osnia held a suitably royal feast in honor of his daughter's birthday; and after the gentlemen who served him had eaten well, and had drunk yet more zealously— in the large hall hung everywhere with those strange banners which Rudolph the Lame took from the King of the Land of Shadows in his last battle, among the cliffs of Toysan—these gentlemen were now making their brags, as an entertainment for the Princess Sonia. So the one told of his warfaring, and then the other excelled him in confessing to superb and unequalled exploits in battle. Seventeen of them thus outbragged the other. Then Volmar, the dark wanderer said:

"You have taken cities and heathen lords and such-like other toys, it may be. But I have taken the fancy of a Christian princess, and that is a fairer thing to be having."

"Come," said King Ludwig, frowning, "but what sort of Christian, much more a princess, would be giving her fancy to a sot and a shock-headed vaga-bond?"

"She is the most wise of all princesses," replied Vol-mar, "in that she has perceived my merits. She is the most lovely of princesses that are now alive."

"Be silent, dark tippler!" cried out Earl Othnar. "There is no woman anywhere more beautiful than our Princess Sonia."

Then dozens of yet other gentlemen arose to pro-test angrily that this patriotic tenet of the kingdom of

Osnia was a true tenet and remained a mere axiom among intelligent persons.

Volmar, who was now drunk to the point when all which a man desires appears plausible, swayed on his feet a little; but his glazed dark eyes did not turn from the Princess Sonia, where she sat beside the King her father under a gold-fringed cloth of estate.

She was very nobly dressed this evening, in a close gown of crimson and gold. She wore a diadem of gold inset with rubies; about the neck and the hem of her gown showed a strip of ruddy fox fur. But her face was like the new moon, Volmar reflected, so thin, so clear, so bright, so unapproachable, was its loveliness.

"It is true," said Volmar, with a judicious hiccough, "that there is no person more beautiful than Sonia. Nor is there any princess more wise than is Sonia. She has, for a woman, really remarkable powers of penetration. She has perceived my merits, where even I did not perceive them. And in return for my merits, gentlemen, she has given me her fancy, and until life ends, she will be remembering me with love."

All they who heard him had heard, at first, in mere wonderment. That at a king's banquet any male person should boast of his high and peculiar standing in a lady's heart, appeared, to the chivalrous gentry of Osnia, a performance as incredible as that, in the same circumstances, any self-respecting gentleman would omit to lie about his high and peculiar standing in warfare. In brief, the rules of polite usage had been violated; insulted decency shrieked for vengeance; and every nobleman's sword was now out.

But the King stilled them. "With your swords, gentlemen," said King Ludwig, very handsomely, "it is permitted you to kill yet other gentlemen. But not dogs."

Well, and at that, all the nobility of Osnia necessarily dropped their swords in order to applaud the antithesis.

Then the King said, to Caspar, the captain of the royal guard:

"Take away Volmar the dark wanderer to a dungeon. This day is sacred, inasmuch as it is my daughter's birthday: no bloodshed must mar to-day. But at dawn to-morrow, when this hulking beast is sober, and awake to his own infamy, do you cut off his head, and bring it up to me with my breakfast, so that I may be sure his poisoned tongue is silenced forever."

"My king and my father," said Sonia, speaking angrily, in a young girl's unthinking way, where the experienced, sage King had spoken with deliberation, "it is not proper that you should let your great modesty check the keen judgment and the fine eloquence which the whole world admires!"

"I have no doubt that you speak with entire justice, my daughter; but just what do you mean?"

"I mean, sire, that we all know you are thinking, and are eager to be saying—in your own superb fash-

ion, such as the rhetoric of no other king equals—
that it is not right this braggart should meet death
honorably under the clean axe-edge. It is not right
that his lying tongue should be brought back into the
palace it has defiled."

"Nevertheless—" said King Ludwig.

"Oh, but I agree with you," the Princess assured
him. "I did not understand this matter until you
expressed it thus nobly and forcibly."

"Yet—" said the King.

"But you, sire, as you must permit me to tell you
frankly, have compounded the fine honey of your
eloquence with the firm hand of your wisdom."

"Ah, but have I indeed, my daughter?"

"Very certainly you did that, sire, when you declared this insane slanderer ought to be hanged, and
then buried whole in our dung-heap, because it is
only in a dung-heap that such filth belongs. And I
quite agree with you."

"The wrong was yours, my dear daughter," replied King Ludwig, indulgently: "and even though
you have somewhat forestalled my remarks, apart
from mixing your metaphors, it is proper that the
punishment of your wrong should be whatsoever you
desire. So you may do with him what you like."

"Do you mark that, Caspar," said the Princess; and
the gray captain answered:

"I hear, Lady, and I obey the King's saying. I shall
do with this Volmar that which you order."

NINE

* *

DOOM OF A LIAR

*

So was it that Volmar—whom the Master of Gods, then passing as an errant philosopher, had begotten upon Rani, the South Wind's third daughter—spent this night in a deep dungeon, without any comforters except a pitcher of water and three rats. But at dawn, Caspar and five soldiers, each armed with a musket, bring Volmar into a field to the back of the palace, with a rope about his neck and with his hands bound behind him.

Well, and that, he reflected, that was a most uncomfortable way in which to be walking, on this uneven meadow land, where the new grass showed sparsely. You stumbled perforce; you appeared undignified, not to say drunk; nor, when walking thus, could you keep your broad shoulders handsomely erect.

It seemed silly to be annoying the last moments of a gentleman with these small inconveniences: but all professional soldiers were hidebound and unimaginative people who went always by routine, Volmar reflected gravely. Even his loved commander and

lion-hearted friend, King Aluric of Atlantis, had at
bottom possessed no real imagination, Volmar went
on in profound meditation, as, for that matter, the
dear fellow's verses showed somewhat plainly, now
that nobody was afraid of Aluric any longer, with
blond blustering Aluric safely buried in the Place of
the Sea God, as indeed were most of the persons whom
you had known intimately, although no one of the
others, of course, had a fine tomb in a heathen tem-
ple, but rather they were lodged helter-skelter in
every quarter of earth, in all sorts of mortuary circumstances—even if no one of them lay snug under a
dung-heap,—because both as a poet and as a soldier
this Volmar had adventured so widely, and so noisily,
and so enjoyably, that for it all to be ending within
the next ten minutes, in the field just beyond that
privet hedge upon which a bluebird perched, appeared simply silly.

No, Volmar decided, as he stumbled on toward
death, he could not give his approval to the hanging
of Volmar. The entire business was silly. It was peculiarly silly that this bluebird had come to inform
people spring was now near at hand, quite as if that
mattered, when everything would be over, within the
next nine minutes, for this Volmar, for this not ever
explained and incomprehensible Volmar, who seemed
somehow to have become a stranger to you, and a
somewhat admirable stranger, if you judged honestly,
inasmuch as Volmar had rioted, and had sung, and

had fought, with the best of earth's gentry, all the long bright way from his first callow freedoms to this thick privet hedge which you were now stumbling through sidewise, with the twigs tickling your nose at a moment in which you were not able to scratch it, because of the absurd military routine that tied up your hands behind you when you could not possibly risk your last flickers of being a devil-may-care fellow by asking stupid, splendid and pious old Caspar to scratch your nose, like a dry nurse.

Then of a sudden Volmar's bemuddled thoughts became clear and bitter, because upon the farther side of the privet hedge he had found a cloaked woman waiting.

"It is even as I said," observed Volmar, jeeringly. "This lady intends to see the very last of me. She cannot bear to think that I must die a knave's death without the spur of her beauty to hearten me now that I cry, Hail and farewell, fair Sonia!"

Sonia put by her blue cloak. "Wicked man, for what reason must you be speaking your lies about me in my father's great hall openly?"

At that, his thick eyebrows went up. He appeared surprised, almost grieved.

"Why, and did I not speak the truth, Sonia, in saying that until your life ends, you will always be remembering me—now?"

She said, gravely: "I shall remember you. That is true. But I shall remember you with my contempt and with my hatred."

"Time will show," replied Volmar. "You will recall by-and-by that I provoked certain death in order that you might remember me always. Turn about, my fair idiot, is fair play. You stay forever in my thoughts, the thoughts which end here; and so do I mean henceforward to stay forever in your thoughts through the long years to come in that quiet while after I have put by thinking and all other sorts of time-wasting. You must always remember, will-you or nill-you, my pretty prude, the drink-sodden Volmar who gave his life in order that you might remember him. With time, you will come to appreciate that very handsome compliment. And about the dead man who paid you this compliment, will-you or nill-you, Sonia, you will think, at first, with curiosity, and, by-and-by, with some tenderness."

She regarded him for a pensive moment, looking up at him sidewise. She smiled thinly, in replying to him,—

"You have a knowledge of women, dark Volmar; but not enough knowledge."

"I do not pretend to omniscience, Lady. I say only that all which a hale youngster could learn, during the bustling days and the not unbusy nights of some fifteen years, I have learned about women in fifteen kingdoms and in more than fifteen kingdoms."

"Lewd Volmar," she said, sharply, "now your debauchery ends. It ends by your being given into my hands, so that your punishment shall be as I desire."

She paused. Her eyes were bright and hard, her lips a straight line. She said:

"I condemn you to live. So do you loose this long-legged sot, Caspar, and let him go free into exile without any hurt save the sting of his self-knowledge."

Volmar cried out, in a changed voice: "I will not accept your mercy! I am too vile!"

"Nor would I grant you any mercy," the girl said, "if I did not know that the sick vanities which fester in your drunken thoughts must make of anybody's mercy a bitterness. For this reason do I punish you with my mercy,—Volmar, the braggart and the fool, the defamer of ladies, the babbler of a sot's lies! I order that you shall live on in your soiled infamy, and be known everywhere as Volmar the Drunken Liar, and have no place in my thoughts."

Obeying her, the soldiers had untied Volmar. He stood clutching and unclutching his numbed fingers, and looking down at Sonia with a flushed face in which rage mingled with amusement. He said, jeeringly:

"You have conquered for this while, Lady. You have tricked first your father out of satisfying his just anger, as now you trick me out of satisfying my dislike of your mincing, prim-mouthed hypocrisy. It is my one comfort, Sapphira, that your early rising and your glib deceits of everybody proclaim that, after all, you must think about me a great deal."

A patch of red in each cheek showed him that Sonia too had a temper to lose.

"I think about no man living, Volmar the Drunken Liar, in the foul way you leer over. I keep instead my clean heart for that man who shall prove worthy of it; and as yet I have seen him nowhere."

At that, Volmar cried out, under the lash of her scorn, and in the anger of his humiliation:

"Do you not let your itching need of a young man wide awake in your bed be bothering you, most detestable of women! No; for you have given me dishonor and the eternal sting of self-knowledge. But I, Volmar, the son of SMIRT, I shall requite you with a fine stalwart young husband to cool your hot prudish lusts every night and all night long."

"My husband, lewd foul-tongued Volmar, shall be of my own choosing—yes, and he shall be a man of clean honor and a person as unlike you as I can find anywhere in the whole world."

"Your husband shall be of my choosing," returned Volmar, furiously.

"He shall not be!" said the Princess, stamping her foot.

"But indeed he shall be, Sonia! Yes, and moreover, it is he, you bad-tempered creature, who will have to put up with your eternal arguing about everything until you have driven the man quite insane."

59

"Why, then," said the Princess, "there will be a pair of you."

Volmar answered, with a demented loftiness: "Whether there be a pair of men or a round dozen of men who deplore your existence, Sonia, I at least do not mean to argue with you. No; for what I have said, I have said. You shall marry the man whom I pick out for you, this thing I swear by high heaven and by all the gold-slippered saints in it; and that is an end of the matter."

"But that, Volmar, that is not an end. It is only another bragging oath; and what sane saint anywhere would be giving his heed to the oath of a drunken liar?"

Volmar said, gloomily: "I do not know. But I mean to find out."

So was it that Volmar was again free to wander at adventure, jeeringly observing the world's ways. There was in his mind a difference, however, as he rode out of Osnia with no temporal possessions except his horse, his long sword and the two pistols at his belt. He was much fretted by the downfall of his drunken plans, because, just as he had meant to live always in her thoughts, so now in his thoughts was always Sonia.

And besides that, in plain fairness, Volmar had decided, he must henceforward obey this abominable creature in regard to changing his name. When he came now to any castle, or to the court of a king, he must now bid the porter announce him as Volmar the Drunken Liar. Yes, it was this title—which was not, to Volmar's opinion, captivating—that the South Wind's own grandchild, and a son of the sublime Master of Gods, would hereafter have to make the best of, damn the prim slut!

*   *

TEN

THE BROWN PRIEST

*

They relate how Volmar came, in the shadow of five great oaks which had seen the dawn of history, and had borne acorns before human wisdom begot any large wars, to the home of a brown priest who lived alone in this quiet place. They say that this holy man had not any companion except a notably colored huge ram. This ram had bright yellow wool and a crimson head and rather dark blue horns and green feet. They tell also that to this priest Volmar confessed all the sins of Volmar; and thus spoke about that consuming hatred which Volmar now entertained toward the Princess Sonia.

"Come," said the priest, who was called Belial, "but hatred is not the most becoming exercise for a gentleman's faculties. In fact, hatred is by many theologians ranked as a cardinal enormity. This affair is grave."

He reflected over it sadly; and then Belial said:

"Yet, after all, it was with untruthful words that you offended against decency and honor and religion likewise. So it seems only fair for you to atone with untruthful words."

"That is good sense, beyond doubt. But your meaning, sir, is beyond understanding."

"Sit here," said the holy man, "and I will show you my meaning."

Volmar sat down on the shining black stone which was carved like a toad's head. Then, just in front of him, brown Belial kindled a fire of cedar-wood, and he sprinkled a red powder upon this fire, saying:

"In the name of Belial, may the Horned Lord command thee and drive thee hence, Raphael! In the name of Belial, may Chavajoth command thee and drive thee hence, Gabriel! Let us labor in peace, Michael! By the Needle, and by the Werewolf, we deny to you ever-meddlesome three the fine fruit of our labors."

Now the fire cast out lazily a thick smoke, which ascended, and which divided into colors; and then these colors took form. Thus before Volmar was made the appearance of an orchard revealed in the shadowless, very clear first light of dawn. Through the flowering apple-trees came a cloaked man; and pausing before a window, he spoke, in a thin far-away voice.

It was of the dawn that he spoke, as a dream speaks, telling about the evils and the doubts bred in the night time. One had for guide at this season, his thin voice declared, only the aloof stars twinkling about their own affairs frostily; or, it might be, one was misled fitfully by the untruthful moon, a furtive and blemished being, a provoker of lunacies, a known aider of thieves, and a most notable equivocator, so dubious even as to her own name that none knew beyond question whether it were Phoebe or Diana or Cynthia or Lucina.

Volmar remarked, "Pooh!"

Such dubieties (continued the cloaked man, still speaking as a dream speaks) were contagious; and they made uncertainties pandemic: for unfaith prospered everywhere under the weak rule of this watery sceptic; so that the lover when absent overnight from his beloved was not always absent from jealousy. Ohimé, but at night even the wise dead were betrayed into doubts of their own blessed condition, wandering about as lost ghosts, at odds with all common-sense, because these deceased persons had been tricked, by night's doubtfulness, into relinquishing the well-earned repose which they had purchased by dying.

"Stuff and nonsense!" said Volmar.

Night, said the far-away thin voice, was fallacious; night coldly prevaricated; night was not to be relied on: but with each dawn came warm certainty. For Sonia arose then, in common with that lesser luminary the sun. And before her radiance the guttering stars died out like the spent candles of dark falsehood's ended misrule, and the whey-faced moon fled, with the timidness of an exposed swindler, before the veracity of Sonia's beauty.

Well, and at that, an exasperated Volmar cried out, "Bosh!"

But in the smoke picture the window above the tall cloaked man had opened a little way, and a woman's white hand dropped from this window a white rose. The cloaked man pressed this flower to his lips, and Volmar saw that this man had the dark face, the petulant gross mouth, and the heavy eyebrows of Volmar.

"You perceive," said the priest, "the good will of this good-hearted simpleton is to be won easily enough if only one goes about it in a manner sufficiently high-spoken."

Volmar replied, with a poet's candor, "I have made dozens upon dozens of better morning-songs than is this labored twaddle in disrespect to the moon."

"Oh, but very truly!" agreed Belial, with a quickness which showed him to be the prince of critics. "And any one of your superb poems, when once it has been a bit pulled about, and has been adapted properly to this Sonia's big brown eyes and her fine skin and her plump high breasts, and to yet other luxuries of a gentleman's sleeping apartments, will serve you to admiration."

"But," said Volmar, "but I do not desire a white rose, or any other maudlin reward, from a creature so detestable."

"Yes, that is quite understood. It is only for your soul's health, which is now imperilled by the great

65

sin of hatred," replied Belial, "that I would urge you to lie your way into her good graces. What follows, you may regard, should you so elect, as a penance. In any case, do you look again."

Obeying the soft, the grave, and the yet somehow dangerous voice, Volmar saw that the magical smoke picture had taken on more subdued colors. Still the same orchard was visible, with the difference that you saw it now, a little while after sunset, in a rising golden-tinged twilight which revealed indecisively the discolored leaves of autumn and the ripe apples upon every tree. A man stood there, beneath Sonia's window; and he spoke, as a dream speaks, saying:

"Lady, I would that, as my words mount up to you, so likewise my thoughts might aspire to enter your presence. But they dare not. You appear to me too fine and too holy, upon this stilled evening, in which, like those western clouds, my thoughts yet keep a pink tinge of flesh. When I consider you, then my love vanishes, because, like a more gentle Gorgon, your cool glance petrifies love into worship, and you chill all un-Christian desires. You enforce me to live either as a monk or as a pagan.

"So do I become a pagan, now that daylight dies and the flaring star of Venus reigns alone and low and strangely lovely in the green void sky. Than Venus there is no power more strong or affable. We wait together outside your window, Venus and I, in this yearning silence: there is no sound in the orchard except my sad speaking. The beauty of Venus is great and clear and kindly and inaccessible: beholding her, I think perforce about Sonia; and I lament that to such beauty I may not ascend, not even in my thinking.

"No; I may not ascend. Yet it may be, ah, Lady, it well may be that this Venus still stoops earthward, now and then, upon her amicable missions of charity, and that she meets amicably with a more modern Anchises or with some stripling Adonis. In a mere goddess such charity is allowed; and for this reason, Lady, I would that you too were a goddess, and not a stone-cold saint enshrined in your remote purity, denying to any man the proud jewel of your heart, that diamond-like jewel, which is flawless and splendid and very hard."

The appearance of Sonia now stood at the window. She beckoned. The man's figure climbed up to the window and entered it: but he looked back, as though to make sure no one was spying on him, and in the golden-tinged twilight the man's face was the face of Volmar. Then this appearance of Volmar closed the latticed window, and nothing more was visible in the smoke wreaths.

"So," said the priest, "do you abandon your hatred, Volmar, and we will see to it that this false seeming becomes a true seeming. You have but to give me a little gift in tribute to my master, and he will ensure that you enter this same bedroom window in just this way. The Horned Lord will make true the words of your drunken boasting; and he will thus remove from you for all time your dishonor."

"That is good sense," Volmar agreed. "For when I have not any longer lied, why, then—in so far as I can see—I shall not any longer be a liar."

"Moreover, Volmar, you will then be at liberty with a clear conscience to expose the girl's worthlessness to everybody. You can in this way satisfy, not that hatred which is a sin, but that praiseworthy abhorrence of a wanton woman which is a virtue."

"You are still speaking good sense, as well as good piety," said Volmar, "and yet, somehow, I do not like it."

"Nevertheless, my son, you ought to be very grateful to the sound reasoning which has shown you how, at the light cost of a little fornication, to be rid of all dishonor as well as of the great sin of hatred."

"You speak smoothly," said Volmar, with a fretted sigh, "and I admit there is no flaw in your argument. Through her dishonor alone may my troubles be healed. Yes, Belial, you point out to me a way in which at one stroke to retrieve my good name through the ruin of her good name, and to re-establish my veracity by destroying her virtue. Moreover, you have the appearance of a holy and amiable person. Yet your feet are the feet of a huge bird, of a fierce bird of prey."

"Ah, yes, Volmar, for my master has put that sign upon all his priesthood. It is but a divine idiosyncrasy, a mere matter of ritual. Let us not think about such pedal peculiarities, or any other light trifles, now that you are about to exchange hatred for love and your dishonor for the respect and the envy of everybody."

But Volmar arose, scowling, from the dark sleek stone which was carved like a toad's head; and to the holy man he replied with harsh stubbornness.

"No," said Volmar; "I will not traffic with you and your piety and your good sense and your soft chamberings. I prefer to keep my dishonor and my wicked hatred of this detestable woman. I will make no terms with her, nor with you either. I decline to dishonor the abominable creature as a fit punishment for preserving my life. To the contrary, just as I threatened, I mean by-and-by to marry her off, in all honor, to that unfortunate person who most nearly deserves her."

*   *

ELEVEN

GRIEF OF THE SOUTH WIND

*

They tell now that the next person whom Volmar met was a huge shining horseman in late middle life. He was not clad meanly. Instead, his fine golden armor was adorned everywhere with rubies, as was also his triangular shield of gold; and on his breastplate of gold blazed yet other rubies. His saddle was bordered with gray eagle feathers; and trappings of red silk and of yellow silk made splendid his tall golden-colored horse. Thus handsomely fared the stranger who cried out, to dark Volmar, in friendly tones,—

"Hail, Volmar! for after all, blood is thicker than water."

"Well, sir," replied Volmar, "inasmuch as you know me far better than I know you, I dare not dispute your striking and profound observation. Moreover, you appear to be a divine personage."

"And why should I not be a divine personage, Volmar, inasmuch as I am your own dear Grandfather, the South Wind, come to arrange about your marriage?"

"Hah," said Volmar, "but it is to the marriage of somebody else that a sworn oath commits me."

Nevertheless, they embraced. And what happened after that has not ever been recorded with any real clearness, because Volmar was forthwith carried up, they say, into an inconceivably high place, to speak about which the powers of men's language have never been adequate.

It was a fertile level land, rich in broad meadows green as an emerald stone, with many blossoms falling upon the sweet-smelling orchards, where larks poured out their song tirelessly, and glad blackbirds were singing and always singing, and bees went about their little labors without ever ceasing. In the pastures of this land grazed golden horses and crimson horses and horses that were colored like the blue sky. The people of this land were a gentle and light-hearted people. There was no land more fair or more peaceful than Auster. And over Auster ruled the South Wind, living tranquilly in a large wonderful house, builded out of shining bronze, which stood among apple-trees that flowered perpetually with white and with faintly pink blossoms, and among pallid, darkly-speckled sycamore-trees that wore forever in Auster their first sparse leaves, which during the spring-time are gray rather than green.

Well, and all the inhabitants of this high and lovely place were friendly to Volmar, their near kinsman, inasmuch as they too were akin to the South Wind.

And the South Wind required it of him that Volmar should marry one or another of the women of Auster, so that the family of the South Wind might be continued respectably by his grandson, in this inconceivably high level land where the beauty of spring-time lasted forever.

"But my prayer-book teaches me, sir," replied Volmar, "that baptism precedes matrimony. And of these ladies whom you desire me to marry the like has not yet been born, much less christened."

For he beheld now to every side of him those women whom poets alone have beheld—howsoever briefly, and in a spring-time which did not last forever,—and by whose wonderfulness the life of their beholder has thereafter been robbed of every sharp savor. All poets have glimpsed the women of Auster; and a very few poets have contrived to ensnare in words a frail shadow of these women's loveliness; but the life of each ageing poet has been haunted, and in some sort it has been laid waste, by his memories of that glimpse which made his lost youth miraculous now and then; and which gave to his name immortality, it might be; but which forever afterward delivered over his heart to a long loneliness, by causing all flesh-and-blood women, either as his wife or his mistress, to appear unsatisfying.

Well, and to dark Volmar's finding, very beautiful were the women of Auster, and very wise, and very tender, and pleasingly mirthful. There was no fault in them. And yet was theirs not a cold perfection, but a variable and a many-faceted excellence in all graces, so that each one of these women was, in herself, a host of exceedingly dear women, who stayed adorable at every instant, but not always for the same qualities. In brief, the women of Auster were as variable as the air of which they were born. But they varied never in being more fine and more noble in their form and their coloring, in their wit and their graciousness, than were the women whom human flesh clothed and restrained from perfection.

Now these ladies regarded their dark earth-born cousin with kindness; and the South Wind was bent upon Volmar's marrying whichsoever one of them Volmar might prefer.

But Volmar said: "No. With no one of these fine sylphs do I either desire or intend to cohabit."

"Pish!" said the South Wind, "and likewise Tush! and moreover, Why not?"

"Because," replied Volmar, "I find their perfections uncongenial."

"Bah!" said the South Wind, "but your reason is not reasonable."

"Yet, Grandfather, I do not aspire toward ladies that are more lovely than are any ladies that ever wore warm flesh."

—To which the South Wind returned, "Fiddle-dedee!"

"I dislike these sylphs, for example, because they

live untroubled with pimples, or even with enough biliousness to result in a sour breath; and are not ever subject to belching."

"You become coarse, my grandson. We of Auster prefer sentiments which are properly elevated."

Then Volmar said: "Yet these women lack blemishes, Grandfather, to an extent which I find fatal to deep affection. They are flawless. No moles and no blackheads, and not even any broken blotched veins, disfigure their bodies, so far as I have yet investigated their bodies."

The South Wind coughed disapprovingly. He—as a gentleman of the old school—after his well-earned respose upon nine thousand and twenty-eight bosoms, considered these investigations to be a matter of course, but not a matter of conversation.

And Volmar paused before that admonitory cough. He grinned somewhat, in the same moment that he continued to regard this fine-looking, divine, grave, stupid, and very dear old gentleman with sincere fondness.

"Yes, and indeed, Grandfather, I could name a great many other feminine frailties to which the women of Auster are not subject; but it would be more kindly of me to spare your old-fashioned and superb romanticism. We will let it suffice that I have not anything in common with these fair paragons. Such are the women about whom young poets dream, and to whom they address rhapsodies: but at my age one is no longer a young poet; at my age one prefers a few imperfections, as being far more companionable to live with. So I cry a fig for the women of Auster, because such lovely and all-admirable beings are not the desire of my heart."

"You annoy me, Volmar," replied his perplexed grandfather, "by this morbid dwelling on the distasteful. You repel me by preferring the second rate to the best."

Thus speaking, the old gentleman refreshed himself liberally, with bubbling bright green wine, which he drank from out of a great crystal goblet rimmed with a broad band of gold. He asked, in divine scorn,—

"What is it, then, that your so famous heart does desire?"

"Under the correction of experience, sir, I imagine that I desire—I mean, of course, in due season, because there is no real hurry about it—a true mate, both in my frailties and, if the need rise, in my appetites as an animal. For I, Grandfather, I am weak, I am foul, it may be. At any rate, I am not perfect, no matter what you might think, sir, on account of your natural partiality for me."

"Hoh!" said the South Wind.

Then Volmar said, "So I prefer a true mate, of a reasonably inferior nature, to whom neither my modest best nor my somewhat immodest worst will appear contemptible."

"You disgust me, Volmar," declared the grieved

75

South Wind: "and yet truly you cannot help being the son of a great but gross-minded god"—here he bowed reverently—"the sublime SMIRT. Ah, but it was a luckless hour for everybody concerned in which that omnipotent person took an advantage of my dear daughter's innocence and of the hospitality which she gave without any stint to every sort of philosopher in her own bed!"

Thereafter the South Wind sighed. He looked rather despondently at this shock-headed grandson for whom he had planned a divine future thus fruitlessly: but there was no understanding this younger generation, he reflected; and they must go their own way, unaided by their elders' wisdom, to destruction.

Yet the old gentleman continued, affectionately enough:

"No, my poor Volmar, you are not suited to dwell in, far less to rule over, the kingdom of Auster. And so, be off with you. Avaunt! Scat!"

"Very willingly will I avaunt and scat also," replied Volmar. "For these sylphs are well enough; yet I do not desire them, any more than I desire the dead Witch of Endor, or the three Furies, or that hateful Sonia, who is the most detestable of earth's women. How then can even a drunken liar pretend to care about the women of Auster one way or the other? And besides, it is quite time that I picked out for the abominable, smug, bad-tempered creature her unfortunate husband."

Thus did it come about that no magic of the upper world was able to hold Volmar. Instead, just as he had evaded, in the home of Belial, the dictates of religion and honor, so now he derided the proud service of beauty and of perfection, holding high his wild dark head; and he returned to the middle earth which had borne and nurtured, among its other fauna, that errant philosopher who begot Volmar.

*   *

TWELVE

MR. SMITH AS TO KEYS

*

They relate next how Volmar met with a pedlar, a majestic but affable person, having incredibly steadfast eyes. This pedlar sat on a mile-stone (which was inscribed "4 Ms. to Garian") , upon the southern outskirts of the forest of Branlon, smoking a cigarette; and he was peddling small magics.

"Of what nature are these magics," asked Volmar, "which you peddle in the lands beyond common-sense, wherein all magics are more common than huckleberries or than handsaws or than hard-headed women?"

"Why, at this season, sir, as it happens, I am marketing the products of a very special magic. These little leaden keys"—explained the pedlar, spreading open his pack—"when they are used idiotically, enable people to escape from the color and beauty, the noble language and the quaintness and the affluence and the contentment, of their lives here, and to enter into quite other lives which are uniformly unpleasant, and which customarily are degraded in their pursuits."

"But to seek out any such ignoble existence is, quite certainly, idiotic," Volmar agreed.

"My customers, sir, are human. It comes to pretty much the same thing. So these knicknacks remain exceedingly popular everywhere, among the nobility and gentry, to whom the wit and fancy and wide erudition of their creator have denied sordidness and all serious calamities. For these dull-colored keys are strong amulets, I must tell you, which enable the light-hearted and quaint and the so nicely dressed nobility of these parts to lead, if but for an hour or two, the lives of yokels or of convicts or of bankrupts or of diseased pimps or of broken-down harlots; and they one and all come back from these little outings into stupidity and squalor very much refreshed."

"But do the people of Rorn, and of Ecben over yonder, love ugliness? and cherish discomfort? and desire infamy?" asked Volmar.

Well, and he got his answer first in the form of a smoke puff and then in the words of a similar philosophy.

"The nobility and gentry of the lands beyond common-sense," replied the pedlar, "are necessarily all poets at heart, if not in rhythmic performance. For this reason they must necessarily desire that which they lack and contemn that which they possess. Such is the foible of all poets; and since time began, nobody, in so far as I know, has ever found any real cure for this foible."

"I believe that is so," said Volmar, humanly deducing the universal from his own special case.

"My dear sir, but beyond any doubt it is a fact; and all facts are of considerable interest to a sound logician."

"Possibly," said Volmar.

"When I say 'considerable,' " the pedlar explained, "I mean worthy of being considered."

"I can grant you that," Volmar said generously.

"Yes, but," asked the pedlar, "but how many people ever do consider anything or anybody thoroughly, and quietly, and *sub rosa*, and in particular, *sub*—as I have heard learned persons describe this special angle of vision—*specie æternitatis?*"

"Indeed, I know as little about that matter as I care," replied Volmar; and he asked afterward,—

"What is your name, O most talkative pedlar?"

"I am called nowadays Mr. Smith."

"Well, Mr. Smith, I desire none of your abominable leaden keys, nor do I insist upon any more of your endless talking. Instead, I go seeking the near road to some noble adventure."

"Ah, but, sir," this Mr. Smith told him, "our gentry have put by all other adventures in order to look for the most excellent princess in the lands beyond common-sense, now that our young King Feodor of Rorn declares he will marry no other person."

"Hah, Splendor of God!" cried Volmar.

"That is an exceedingly handsome oath, dark sir,

to which, as I now recall, William the Conqueror was very much addicted. Yet an equally great monarch, King Louis the Eleventh of France, used to swear 'by God's Easter!' Certainly, this King Louis was a wise man; but he was no wiser than Socrates, who customarily swore 'by the Bitch!' And Zeno, another notably wise person, who founded the sect of the Stoics, chose to swear 'by the Caper-tree!' Tastes differ, you perceive, even in profanities, among the very best people. So, what, after all, my dear young sir, just what does your exceedingly handsome oath signify?"

"It signifies that I know this princess," replied Volmar; "and that I find her the most detestable of women; and that your unfortunate King shall marry her if, after I have once seen the man, I think this impudent, wife-seeking, crowned, very wealthy Feodor deserves any fate so dreadful."

"'He shall marry her,' you remarked," said the pedlar; "and that likewise sounded most splendidly. Yet who are you, my young Hector, to compel a king?"

"I am Volmar, the son of SMIRT, a most famous philosopher, who was worth ten of your Zenos and your Socrateses."

"So, so!" said Mr. Smith, in urbane surprise; and for some while he looked at Volmar pensively. Then the pedlar smiled, saying:

"The arts of Urc Tabaron are dependable. And since you term SMIRT a philosopher, I infer that your mother must have been Rani, the South Wind's third daughter."

"That is true, Mr. Smith, although I do not in the least follow your logic."

"Ah, but I follow you, big, blustering, shock-headed son of SMIRT, now that you go single-handed to impose your will on a king," replied Mr. Smith, admiringly.

"Very well," said Volmar. "Do you come with me, and I will show you just how to do that."

*   *

THIRTEEN

THE KING WITHOUT STAIN

*

So then, as young King Feodor sat with his counsellors in his palace of white stone in the fair city of Garian, the porter came to ask audience for a pedlar and a drunken liar in regard to the King's marriage.

"With what mummery," said the King, "are we interrupted in our talk of this marriage? Admit them."

This was done. Volmar bowed civilly enough—for Volmar—toward North, South, East and West, and after that he bowed to the King.

Then he looked very hard, across the broad table of fair white oak, at King Feodor. Volmar thought, first of all, with a poet's irrelevance,—

"Life is going to bruise and to hurt and to damage this fine boy most damnably."

His second thought was: "I have found my man. Here is a king without stain. I love, I hate, I revere, I pity, and I can just manage to sneer at, the manifest virtues of this superb crowned youngster in his ermine and his purples of two shades. Yes, here, beyond doubt, is that damnable Sonia's fit mate."

Aloud, he said, jeeringly: "Hail, sire! And do you contrive a royal reward for Volmar the Drunken Liar, now that he brings you fair tidings as to the most excellent princess in the lands beyond common-sense."

The King replied: "Ho, drunken liar, but that all-perfect lady appears to be perplexingly plentiful. Here, upon this sheet of parchment are listed, in letters of gold, ten royal spinsters and two widows, each one of whom, this or the other of my twelve counsellors assures me, is the most excellent princess in the lands beyond common-sense."

Volmar said: "I do not know whether your counsellors are bribed men or self-seeking men or mere idiots; but I do know that in no king's palace may that woman be found who is fit to live as a chambermaid to Sonia, the daughter of King Ludwig of Osnia."

"Her name is not here, Volmar the Drunken Liar, among those twelve women whom my counsellors declare to be the most excellent princesses in the lands beyond common-sense."

"Then, King, you are counselled by such persons as outrival Volmar in their untruths and their shamelessness."

Thus speaking, Volmar turned to observe the King's counsellors; and he found them a noble company. Four of these learned men wore scarlet robes adorned with peacock feathers and with the heads and breasts of gaily colored birds imported from Persia. Another four went in robes of Tyrian yellow bordered with a fringe of cedar bark. And the other four had sea-green robes, heavily quilted, which were trimmed with the fur of the dormouse and of the marten.

Volmar scowled at the entire dozen impartially. From his left hand he removed his glove, and he flung it down before these gentlemen, saying:

"I, Volmar the Drunken Liar, demand the Judgment of God. Let him among you fine counsellors who declares that Sonia is not both the most excellent and the most hateful princess in the lands beyond common-sense now lift my glove. After that, we will fight, either with swords or with pistols or with battering-rams—or, if my opponent so prefers it, with sharp knitting needles—until the one or the other of us is dead."

"God being that which the wisdom of all better-thought-of people assures us He is," the King answered, "your offer appears reasonable; your choice of weapons bespeaks your broad-mindedness: and a Christian monarch must admit the Judgment of God."

Then his counsellors said: "Nay, sire, for high Heaven's sake, let us not be dragging Heaven impiously into any question of the realm's public welfare. It is expedient, for this reason or the other reason, that some one of these dozen princesses be declared the most excellent princess in the lands beyond common-sense, and that you should marry her on account of her super-eminence, whether she has it or not."

"But," said the King, "Volmar the Drunken Liar has appealed to the Judgment of God."

His counsellors answered: "Nevertheless, we uphold our own judgment; for the harsh conditions of human life have forced us to learn a great deal more about statecraft, let us assure you, than the Eternal Father has any need to be knowing in His enviable estate as an absolute monarch in paradise. As for this Volmar, we think him less fit to adorn a counsel chamber than the city jail."

The King looked on their twitterings thoughtfully. Before this all-impudent black crow of a Volmar these counsellors were like fluttered humming-birds. Then the King turned toward Volmar the humorously grave face of a young poet. He smiled, confidentially. And Volmar knew of a sudden that Volmar exceedingly loved this fine lad.

"You at least," said King Feodor, "you proclaim yourself to be a liar before offering your counsel. I admire that gambit. So do you now tell me about this Sonia."

Volmar smiled back at him. That Volmar winked at King Feodor may be dismissed as a legend not wholly substantiated. Then Volmar spoke about such of the tricks of Sonia as he most hated, denouncing her heart-troubling looks and her inconvenient piety and her wheedling soft kindness toward everybody and her high-spirited intolerance of warm human iniquity. The King listened with attention.

"You have told," said King Feodor, by-and-by, "of that woman who shall be my wife, if indeed I can learn to be worthy of her."

"That," Volmar replied, "you can never do, so unmanlike and so high-minded are the ways of this brightly colored idiot's living. Yet in your appearance, and in your wealth, and in your worldly estate, and in the clean soul which you still keep, I esteem you to be less unfit to marry this detestable woman than is any other man now breathing. With that we must be content."

The King answered, "Your approval gratifies me."

"Oh, but I have found many kings to be decent enough people when they are properly handled," replied Volmar. "I am not narrow-minded about royal persons. Some of my best friends are kings."

"Meanwhile," young Feodor continued, "if it indeed has so happened that truth has been brought to my court by a stray pedlar and a drunken liar, it is right that this pleasingly inappropriate couple should bring beauty also. You two shall be my ambassadors to the court of Osnia."

They passed then into a six-sided hall which was paved with marble of two colors, and of which the walls were covered by pallid green tapestries embroidered with basilisks and wyverns and hippogriffins worked in threads of pale gold and of silver, the eyes of each monster being made of seed pearls and emeralds. There six trumpets were sounded. Then the young King ennobled Volmar and Mr. Smith, making them respectively the lords of Druim and of Achren, and assigning to each of them a suitable estate.

"—With the proviso," King Feodor added, "that if you do not bring back the Princess Sonia to be my wife, each one of you shall be sewed up in a sack of quicklime and cast living into the sea, so that you may be both burned and drowned. That only shall be your inheritance tax."

Then he sent these two to be his ambassadors in the realm of Osnia. And Mr. Smith put aside his pedlar's pack, remarking that his stock of small leaden keys did not harmonize with his present estate as Lord of Achren.

*   *

FOURTEEN

OBSERVATIONS IN OSNIA

*

You are welcome, fair lords," said King Ludwig, "and to no living well-to-do monarch would I give my dear daughter more willingly than to the young King of Rorn. Yet, so far as goes my decision, the making up of my mind must rest, as it customarily does rest, with her."

"But that, your majesty," observed Mr. Smith, the newly created Lord of Achren, "that is hardly the approved way in which we shrewd plenipotentiaries set about the arranging of any royal marriage. No, for we must first have protocols, I believe—whatever they may happen to be,—and indentures, and treaties, and diplomacies, and compacts, and perfidies, and affidations, and a large lot of signatures, rather than a mere girl's mere say-so. Let us do things in order and with proper ceremony."

The King answered him, compassionately, "Nevertheless, my Lord of Achren, I can detect in you the chastened, the optimistic, the even adventurous air of a widower."

"It is true, your majesty," replied Mr. Smith, "that, in my time, I have lost a wife or so. If I do not speak a bit more definitely as to these inexpressible distresses, that is due to no lack of candor, believe me, but simply to the fact that I was not ever very good at arithmetic."

"Talking then as one widower to another," the King continued, "let me assure you that Sonia takes after her sainted mother in everything,—except, now I think of it, people have been kind enough to remark that her intelligence and her keen sense of humor and her sweet disposition come from my side of the family."

"I can quite understand your majesty," declared Mr. Smith, with a magnanimous sad sympathy, "for marriage, howsoever steadily it may deepen discomfort and heighten the bitterness of an argument, does broaden the mind."

"Do you think so, my Lord of Achren? Now, to the contrary, it was my experience that marriage made a man feel rather too much like a goose."

"In fact, your majesty, the goose—or, in any event, the gander—does prefer a seraglio—"

"No, no, but I did not mean that at all."

"Yet it is true," Mr. Smith went on, equably, "that, irrespective of the gander's gay gallivanting, a pairing for life—and, in brief, a true marriage—is the custom of many birds. I except of course the Gallinaceous family."

"Indeed, and why should you not except them?" said King Ludwig.

"But not," Mr. Smith stated, with firmness, "the majority of Mammals. The union of the male and the female is of a durable and monogamous character among gazelles, moles, squirrels, whales, hippopotami, seals, reindeer, and, in all probability, wolves."

"Your observations," replied King Ludwig, "are no doubt truthful; in any case, they arouse in me an interest more easily perceived than described. Yet after all, my Lord of Achren, just what have the family affairs of wolves and gazelles and squirrels to do with my daughter's marriage?"

"All facts, your majesty, are of considerable interest to a sound logician—"

"Yes, but—" the King interrupted, as with both hands he distractedly rumpled his gray hair.

"And when I say 'considerable,' I mean worthy of being considered—"

"It is far more to the point," the King answered, "to consider what Sonia considers in regard to those considerations which have prompted me to consider favorably the considerate offer of the King of Osnia. And if my talking is mixed up, why, that is simply because you have considerably upset me, my Lord of Achren, by ding-ding-dinging away until the not-ever-resting sound of your tongue has almost led me to believe that my dear Sonia's sainted mother has brought back all her hard-headedness out of paradise to bemuddle up the entire matter. So, in God's name, let us now stop talking, for this while, about your whales and your gazelles and your ganders."

They summoned Sonia. She came. She walked as daintily as a white hind, Volmar reflected. It was not suitable that the eyes of this repulsive young prude should be as clear and as steady as the eyes of a falcon; or that the whiteness of her skin should dazzle your own eyes; or that it should trouble your thoughts also, with speculations as to its probable softness.

Well, and when she had heard the King of Rorn's message, she smiled very graciously upon his two ambassadors. That she did not recognize Volmar, in his bright finery, was a fact so self-evident that the new Lord of Druim could almost, but not quite, believe that in sober earnest this abominable woman did not recognize him.

"Your master," she declared, modestly, "has honored me beyond my poor merits. My gratitude shall repay his generosity. And it is a good omen, my Lord of Achren"—she said, to Mr. Smith—"that in many dreams I have seen your face before this fine fortunate morning."

He returned, "That is likely; for I live in many dreams just at present."

"Now I," said King Ludwig, "I find more of the familiar in the face of my Lord of Druim. He has somewhat the look of that Volmar whose loud tongue fetched him at long last to our dung-heap."

"It is possible that my Lord of Druim is thus afflicted," replied the Princess; "but I cannot judge the resemblance, because I have quite forgotten this Volmar, and he keeps no place in my thoughts."

She made ready then to depart with the two ambassadors; and after them followed the usual dowry of a princess of Osnia, in the form of twenty-nine oaken wagons laden with white silver and red gold and with precious stones of eleven kinds.

*   *

FIFTEEN

REMARKS ON THE FRONTIER

*

But how, pray, should a mere braggart and a foul-mouthed liar come to be Lord of Druim?" the Princess Sonia demanded of Volmar.

They had now quitted her father's kingdom, turning toward the stony uplands of Laczo, where the strong fortress of Toysan stood gray and turreted on a gray hill.

Volmar replied, "It was the inspiration of a young poet, O most detestable of women, to decree me a nobleman because I brought to him truth; and because I promised to bring him beauty also, riding beside me, upon the saddle of your horse."

"So!" said the Princess, without seeming displeased by his candor beyond the point whence forgiveness might be hoped for. "And what manner of man is this misguided young poet?"

Volmar told her: and as he spoke of her husband that was to be, he talked with a noble fervor. In his time Volmar had foregathered indulgently with eight kings and with scores of fine warriors and with at least three world-famous poets whose songs Volmar admitted to be so-so: but no one of these applauded persons had ever captured his fancy as did the greathearted, grave, innocent, young Feodor who was king over Rorn. And in consequence, Volmar's speaking, as it were, now clapped the hands of enthusiasm to the ribs of dejected reason, in order to play leapfrog upon the extreme limits of eulogy.

"I can but assure you, most fortunate of women," Volmar perorated, "that for your special benefit Galahad has come out of his legend to live again on this sinful earth."

"Every woman must admire Galahad, of course," remarked Sonia, without any remarkable conviction. "I am not certain that every woman would want, quite, to marry him."

"But, you ungrateful creature, no sane woman could demand more in the way of a husband!"

"My point is, Volmar, that a sane woman might conceivably beg for less. So! and has your young master no faults at all?"

"He has none," said Volmar.

"Oh, very well! Then I am blessed very far beyond my deserts," replied Sonia, "and, it may be, a little way beyond my wishes."

But at this time they were interrupted. For they had now passed, by a narrow road through some brooks and marshes, into Tarob, a kingdom which Mr. Smith had visited, in the capacity of a pedlar, before to-day.

He was thus able to inform his companions that Tarob was a place famous for its fine pearls, a place where the houses were all roofed with turtle shells, and a place too where the King was not permitted to beget any children. Should he break this law, then the King must be thrown down into a pit in which had been placed a tigress, an asp, and a wild stallion.

—Which reminded Mr. Smith of the fact (a fact which he regarded as being of considerable interest to a sound logician) that kings were very often subjected to such rules of etiquette as tended to emphasize the unique social position of a monarch rather than to increase the comforts of his existence. Thus as in Egypt (Mr. Smith pointed out) the Pharaohs were permitted to eat no flesh except that of the calf and of the goose, so in Ireland the Kings of Connaught were commanded not ever to wear speckled garments, and the Kings of Ulster were forbidden to attend a horse fair. In Madagascar the King was not allowed to enter a boat or to cross running water—upon, doubtless, a variant of the same principle by which in Dahomey the King was at once dethroned and killed if he looked at the ocean. Most hidebound of all monarchs, however, Mr. Smith estimated to be the Mikado of Japan (or, to speak properly, the Tenno, inasmuch as "Mikado" was a metonymy, and meant actually "the exalted gate," Mr. Smith paused to explain), who was not let ever to place his foot on the ground; who must be bathed by other persons during his sleep; and whom the laws of his kingdom forbid ever to trim his hair, his beard or his finger-nails.

The instructive remarks of Mr. Smith were truncated, at this exact moment, by the King of Tarob himself, who came riding out to meet them attended by seven trumpeters and a troop of fine-looking boys. He wore a violet-colored satin tunic fastened about his waist with a belt of chastity, to which the keys were attached; his mantle was of gold tissue embroidered with purple moons; and on his proud head was a large scarlet hat embroidered with prancing golden lions. In his habiting this King Lithuel the Second was wholly splendid; and his nightly habits concerned only himself and his maker.

Moreover, all his city, and the granite castle he lived in, had been hung with bright-colored banners and tapestries and with red and white garlands. The banquet which King Lithuel tendered, on that clear summer evening, to the betrothed wife of King Feodor of Rorn was incredibly served. None can describe the profusion of dishes, the abundance of meats both stewed and roasted, the variety of fish, the diversity of wines, the performance of the jugglers and the poets laureate, or the dignity of the butlers, because all that Tarob and the King of Tarob's luxuriant imagination could produce of elegance, of splendor, of tact, and of merriment, was to be seen at this banquet.

Said Volmar: "The polite wise world honors every

woman who prevents its monarchs from sleeping too much. Yes, Lady, I have arranged for you a match which well shows my loving-kindness in overlooking your hard-headedness and your bad temper."

And Sonia, apart from making a face at him, replied nothing, at this time.

* *

SIXTEEN

THE QUEEN'S PROGRESS

*

Then in Melphé the betrothed wife of King Feodor was entertained in superb form by Duke Philibert, who by the late murder of his nephew Cosimo the Well-Loved had made firm the Duke's guidance of all social gaieties. So in this place, for her entertainment, was enacted a masque, in which the Seven Virtues and the Three Graces and the Nine Muses tendered homage to Queen Sonia. These abstractions were realized by the duchy's best-thought-of professional harlots, who appeared in very brightly gilded chariots drawn by centaurs, dragons, hippogriffins, negroes, doctors of divinity and camels, and by eunuchs with lovely soprano voices, so that Duke Philibert's hospitality lacked for nothing in the way of magnificence.

Moreover, he gave to Sonia an embossed plate of gold, about the size of a carriage wheel, upon which was represented the history of Helios, and a yet larger plate of silver upon which were shown the exploits of Artemis.

99

"Everywhere the great lords of earth," said Volmar, "have combined with one another to see which potentate can most liberally honor the wife of King Feodor. And so, by arranging this match for you, I have atoned for my misdeeds quite handsomely. Yes, even though I lied in saying that you had given me your fancy, because of that afternoon in the orchard—"

"I do not remember," said the Princess, crisply, "anything which happened in my father's orchard upon that Thursday afternoon, or at any other time."

"And in fact," remarked Mr. Smith, soothingly, "as a betrothed queen, it is your royal duty to forget all such occurrences."

But Volmar cried out, in anger: "Very well, then, even though I lied in saying that you had given me your fancy, and that until life ends, you will be remembering me with love, yet it is I and none other who have got for you, most hateful and most forgetful of women, a young king of men to be your husband. And may Heaven grant him the patience to put up with you!"

"Oho, and besides that, self-seeking and swindling Volmar, you have got for yourself a lordship and the estates which the King will give you when you deliver to him my body."

"You are a lewd-minded woman, Sonia, always to be thinking about your body! And it would much better become you to be thanking me for making you a great queen in well-to-do Rorn. Only last week you were nothing but a two-penny princess in little Osnia."

"You are being well paid for it, you thrifty servant, with your lordship over Druim."

"And besides that," declared Volmar, "I have seen, in Auster, and in yet other places, dozens upon dozens of women with far handsomer bodies."

She replied to this statement, as a digression, by returning to the real point at issue. She remarked, loftily:

"Yes, it is you, Volmar, who ought to be thanking King Feodor for his great foolishness in creating you Lord of Druim, as if anybody could make a silk purse out of a sow's ear; and for so causing me to think poorly of my husband before I had ever even seen him."

"Oh, but come now—!" said Mr. Smith, ineffectively.

For Volmar was shouting, with frank fury: "It is not your body but your heart also that you will be giving to my master, you abominable creature, when once you have beheld his excellence! Yes, you will remember to do that, no matter how much else you may have forgotten!"

"It is you who forget yourself, Volmar, when you dare to bellow at me in that way. Yes, and you forget also everything which you ever said in an orchard."

"Do you stop lying, most untruthful of women! I keep firm my memories! Now may God smite me dead

if ever I have forgotten any least word that passed
between us, or any moment I shared with you, you
wicked silken Sapphira! you king's tidbit!"

"You absurd Volmar," she replied, smiling, upon
a sudden, for reasons which were best known to herself, "and is it certain that I must love this young
Feodor quite as entirely as you love him?"

"But I do not love him, you minx, you jill-flirt,
you harridan! Rather, it is hatred which possesses
me when I look on this great-hearted young champion
and perceive in him all that I might have been and
shall never be. Rather, it is hatred which possesses me
when I think that this man merits all your abominable perfections."

So unbounded was the atrocious woman's unreason that, under the pelting of Volmar's abuse, she
continued to smile happily.

"Come now," said Sonia, "but let us be more wise,
and discuss other matters than the undying dislike
which we have for each other."

"Ah, ah!" declared Mr. Smith, "but, at last, one of
you has said something sensible. Let us by all means
talk about other matters. It is the peculiar blessing of
man that, even though he has five senses with which
to acquire knowledge, and a brain with which to
make reflections, he has likewise a vocabulary with
which to edit any awkward results."

Volmar grunted. Volmar said then,—

"But what is there to talk about?"

"Everything," replied Mr. Smith, with enthusiasm.

—Whereafter he proceeded to demonstrate the at least partial truth of his statement. For Mr. Smith, now that he had touched on the great importance of mankind's vocabulary, began talking about the odd fact that no tribe of American Indians, howsoever large their vocabulary, appeared to have practised any regular system of writing; and he quoted the five theories by which scientists have accounted for the omission. He spoke also of the *couvade*, customary among the Carib Indians, by which, when a child was born, the father was brought to bed instead of the mother; and he passed on to consider the equally strange crowning of Inez de Castro as the lawful Queen of Portugal several years after her death. Why was it, in point of fact, Mr. Smith then debated, that washing was injurious to pearls? and just how far north did the redbird migrate in spring? He deduced that the most probable answers were: (*a*) on account of the concentric layers of the pearl; and (*b*) Massachusetts.

He next mentioned, as a fact of not inconsiderable interest to a sound logician, that Mount Fujiyama was 12,395 feet in height; told why milk boiled more quickly than water; explained the difference between a concerto and a symphony; and he talked eloquently about the dolphin (or *Coryphæna hippurus*) both as a conventional symbol in printing and in candlesticks and as a prognosticator, in marine credence, of fair

103

weather and of white-capped waves and of cloudless blue skies.

Very deeply engrossed by the informative nature of Mr. Smith's remarks, the three of them (in the same instant that Mr. Smith finished telling about how the cushions used in upholstering came to be called squabs) reached a broad muddied river shining like brass in the sunlight. Fording this river, the Amio, they rode up, across fields which were overgrown with blue-flowering heather, into the city of Sorram. This town was girdled with olive-trees and mulberry-trees, and well fortified with white stone towers. Here they were met by the King of Ecben in person, who came piously with an abbot riding on each side of him; and before him walked four clerks, each clothed in long robes of lamb-skin and carrying a leaden sword, because the realm was at peace with all other kingdoms this week.

They attended mass here, first at the convent church of St. Clara, and afterward at the cathedral church of St. Agnan. But the feasting was different in Sorram, because of the old custom of Ecben that the men sat at table with men, while the ladies ate together in another banqueting hall, which was walled with engraved plates of silver that depicted the misfortunes of Alfgar, who had once reigned over this same kingdom.

*   *

SEVENTEEN

PARTING IN ANGER

*

So they came uneventfully, upon the next afternoon but one, to where the charmed forest of Branlon stood between the kingdoms of Ecben and Rorn.

"Let us pause here," said Volmar, when they had reached a deserted smithy.

"You select an uncheering spot," returned Mr. Smith, "where desolation alone woos the regard. And yet, truly, it is well for us to sip, rather than to gulp, our advancement. We need but one step onward, over the invisible line between Ecben and Rorn, to step up in this world rather dizzily. A step more, and we are in the semi-fabulous kingdom of Rorn. Through that step you become a queen, Lady Sonia. A step more, and Volmar and I, with our embassy discharged, and with the uncaptivating off-chance of being sewed up alive in a sack of quicklime dismissed, will become very great lords in reality as well as in title, the each one owning his castles, his desmesnes, his manors—"

"Now but do you stop talking for one half-minute," said Volmar, "if you find such a thing to be possible."

"Why, pray, should the all-envied, proud Lord of Achren not talk at his own will about facts which are of considerable interest to a sound logician?" Mr. Smith demanded; and he continued, equably:

"Also his warrens, his parks, his woodlands, his messuages, his fishings, his peasantry, his *droits de seigneur,* and all the other appurtenances of a snug nobleman. No, my dear Lord of Druim; I shall not keep silence; for admiration finds here its food. In such circumstances it really does behoove us, I submit, to acclaim the wonders of geography; and to applaud without any glum backwardness the injustice of our good fortune. In short, upon this engagingly funereal occasion, which marks the decease of all sorrow and trouble, we ought to step out of Ecben with the solemnity of rejoicing pall-bearers."

"Ah, but for one," replied Volmar, "I shall not step at all; and you two must go forward without me. To become a blacksmith has long been my ambition; it was the dream of my boyhood: and in this smithy I intend to fulfill my desire."

Now Mr. Smith shook his divine head; and he emitted the brief low whistle of a dignified reflectiveness upon the dissatisfying.

"Truly," remarked Mr. Smith, "the arts of Urc Tabaron are dependable. So it is in this manner that he compels you to make your home in Branlon. . . Well! I assent; and yet it does seem a trifle unfair to the all-envied, proud Lord of Druim."

"This thing is in no way reasonable," said Sonia, "that on a sudden the Lord of Druim should become a blacksmith."

The gross eyebrows of Volmar puckered. His face scowled. And he said, sullenly,—

"Nevertheless, Lady, it does not suit me to enter the kingdom of Rorn, now that the woman whom I most dislike of all women living is to be Queen over Rorn."

Then Sonia came to him, with a little laugh which was half a sob; and her eyes were very bright, and all her bright-colored small face seemed wholly wonderful. She took his hand, saying:

"Let there be friendship between us, Volmar, putting the past aside. Out of that ancient lie which you spoke in my father's hall has come for you a wide lordship and much wealth, and for me a kingdom and a champion without any stain to be my husband. The old evil has turned somehow into good; and so let our sharp enmity turn now into friendship."

He replied: "I have got for you a young king of men to be your bedfellow. And now"—his face changed—"now that I bring you to King Feodor's bedside, I perceive that I detest you more than I had suspected, Sonia, O my lost Sonia, and I cannot go forward to witness your happiness."

She appeared startled and a little troubled. But she said only,—

"You speak in riddles, Volmar."

"Indeed," said Mr. Smith, "I believe that the Lord of Druim speaks of a most ancient riddle. And I could give a guess at its name."

"It is called hatred," Volmar returned. "I dislike this woman so much that I am not content to be a well-thought-of baron, and her husband's servant, in any kingdom of which this woman is the queen. I prefer to remain here in Ecben as a blacksmith or, if the need be, to go as a vagabond into wild places where I shall not be seeing her detestable face or be thinking about her golden-brown eyes and her hateful milk-white body. So do you ride forward with her, Lord of Achren. Do you deliver her soft, sweet, dear, damnable, paltry abominable body to King Feodor. And I will await your return here in this smithy."

Long and steadfastly the Princess looked up at Volmar. Her large eyes were not friendly now. There was in them only a doubtfulness and a half-frightened wondering. She said then:

"O most perverse and most stubborn man, I am well rid of you, for your ways trouble me beyond endurance. So I will go now to become a crowned queen in whose thoughts there is no place for a drunken liar."

*　　*

EIGHTEEN

THE TRUTH OF IT

*

Volmar sat late at the door of his smithy. There was no moon; darkness lay about him; but overhead all the stars of heaven seemed flaring and vibrant, in the while that Volmar regarded them and thought gravely about celestial deficiencies. Yes; it was undeniable that the Great Dipper needed a very much brighter star in the place of Megrez, so as to keep the outline of the Great Dipper distinct and uniform, nor did it appear pardonable for Orion to be wearing his sword on the wrong side, or for Cassiopeia, who was a great queen, but you must not think about queens, to have a chair which was rickety and back-breaking to sit in, even though these celestial blunders were not the concerns proper to a blacksmith, who must not think above his station, who must not think about the most lovely and dear of all human faces, but only about horses. Yes, you must think very resolutely about horses.

There had been Pegasus, and Caligula's horse, and the Wooden Horse of Troy, and Mahomet's horse, and Alexander the Great's horse, and the nightmare, and Balaam's ass, although the true nightmare would henceforward be to dream about the most lovely and dear of all human faces, knowing that you would not ever again see the detestable creature, and quarrel with her, and provoke her so that a clear patch of red would flare on each of the high cheekbones deliciously. But no horse was of that delicious delicate color, about which a blacksmith had no more reason to think than he had to think about the doings of a king and a queen when they in bed together, oh, God, but you could not endure the thought of those royal doings! You could only long to break, and to hurt, and to torture unhurriedly, without killing either one of them, until you had quite requited such lechery. So you must think about other matters, if but for your own sanity's health, Volmar decided; and he groaned aloud.

"Well, at all events," said Volmar, "there is more happiness in Rorn than there is in my smithy. And I have served for their own good the King and the Queen of that kingdom loyally."

"But there is no queen in Rorn," said a tiny voice.

Then Volmar uttered a half-frightened cry; and his arms clasped about Sonia before he had recollected this was a person whom he peculiarly hated. He thrust her away from him, and he shouted,—

"Why do you return to be plaguing me?"

"It was merely," said, in the darkness, the urbane voice of Mr. Smith, "that the new Queen of Rorn, just before we reached Garian, thought of a fact which might ease your conscience. So she has mercifully returned to tell you about that fact, because all facts are of considerable interest to a sound logician."

"It was merely," said Sonia's voice, "that, as we were riding along, I thought about the bold lie which you told in my father's great hall publicly."

Volmar said: "I have paid for that bragging lie with a life's failure. Because of it, I, who might have been Lord of Druim—yes, and a not ever troubled demi-god in Auster likewise—stand here, a mere black-smith, without any honor in this world, and with a dead heart inside me. That ought to content you, Sonia."

"The wealth and the high station which you have flung away, hard-headed Volmar, content me,—ah, but quite utterly do they content me! Yet you said then that I had given you my fancy, and that until life ends, I would be remembering you with love."

"I spoke infamy, babbling a sot's drunken lies," replied Volmar; "and so, after all this while, you must be returning to remind me of my infamy. That is very like you, most hateful of women."

"Oh, stubborn and most foolish of all living crea-tures, save only one creature, perhaps," replied Sonia, laughing somewhat ruefully, "but it occurred to me, just as we were riding along, and when there was not much else to think about, that you had spoken the truth."

He cried out, hoarsely: "Do not tempt me, Queen of Rorn! Do not mock my exceeding folly!"

"But here is no Queen of Rorn," her grave sweet voice declared, steadfastly, and without any hesitating, in the kindly darkness. "Here is only a stubborn and a very foolish girl who dislikes you and your childish blustering weakness, O my dearest, with all her judgment, and who yet loves you—Volmar the Sober Truth-Speaker—with all her heart."

"There is no reasonableness in her love," he returned, sombrely, "because there is no reasonableness in me, and not much control over myself either."

She admitted this, saying—with a small, wonderful, low outburst of laughter,—"No."

Then the man said: "If there be any happiness in the time to come, Sonia, that will be a miracle and no less. Out of the dark I cry to you, my one love: and I say, Beware of Volmar! I say that I shall strive to be worthy of you, O my dear Sonia. And I say also that I shall fail. I cry to you, in the while that my arm goes about you, Do you leave me, Sonia! Do you not put any faith in Volmar!"

She replied, with strange soberness: "And I also shall fail you, perhaps. I shall turn even more quick-tempered, it may be; and when I am angry, why, then no doubt, I shall talk endlessly about the grand Feodor whom I might have married. Yes, that is very likely, Volmar; we both know far too well how to hurt each other: and the veiled future frightens me as I speak here with you, thus truthfully, in this deep darkness. We shall have our one hour of happiness; and after that will follow, as I fear, O my dearest, our black misery, black as this darkness."

"Do you be wise, Sonia! for in Garian a fine throne and a young king of men await you."

"But in this ruined dark smithy, Volmar, I find love and you whom I choose without overmuch hope-fulness—and yet without any faltering either. There is no joy in my heart, O wild-hearted Volmar, now that I lay this cold hand of mine upon your hot large hand, but only a distrust of you and of your doings in the bleak time to come, and a strong need of you. Even from that first day of ours, in my father's orchard, it was true that I had given you my fancy along with my distrust. Yes, and it remains true, O very dear, weak, loud-tongued Volmar, that until my life ends, I shall be remembering you with love,—at all times of course, except when we are quarreling."

Then Volmar said, "Do you go away, Mr. Smith, and leave the two of us doomed persons together."

"Indeed," replied Mr. Smith, "I suspect that Urc Tabaron has been a little rash in this special match-making. Nevertheless, my dear boy, I obey you."

PART THREE

THE BOOK OF ELAIR

* *

*

"Consolidation of the railways of Evain, comprising 3,028 miles, formerly operated by twenty-six companies, into one operating company known as the Stairth & Branlon Rapid Transit, Inc., was completed early in 1932, under the direction of seven financial genii. The authorized capital in 1934 was £38,911,604; gross receipts £4,979,809; operating expenditures £46,154,181. Vessels entering the five ports of Evain in 1934 numbered 13,629 (including sailing vessels and the galleons of romance) of 8,682,470 tons."

*   *

NINETEEN

HOW THEY QUESTED

*

Now the tale speaks of the second magic of Urc Tabaron, telling how Fergail, the young Queen of Evain, let it be known in the lands beyond commonsense that she would become the wife of him who brought to her the charm, or the elixir—or, in brief, a thaumaturgy of any sort—by which her youth might be made steadfast.

There was no woman more comely than Fergail. Her wealth in oaken houses, in tilled lands, and in white and black cattle, was beyond counting; so likewise were the numbers of men that wooed her. But now, because of the second magic of Urc Tabaron, now in the mind of Fergail moved a gray thought of how patiently time waited to despoil her of all such pleasantries; and in the Queen's silver mirror smiled back at her a fair-colored assurance that so long as youth lasted, in a worldful of persuadable male creatures, Fergail need lack the fulfilling of no desire.

She summoned her druids. In their presence she laid both hands on the private parts of the image which was called the Red Stallion of Stairth, and she made publicly that oath which only the queens and the kings of Evain might make, and, breaking which, they also must be broken, into four pieces. Fergail thus made her oath to marry the champion who should procure for her a dependable magic by which, in derision of time's malice, her young beauty would be made perpetual.

Hearing her, Elair the Song-Maker laughed high-heartedly. He got ready his horse, his sword, his fine harp of maple-wood, and his pistols. After that, he rode out of Evain, well armed in all respects except that upon his head showed a wreath of rowan berries in place of a helmet. He rode eastward, thinking always about the sea-green color of Fergail's eyes and about the red color in the curved lips of Fergail and about the clear gold of young Fergail's hair. There was not in this world her twin for loveliness.

Thus likewise, upon the highways and down the pleasant lanes of the lands beyond common-sense, rode yet other enamored horsemen. Among them were kings and princes, a brace of fine emperors, and many dozens of lean poets and burly men-at-arms, each one of them led by his desire of Fergail and by memories of her bright beauty. To all these came adventures, and to some of these came death, in their searching for a magic which would make eternal the dear youth of Fergail: but with none of these men have we any concern.

HOW THEY QUESTED

The tale follows Elair the Song-Maker, whom the Master of Gods begot upon Airel, a conversation woman; and the tale narrates how Elair rode out of Evain, looking for Urc Tabaron and for such aid as this wizard had once given in the old days to Elair's mother, Airel of the Brown Hair.

TWENTY

*   *

LANDS BEYOND COMMON-SENSE

*

Now in those days to be a young champion riding at adventure through the traditionary lands beyond common-sense, upon that immemorial business of a champion, the pursuit of a quest, was a fine calling, with few idle moments in it. The countryside abounded in matters of interest; and the local doings afforded to the wayfarer every one of the more handsome improbabilities of romance.

There was hardly a bush by the roadway but concealed, until you had come to it, a meddlesome sorcerer, or a dragon unamiably prepared to have lunch with you, or a metallically clothed gentleman, with his visor down and his lance ready, politely desirous of a combat to support the contention that his lady in domnei was the most fair and worshipful of this world's ladies. Nor was it only in the meadows and the lowlands that adventure prospered, because upon at least one hill out of every three hills stood a castle which either diffused, or else was beset by, this or the other kind of enchantment.

Of these castles some were square-shaped, gray stone fortresses, having at each corner a round tower capped with a shining, steeply pointed lead roof; and about such castles were moats filled with clear water in which swam red fish and white fish. Yet other castles, builded throughout of marble, arose to a superb flowering into pinnacles and into vaporous looking domes, which seemed like huge bubbles moored overhead; and these castles stood among very broad terraces of marble which were guarded only by large lions carved variously in the old purple porphyry of Egypt and in the green porphyry of Greece. Still other castles, erected by architects more ambiguous, were to the eye of the traveller just shining black precipices, with remote clouds floating—in an indescribably sinister manner—about and into their lower windows. But in each castle lived wonder and beauty and danger.

And about the highways also roved these three, so that at every bend of his road the glories and the prettiness and the quaint horrors of myth now jostled Elair's passing. To begin with, from a broad clump of elder-bushes, a centaur arose, tilted back rather remarkably until his hind legs were up, to grin at Elair in pleased surprise. Then witches, bloated with dropsy, croaked to him like foul frogs, telling about the worshipped joys of their wickedness. And a golden cat sang to Elair the strange tale of this cat's love for a wood nymph and of her partial response to this love.

To Elair came Luridan, in the likeness of a slim boy who was rather unpleasantly beautiful. His eyes sparkled under delicate arched brows; his lips were like coral. He chaunted those fatal songs which, under the name of Behelah, he had made very long ago in Jerusalem, in the days of Solomon; and Luridan chaunted also the poems and the false prophecies which he made in Cymry, where he was called Wadd. All these were most poisonous songs which tempted their hearer to follow after Luridan to a foreknown but delicious destruction. But after Luridan now followed, instead, a great tawny man, having the thighs and the legs of a goat; and this Balkin, who was Lord of the Northern Mountains, made safe the road of Elair, with a large flaming broom, which swept away Luridan and destroyed his bad loveliness, for that while.

A young emperor, in a purple robe embroidered in scarlet with the twelve signs of the Zodiac, each displayed upside down, whispered to Elair about that desire which had drawn down this lost whisperer into the Place of the Crocodiles, and about how that desire had been satiated in a musk-smelling twilight. In a pavilion of shining stone, having a cupola of alabaster, and containing a pillar of fretted gold upon which stood the figure of a golden bird with a diamond serpent in its beak, a naked dark woman, who was wholly beautiful except for the fact that her feet were affixed backwards, clung to Elair's elbow in the while that she lamented the ill bargain which had procured for her an immortal soul. And a crowned maiden came to him in such royal robes as were once worn in Babylon, carrying a cushion of green velvet. On it lay a stone which shone with a great light. Behind her walked six maidens in white robes, who carried torches of transparent glass in which burned balsam. They told him of the stone's virtues, offering it to Elair at a price which he declined to pay.

And in Nettan, Elair rode for some while with a company of such beings as hunted the unicorns of Nettan. All these, of course, were deaf-mutes, with long yellow hair; and they wore, as was customary, their mantles of green and bright silver shoes. They carried bows made from the rib-bones of their mortal enemies; their arrows were of bog-wood tipped with white flint and dipped in the dew of hemlock; their quivers were fashioned of snake-skin. Such was the appearance and the gear of these deaf-mutes; but of their needs and of their doings, among the rose-colored cliffs of Nettan, perhaps the less said, the better.

Moreover, with the affairs of one or another royal family—families which to a noteworthy degree inclined to consist of a golden-haired princess, of three princes, of two brunette step-sisters, of an industriously abominable stepmother, and of a king with a weakness for asking riddles—the incidents of travel involved Elair time and again.

And Elair the Song-Maker liked it all. Elair entered

with such wholeheartedness into the traditionary avo-
cations of a young champion embarked on a quest
that, were his combats, his imbroglios, his temptations
(all which he resisted nobly), his traffic with super-
natural creatures, his destructions of monsters, his res-
cues of harried innocence, and his unimaginative dis-
plays of the more superb virtues in general, all written
down in this tale, the depressing result would be one
of the longest books to be found anywhere in the
libraries of an already sufficiently afflicted world. For
great-thewed Elair had every heroic attribute, such
as altruism, and bravery, and courtesy, and dulness,
and earnestness, and fidelity—and so on, down through
the entire alphabet, to and including zeal. Each one
of these attributes he displayed, over and yet over
again, in the while that he quested after a magic which
would make steadfast the youth of Fergail.

Well, and he inherited, now and then, from the depraved ogres and tyrants and sorcerers whom at odd
times he killed, a number of wonder-working trinkets.
But no one of these charms, it so happened, served to
secure youth's eternalness. Elair the Song-Maker got
only a resistless sword, and a talking harp, and a blue
pigeon which at its owner's request would lay instead
of eggs three large pigeon-blood rubies; and he got
also an ever-filled purse (which was made from the
skin of a mantichora), and one or two other marvels.

But each one of these marvels Elair the Song-Maker
left punctiliously beside the corpse of its late owner.

"The son of sublime SMIRT should rely on his own worth and his own powers," said Elair. "As SMIRT's son, I may not becomingly depend on such cheating kickshaws to make my way in the world. Yet as a lover, I have sore need of that magic which will make steadfast the youth of Fergail, and so win for me the beauty of Fergail, to whom I have sworn eternal fidelity."

* *

TWENTY-ONE

WOMEN BY THE WAY

*

At one time Elair came to a thick hedge of fire-thorn bushes, which was so tall that it reached up high above his rowan-crowned black head as he rode toward this hedge; and there was a mistiness all about the place. But he found an opening, and he got through it into an open space that was overgrown with ferns and small purple flowers, and in this meadow he saw a tent of red satin. Beside the open door of this tent stood a pear-tree in full blossom—which did not seem reasonable at this time of the year,—and on a branch of this pear-tree was hung a hunting-horn of silver.

Elair sounded this horn defiantly. Out of the tent came at once a great black man. He had bright yellow hair and sparkling red eyes, and he carried a large iron club studded with nails. So Elair had drawn one of his pistols when a sweet voice spoke, from inside the tent, saying,—

"Do you go away, Gabron!"

And with that, the black giant grinned. He panted seven or eight times, like a very friendly and much magnified dog, in the while that he turned himself into a black cloud; and he so vanished.

Then Elair put up the pistol, which was not the weapon one needed. He went laughingly into the red tent; and he stayed in that place all night, among great pillows of swans' down, in a broad bed made out of yew-wood and ivory, with an immortal woman, who was called, as she told him, Morgaine la Fée.

And another time, after Elair had come to Abradas, the old Emperor Basil and the young Empress Eudocia asked for one of those songs which had brought famousness to Elair the Song-Maker in all the lands beyond common-sense.

"Hearing," remarked Elair, tolerantly, "is obedience. But about what shall I sing, O sublimities and twin radiances of the age?"

"The theme does not matter," said the old Emperor, whose views as to art were, of course, of an old-fashioned and frivolous type. "The treatment alone matters. Do you sing at your own will, Elair, about anything under the sun, so that you favor us with a fair taste of your quality."

"Before any audience so exalted," replied Elair, with continued politeness, as he took up his fine harp of maple-wood, "I may not rationally stoop thus low for my subject matter. It follows that I must sing about the sun's self."

And he did. In fact, before a king and a queen, Elair almost always sang this song about the sun, because it was so easily altered to fit any royal couple as to make them think this song an impromptu inspired in that very moment by their own excellence.

Now in this song Elair duly applauded the sun, as a ruddy and all-domineering overlord, ruling everywhere under the permission of his betters in Abradas; as a power of supreme majesty and stateliness, affable and benign and very famous in the myths of all nations; as a fine mathematician, who figured out the Solstice and the Equinox and the Sidereal Year without ever making an error; and yet as a most dreadful adversary, who faithfully smote his unfriends (so said all learned astrologists) with pimples, with palpitations of the heart, with cramps, with infirmities of the brain, with catarrhs, and with putrid fevers, in the while that the sun invaded each earthly kingdom every day, in search of no man might say what, like a gold-armored and all-terrible emperor, whose abilities were but slightly inferior to those of the great Emperor Basil.

In reply to this adroit compliment the old Emperor bowed gravely his white head, upon which was a shining crown with ten rubies in it.

Thus (continued Elair) thus intrepidly fared the sun, that all but omnipotent sun, whose self-complacency was yet checked by the glory of Basil, and whose splendors became mere futilities before the bright face of Eudocia, inasmuch as this Empress outshone the sun in beauty and in all other supremacies such as quickened holiness and high thoughts, where the sun (a mere market gardener, in comparison) thrilled seeds toward vegetating or, like the pursuer of a trade far more unmentionable, nudged the beasts and birds and insects—oh, but even the cold-blooded fish—into beginning a fresh love-affair every spring, at or about (through a coincidence oddly appropriate) the advent of All Fools' day.

The Empress had blushed; but she smiled also, as she looked down modestly at the point of her little green and white shoe.

Hey, but beside Basil was not this Phoebus a snuffed candle! Elair jeered, in his peroration. Alas, the speckled, the gross, the lechery-whelping Phoebus! the lumbering, lewd, gaudy pander to all zoölogy! tickling no less the huge elephant and the oily whale than the light gnat and the timid, tipped-tailed wren with his all-embracing lubricities! Into what shielding eclipse, or what bolster-thick snow clouds, might this round-faced and tawdry and tinselled vagabond vanish when the chaste and all-holy Eudocia appeared?

Their majesties both applauded.

Well, and after that, the young Empress Eudocia took a fancy to Elair; and she carried this fancy to such an extent that Elair himself noticed it, rather unavoidably. She coaxed him to sit upon her husband's throne; upon Elair's black head, over the wreath of rowan berries which he wore on account of his obligation, she put her husband's gold crown with the ten big rubies in it; and in the hand of Elair she put her husband's sceptre.

"For you, my dearest," said the fair Empress, "are the best song-maker in the whole world."

"Come, woman of the sweet lips, but let us not exaggerate, because even though I have not met him anywhere, still it may be that my equal does exist," replied Elair, modestly, as he removed her from his lap.

He then looked, with some little embarrassment, about the vast lonely throne room. This hall was barbarically painted everywhere with tall savage saints, each having the wounds and the blood of his martyrdom yet on him, but each wearing a breastplate or a necklace inset with precious stones; and the look of this holy company in general was of a character to chill the more tender emotions.

But Eudocia did not mind any mere saints. She continued, fondly embracing Elair,—

"Yes, and you are likewise the joy of my eyes and the flower of all beauty and the large consoler of my soul."

"Hah, but you are a crowned empress; and such talk does not befit your present station, madame," Elair replied, severely. "These remarks are much better suited to your bedchamber."

"I agree with you, desire of my heart," the Empress

answered, with a becoming humility; and she at once led him thither.

Yet the very next afternoon Elair parted from her, in unconcealed disapproval, because she had hired three able-bodied clergymen to drown the old Emperor Basil in his bathroom, so that Elair might become her second husband.

"The amenities of social life, the license of a poet, and that politeness which every young gentleman owes to all personable and inadequately married young gentlewomen," remarked Elair, "are one thing. But murder, madame, a prosaic murder in the purely utilitarian atmosphere of a bathroom, is quite another thing. No, you sad, silly, and too impetuous fond darling, I have no least desire to be an emperor. No, I have but one desire in this world: and the name of that desire is Fergail."

And yet another time, as Elair rode along by the broad bay of Meroë, he found four girls dancing there mother-naked on the smooth sand, and beside them lay five jackets made out of white feathers. When the girls saw Elair they screeched and they twittered, like frightened birds, in the while that they hastily put on these feather jackets. In this way they were all four changed into sea-gulls, and they flew away hurriedly. Now but one feather jacket remained; and Elair hid it in the tall beach-grass.

He saw then where a fifth girl lay asleep and unclothed in the sunlight. He awakened her amorously. She was much surprised; but matters had already gone so far that she amiably aided their conclusion before asking who Elair might be.

He told her his name and his parentage. When the proprieties had been thus observed, she began to display a naturally affectionate disposition. And it was a happy day of which Elair spent the sunlit remainder with this girl, who proved to be a daughter of King Morskoï.

"Now do you come with me, dear lover," said the girl Astrild, toward evening, "into my father's kingdom in the far isles of the ocean. For there is nothing of sorrow or of evil in that place, and all its colors are shining. Age will not ever take away your comeliness in the land of the Water Tzar, and his glittering people live safe beyond the gaunt reach of death."

"No," said Elair; "ah, no, my dear, but I was not meant for this paradise."

"Yet in my father's kingdom, O man of boldness, there is no care and no sorrow. All persons remain young there; the color of the wild rose is in their lips and in their cheeks. Gray hair does not chill their imaginings. A small wrinkle or a loose tooth would be a thing to be wondered over in that place forever. Yes, and among this beautiful people without any blemish we may retain for all time the fond joy of our love. For the ways of the Water Tzar and of his fine kingdom are not the ways of this gross earth. Love also keeps love's youth in that kingdom. But in your mortal world, Elair, love turns into a disliking as ruinous as flame; or love vanishes like a bad-smelling smoke; or, at best, love can but smoulder out into the ugly and dusty ashes, the gray cinders, of a nodded-over hearth-fire."

"That is not true about the love of a poet," replied Elair, as he yet again embraced the girl ardently, "because in the love of a poet there is no varying whatever; and neither time nor chance will ever shake my fixed love for Queen Fergail. For this reason I cannot go with you, core of my soul, to become forever happy and forever immortal. O woman of soft words and of fair breasts, you are the delight of my body. My eyes worship you. But my faith and my heart aim otherwhither."

Weeping a little, the gentle, very lovely, golden-haired daughter of Morskoï kissed Elair for the last time, saying,—

"Farewell, dear mortal lover, whose equal at love-making, and at pig-headedness also, I have not ever found!"

After that, Astrild put on her charmed jacket of white feathers; she too became a sea-gull; and she flew away eastward across the broad tumbling waters.

Though indeed (as Elair reflected, with a poet's concern for such trivialities) "tumbling" was hardly the word; nor were there any words in which you could speak with adequacy of the sea's heart-stirring multitudinous movements and of the color and of the glow and of the unexplained beauty of this moment, which for no very plain reason was a sad moment.

From behind him the low sun cast Elair's long slanting shadow across the brown sands so far that the last turbid scrabbling of the waves now caught and now released the head of this shadow. The incredible deep blue of the sea was becoming green. It was taking on the color of the dear eyes of Fergail. The great waves arose without any hurry, in very long obscure straight lines that moved implacably shoreward; and then curdled and, with a majestic sportiveness, half lazily, tumbled over into white foam which was made radiant, and was made almost pink, by the low sun. The sunset in the same way made radiant and made almost pink the white body of the departing sea-gull, which but an instant ago had been the fair body of Astrild,— although her slow-moving wings, when you saw them thus, from below, seemed to be dark gray.

These things alone Elair noticed; there was no sadness in these things; and yet to see them made sad his young heart, he did not know why.

Well, and at yet other times Elair met with yet other women; and he treated all of them civilly, as became a fine lusty poet in the pride of his youth. But at no moment did the heart of Elair waver in its unalterably fixed love for Fergail; and in his thoughts stayed always the sea-green color of her eyes and the red color of her curved lips and the clear gold of her hair, because in all this world Queen Fergail had not anywhere her twin for loveliness.

* *

TWENTY-TWO

TALK WITH A TIPPLER

*

Thus Elair rode through the breadth of three improbable kingdoms, dealing death to those men who opposed him, and accepting with vigor the kindnesses that were proffered him by noble ladies; and it was in Melphé that he killed the great Worm of Winden.

He passed thence, beneath acacias and sycamore-trees, where the road ran through green fields which were nourished by canals. Here he saw buffaloes grazing; and flocks of silvery herons; and sometimes a lone pelican as it budged lumberingly about its fishing. Moreover, two very large whitish-colored eagles startled him, by soaring up from the side of the roadway, just as Elair came into Ecben.

Well, and in Ecben he found the city of Arleoth to be making ready for a public holiday, on account of a witch-burning that had been arranged, by the Bishop, for the next afternoon.

This much Elair learned from a shock-headed blacksmith, called Volmar, whom Elair met in a tavern. There they fell to drinking together, because

Volmar had already disposed of two bottles of this tavern's wine, and was ripe to assure Elair of the wine's palatability.

"His grace the Bishop acts upon private information," said Volmar, "and has not yet disclosed what woman will be honored with the main part of to-morrow's entertainment. But in such matters he is equally thorough and well-skilled and economical. He understands, I mean, how to perfect any woman, howsoever inexperienced, in the rare accomplishment of entertaining several hundred of the best people for an entire afternoon."

Thus speaking, Volmar refilled his glass.

"She will first be weighed, I suppose, against the parish church Bible," Elair hazarded.

"Oh, yes; and then stripped to be searched for any such private personal marks as may have been made by her familiar spirit during their shared practice of the indelicate. That is always a popular feature, for our Bishop selects his witches as young and handsome as may be."

"Do you torture hereabouts?" Elair asked.

"Not until after the woman has been swum in the Cathedral lake," replied Volmar, when he had emptied his glass. "No, for we lost two women, who were so exhausted by torture that they drowned, and thus robbed us of a really good burning. The public hissed the performance, I must tell you. So nowadays we duck first and we torture afterward—but not ever, by the shrewd Bishop's philanthropic orders, very seriously."

"I perceive your meaning, Volmar. After the woman is half drowned, you revive her with your pincers and thumbscrews and so on. That enables her to enter more livelily into the true climax of the day's entertainment, which is, of course, the slow burning of her accursed body while she is yet alive and is able to suffer with animation. Shall you take any part in this holy business, Volmar?"

"No, Elair, for I admit that my piety is not all which it ought to be. I admire the high principles of these religious ceremonies, and yet, somehow, I do not enjoy them."

Volmar refilled his glass. He emptied it reflectively. He continued,—

"So I shall return home this evening, riding toward my smithy in Branlon, after I have met that young man with a wreath of red rowan berries about his dark head for whom I am waiting in this tavern."

"But Branlon is my goal also," cried out Elair, "for it is in Branlon that Urc Tabaron lives. Besides that, my hair is dark as your hair; and I am under an obligation to wear a wreath of red rowan berries about my head."

"I infer from these facts," replied Volmar, after thinking over these facts, "that it must have been for you I have been waiting all day in this tavern, at the request of Mr. Smith, the Lord of the Forest, in order

that I might give his message to the young champion
who came looking for Urc Tabaron. Come now, Elair,
but that is a most happy coincidence, which calls for
another bottle."

—Whereupon Volmar himself called for it.

Elair belched indignantly; and then said: "I do not
know anything about this Mr. Smith. He has no call
to be sending me messages. I do not value his messages
at the worth of an old shoe-lace, or of a bent pin,
or of a dried pea in a dead pod. I do not care at all
for the messages of any meddlesome Mr. Smith. What
is his message?"

"I was to tell you, Elair," replied Volmar—and he
shut his left eye, in order to see rather more accurately,
as Volmar poured wine into Volmar's glass,—"that
I am Volmar, why, but, yes, to be sure, I am Volmar,
whom SMIRT the philosopher begot upon Rani, the
South Wind's daughter. And why, pray, should I not
be Volmar if it pleases me to be Volmar? I must ask
Mr. Smith about that."

"This Mr. Smith has more sense in his impudent
messages than I thought he had," Elair answered. "For
I, Volmar, I am the Elair whom SMIRT of the High
Misdeeds begot upon Airel the conversation woman.
So we two are brothers."

"Well, but that is not my fault, Elair."

"It is not your misfortune, either, let me tell you,
Volmar. It is obvious, Volmar, that you have been
drinking with somebody. Do you let me have that

bottle, if indeed you have left any of it. As I thought, it is empty. Nevertheless, I forgive you, my dear brother, on account of that natural affection which ought to exist between us, even if it does not. O my dear brother, do you think we ought to embrace?"

Volmar considered this proposal very gravely; and in considering it, he hiccoughed, as he waved jerkily, toward the tapster, for another bottle of wine.

"It would perhaps be as well for us to embrace," he decided, by-and-by,—"but without prejudice. I admit to you, Elair, that when I think about how many children our divine father must have left here and there during his travels, I do not wish this embrace to establish a precedent. No, Elair; no, I am not prepared to regard every one of my brothers, and it may be, a great number of hulking snub-nosed sisters, too, with complete fondness. No, Elair, you need not argue about it any longer; and I wonder at your obstinacy, you big snub-nosed Elair, because there is a natural fixed limit to all things, even to my fraternal affection."

"Nevertheless, my dear brother, let us respect the conventions in our deeds, whatsoever we may think about them in our hearts," returned Elair, who had always that strict sense of the proprieties which Volmar lacked.

So the two gentlemen embraced each other in due form, a trifle tipsily; and after that, Volmar gave the second part of his message, saying that he came to guide Elair to the house of Urc Tabaron. Volmar then finished the bottle; and the two mounted their two horses and rode together toward Branlon. They entered a little way into the northern part of the forest, and so approached a gray house among oak-trees.

Volmar, whom the fresh air had almost sobered, as it had quite sobered Elair, now pointed out this house from afar.

"That is your goal, Elair; and to go further is not permitted me. So we must part, O my brother, for a brief while or for a great while, just as Mr. Smith may elect."

And with that, Volmar rode away.

"Hah," said Elair, "but this dark-faced thirsty brother of mine is a cool hand. He does not squander his natural affections; or at any rate, he conceals his fond love for me like a stoic. Well, but that hardly matters now that my quest is about to end triumphantly."

*   *

TWENTY-THREE

THE GRAY HOUSE

*

Now the tale tells how all seemed very quiet in the clearing about the gray house; and the small fiery devil who sat upon the roof-tree, meditatively picking his teeth, vanished when he saw Elair. Elair considered this odd, if not positively unfriendly, as he approached the door of the gray house, walking upon a pathway of soft clay, in which the huge feet of Elair left huge footprints.

Well, and when Elair had entered this house, an old man—high-nosed and most nobly bearded—lay dead there, under a sheet of green silk, with a platter of salt resting upon his breast; and beside the body sat a young girl dressed in gray.

"Peace to the dead!" said Elair; "and to the living their share of happiness!"

"Though you are very welcome to see, tall black-haired man," the girl answered, "yet you may not look to find happiness in the house of Urc Tabaron."

"Nevertheless, he is a skilled wizard," replied Elair. "That is known everywhere. And it may be that he will aid me in my quest, as he once aided my mother Airel against the fire-breathing Cat of Macha."

"Urc Tabaron," the girl said, "was a lord of all magics yesterday; he aided many; he was kindly in a fine time that will not be returning. For it was yesterday that his bond ran out, and that his serving spirit took the agreed forfeit. So now Urc Tabaron lies dead between us, tall man; and I, his daughter, am left friendless."

"Then Urc Tabaron cannot aid me after all," thought Elair, considering humanly his own affairs first; but he said aloud,—

"Yet you are not friendless, young girl whose name I do not know."

"I am called Oina, huge snub-nosed man; and tomorrow, or the next day, it may be, when the burghers of Arleoth know about my father's death, I shall be called Oina the Witch; and because of this little people's hatred of my father's wisdom and of his calm friendly ways, my body will be burned living."

Elair remembered now those episcopal activities of which he had heard in Arleoth. But he said only,—

"That would be a great pity, Oina; for you have a well-shaped body."

"It is as Heaven made it, man of sweet words," she replied, modestly.

"It is a body such as, at the fit time, some lucky young champion, and no flames, shall embrace ardently," Elair told her. "I remain here, Oina. The

men of Arleoth will come to this place assuredly, led
by their Bishop. So let us now bury your dead. And
when the Bishop of Arleoth comes out against Oina
the Witch there will be yet other dead to bury."

Elair digged a grave. In it they laid that which Urc
Tabaron's serving spirit had made of Urc Tabaron.
And Elair spoke to the dead wizard, saying:

"May peace be with you, Urc Tabaron, now that
much power and wisdom are not with you any longer.
I had strong need of your magics, to find for me the
Water of Airdra, so that I might win the unequalled
beauty of Fergail the proud Queen. Well, and yesterday you knew how to compound the Water of Airdra:
from them who have tasted this water youth does not
ebb, nor may age touch them. Yesterday you might
well have aided me. But you lie huddled now in a pit,
all witless and badly bitten, with your lean neck
wrung, you whose cunning once helped my mother
Airel to evade death; and for her sake shall your
daughter evade death so long as my sword-arm keeps
its strength, or my pistols yet have a bullet in them."

Oina cried out, "And what talk is this about the
Water of Airdra and about Queen Fergail?"

Elair told her, first, his name and parentage, and
second, the conditions of the queen's quest.

Then Oina said: "Of the Water of Airdra I have
heard my father speak, time and again. But who is

this Fergail woman, about whom I have heard no word until to-day?"

Elair said: "There is no word but falters before the perfections of Fergail. She is a great queen in Evain; she is famed for the bright colors of her body and the lovable ways of her life: but by rights she ought to be queen over the whole world."

Now Oina regarded him gravely. She sighed afterward, saying,—

"And besides this, Queen Fergail is of all women the most fortunate, in that she is well loved by Elair, the son of sublime SMIRT."

"Do you think so?" asked Elair. "Indeed I also, at times, I grant you, I have been forbidden only by some proper modesty from thinking that Fergail might do worse than to reward entirely my entire adoration. For people tell me I have qualities not amiss in a king."

"There is no man between any two oceans who is more fit to be a king," declared Oina.

"Come, come, but let us not exaggerate, my dear child! Here and there, I do not doubt, may be found my equal, or perhaps a person who is even my superior, in some slight unimportant respects such as no sane woman, at any rate, would consider essential to being a well-thought-of king. About that, of course, I do not know."

"And that which a person does not know, Elair, does not matter."

"You speak strangely, small mouse. I know, in any event, that you are a droll child."

"And is that all which you find me, Elair?" she inquired, with grave wistfulness.

"No, my fawn. For you are likewise a most adorable child," replied Elair, genially.

*   *

TWENTY-FOUR

IN REGARD TO OINA

*

Truly, of the women whom Elair at some time had known, and loved in his careless fashion, none seemed to him to have been more innocent or more helpless than was Oina. Very certainly, no woman alive anywhere needed more immediately a defender. So was it that pity overthrew this black-haired and blunt-nosed Elair, who in his day had overthrown the green Worm of Winden and four giants and one sea-monster and two full-grown dragons.

In his heart was Fergail firmly enthroned, as the most beautiful and the wisest and the most worshipful of all earth's ladies. Yet his eyes rested with pleasure upon Oina, the fond child, who, in her small mouse-like fashion, was rather pretty.

Yes, and Oina had her accomplishments, too. That night she cooked for Elair the very nicest supper he could imagine. And he partook of everything with appreciation,—of the thick bean soup, and of the white trout, including the roe, with its sharp-flavored wonderful pink sauce, and of the mutton and the veni-

son, and of carrots, and of spinach, and of a half-dozen
or so onions. He ate then, for his unpretentious dessert,
a large rice pudding, liberal with its currants, and
four apples and several handfuls of walnuts. And in
no king's palace, as Elair remarked truthfully, had
he ever eaten with more zest. The girl was a born
cook.

Moreover, it was heart-warming to talk with Oina,
as he did after their fine supper that night, about the
wide world which Elair had travelled over, and to
recount to her his superb adventures therein, while
she listened admiringly, with her red lips a bit parted
and her soft eyes glowing in the candle light, and he
told about how, at Winden, he had fought with three
worms simultaneously, each one of them larger than
a cart horse. It was Elair's way whenever he talked
about himself to use freely a poet's license.

But the trouble was, What to do with her? When
the best people came from Arleoth, upon the second
day of Elair's stay in the gray house, to dispose of
them was no heavy task. It involved merely the killing of three leading citizens and the slight wounding
of a fat bishop's backside—an operation as respectfully performed as proved possible—before the best
people went away from Elair of their own will.

Yet his problem remained: and a person who had
upon his hands, willy-nilly, the daughter of a known
wizard was in a hard quandary. During the latter years
of his life, Urc Tabaron, so far as Elair could discover,

had dealt only with elemental spirits, a few demons, and a deposed pagan deity called Mr. Smith; so that no human friend anywhere survived to whose kindness Oina might be entrusted. The convent, that ever-open refuge for womankind, was closed sternly to a girl of Oina's far too dubious origin, as to which a bishop would now speak forcefully without pausing to sit down.

In brief, there seemed nobody ready to take charge of her; and yet to leave her alone in this forest was impossible, even apart from the fact that the best people of Arleoth, upon the first news of Elair's departure, would promptly utilize the child's soft slender little body for a fine public witch-burning.

*   *

TWENTY-FIVE

MR. SMITH UPON MODESTY

*

Now came to the gray house an heroic being, of majestic and yet affable demeanor, with a twittering halo of white birds circling about his dark head; and he carried in his hand a long silver staff, having a fir-cone at the tip of it. This person shone, like white fire, until of a sudden the birds left him. He assumed then the hues more proper to mortality.

Afterward, when Elair had asked of this visitant his name and mission, benign Mr. Smith said:

"I am the Lord of this forest, whom curiosity led hither. I desired to see again that son whom SMIRT of the High Misdeeds begot upon Airel the conversation woman in six conversations."

Elair answered the renowned demi-god, "Well, and you behold that son, Lord of the Forest, howsoever unworthy I may be of my sublime sire, who was a supreme master of gods, whereas I am only a supreme master of warfare and of love-making and of minstrelsy."

"Ah, but at least you inherit his well-known modesty," replied Mr. Smith, admiringly, "along with his good looks."

"Meanwhile, Lord of the Forest, I do not understand how you can be seeing me again unless you have seen me somewhere before to-day."

"Now you bring up this point, Elair, that does appear logical," Mr. Smith admitted.

"For you cannot possibly have seen me in this part of the world, Lord of the Forest, which I am now visiting for the first time."

"Yes, that is true, Elair." So then, after thinking over the matter for some while, Mr. Smith suggested,—

"It follows, no doubt, that I must have seen you in some dream or another."

"Yet that does not quite follow," said Elair, puzzled.

"Well, but how else would you explain it?" asked Mr. Smith, with the air of a broad-minded person who has formed his own private opinion, but who remains open to argument.

Such obtuseness rather bothered Elair. Yet he said patiently:

"But I am not explaining it. You are explaining it."

"Then why, Elair, do you not listen to this explanation as carefully as I listen, in the deferred hope of understanding my explanation, instead of becoming loud-voiced and angry?"

"Because, Lord of the Forest—well, because when

I listen to you I do not know at all what you are talking about. Your words are smooth, and they are self-confident, but they do not mean anything."

"Now you become commonplace, tall child of a dream, for I cannot guess how many thousands of persons have said to me that same thing."

"Nor am I the child of a dream," Elair then stated, with a continued vast patience. "I am the unworthy son of that sublime SMIRT who had such tremendous adventures in the old days; and who became a master of gods; and who rode away, in the company of a red-colored devil called Company, upon a flash of lightning; and who so met my dear mother, upon a glass mountain, in a planet which SMIRT owned in fee simple."

It was a précis of Elair's origin which Mr. Smith appeared to regard with urbane but frank scepticism. Mr. Smith coughed delicately, saying,—

"Need I point out, Elair, to a person of your sound judgment, that, inasmuch as happenings of this exact nature do not happen except in dreams, it follows that you, Elair—who were the result of this not wholly conventional rendezvous—must necessarily have been a by-product of this same SMIRT's dreaming, and perhaps of his indigestion?"

"Indeed, but you had far better not point out any such scandal as to my ancestry," replied Elair, angrily.

"So, then, you see for yourself," said Mr. Smith, spreading out his very beautifully shaped white hands.

By this deduction was Elair a bit puzzled. Still, he said, amicably enough:

"Well, why, of course, Lord of the Forest, so long as you leave the entire matter to my judgment, there is no possible room for quarrel— And yet, after all, Lord of the Forest, just what do I see?"

"Why, you see that you yourself do not dispute your origin, on account of your remarkable and your profound intelligence."

"Nevertheless, sir—"

"—For you perceive that origin to be oneirodyniac."

"Oh, but do I indeed, Lord of the Forest?"

"Yes, Elair, you perceive it to be virtually unequalled."

"Well, but—" said Elair.

"And I, Elair, if you will permit me to say so, I rejoice to behold your sanity, your self-control, and your rare poise, after having been confronted by this discovery."

But all these compliments Elair waved aside with a huge hand; and he benignantly answered:

"You are a little bit too flattering, Lord of the Forest. No, no: I would not say quite that."

"Yes, and your not saying it, Elair, is what I have somewhere heard described as the defect of your qualities. But I say it, Elair, because I can say without impropriety all that from saying which you are prevented by the well-known modesty you got from your father."

"Ah, ah! But, then, really, sir—" Elair remarked, from a point somewhere between pleasure and embarrassment, and a good way removed from any least comprehension as to what this demi-god might be talking about.

"Now modesty, I repeat, is a fine virtue, Elair."

"Indeed, I have often heard of it, Lord of the Forest."

"It prevails especially among women, Elair, so the women all tell us."

"Nevertheless—" said Elair.

"Why, but, upon my word, that is true," replied Mr. Smith. "I am extremely glad, my dear fellow, you should have pointed that out. Yes, among women, modesty is very often a most puzzling and incalculable virtue, and a plain virtue of ritual. You are quite right, Elair; and I follow your argument with entire approval. As in Sumatra, for example, the knees, so in Persia the breasts, are the only parts of her body which a well-bred woman will not display freely to the public. In some sections of the United States, such as Georgia and Mississippi—and, I believe, also in certain portions of Vermont—it is considered immodest for a woman to exhibit her navel in mixed company. Yet their modesty incites Mohammedan women to go always with their faces veiled; whereas in China either to display or to mention her foot would disgrace for life any properly brought-up female."

"Still—" said Elair.

"Yes," Mr. Smith assented, "but that also is wholly true. Even where, as in most countries of Central Africa, a gentlewoman is accustomed to go stark naked, and thus exhibits her entire person, she yet manages to preserve a becoming modesty by having her body tattooed with attractive designs. Yes, I am glad that you should have brought up all these facts, Elair, because they are of considerable interest to a sound logician."

"It was merely that they occurred to me in passing, Lord of the Forest. Nevertheless, just what has all this modesty to do with your curious notion about my being the son of a dream?"

"Ah, that concerns your own modesty, Elair. For I say, in all calmness, that most people would be confounded by any such discovery as you have just made, about this oneirodyniac problem. They would become indignant. They would argue. Whereas you, Elair, you confront the inevitable with a composure which I can but describe as marmoreal, and which I envy beyond any describing at all."

"Well, but in this world, sir," replied a quite mollified and a gravely condescending Elair, "one does learn by-and-by to take problems as they come. Avoid haste, that is the main thing. Do not ever let them flurry you. Take them to bed with you, if you like. Remember always that there is no least need to make any fuss over them. Yes, sir, it really does pay, in the long run, not to make any fuss over them. Just turn them over quietly."

"I can but bow to your far wider experience, my dear boy," replied Mr. Smith,—"without venturing to endorse all these sage axioms about women."

"So, do you think I am still talking about women?" Elair asked, a little uncertainly.

"I apologize, Elair. I admit the adroit rebuke. You alluded to them, far more tactfully, just as 'problems.' Yet you very well know how to dispose of them, under any and all descriptions, I can see; and so, one need not worry as to your future."

Thus speaking, Mr. Smith went away; and Elair slightly tilted his wreath of red rowan berries, in order to scratch pensively at Elair's black head.

"The poor lad," said Mr. Smith, "has leaden wits and a heart of gold. Yes, Branlon and the unreasonable small magic of Branlon will hold him, even though it might perhaps be just as well to advise that little gray witch about his footsteps."

But Elair said: "This Lord of the Forest is a queer person. He is, perhaps, slightly insane. He, most certainly, is lewd-minded; and he is infected with much self-conceit. Yet he was not very far wrong when he called them 'problems.' "

*　　*

TWENTY-SIX

THE WATER OF AIRDRA

*

Elair brooded over his problem. The days passed.
Then Elair sighed, and he told Oina that the one way
out of their difficulty was for her to become his wife.
"For I cannot desert you, child. And it is not right for
us to be living together without being married."

"Your will is my will, Elair. But it is that Fergail
woman whom you love."

"It is Fergail," Elair corrected this inaccurate young
person, "whom I worship. Still, I am fond of you.
Your cooking pleases me. And I daresay we would
get on together well enough. Besides that, I have but
a little chance of winning Fergail, because I have not
any notion where a person can find the Water of
Airdra."

"Yet is Fergail the queen of this world's women,
as you have told me time and again, Elair, until I simply cannot stand it any longer, Elair."

"And why, Oina, should I not tell you that which is
true? Yet it is equally true that Fergail must belong,
not to me, but to that lucky champion who shall bring

to her the Water of Airdra, or some other magical drink, by which her youth will be made steadfast."

"Indeed I remember very well," Oina replied, smiling reflectively, as she went on with her sewing, upon a pair of plain gray serviceable hose for Elair the Song-Maker, "how my dear father laughed when he heard that news, asking me how I would fancy this fine queen for my stepmother."

"Ah, yes," Elair assented; "so you lied to me in declaring that you had heard no talk of Queen Fergail!"

For an instant she appeared startled, biting her lip. Then Oina very placidly went on with her sewing.

"It was a matter," Oina declared, with an almost violent lack of interest, "which passed quite out of my mind. For what is this Fergail to me?"

"And after all," Elair said, complacently, "I was right when I thought Urc Tabaron would know this secret if any person knew it. In such deductions I am not often mistaken, because—like Mr. Smith—I appraise matters logically. Well, and do you know, Oina, logic now points out to me that if your father had ever laid his eyes on Queen Fergail, it is wholly certain he would have made her your stepmother, because there is no man so wise or so infirm but his heart becomes a bonfire at his first sight of Queen Fergail?"

At that, Oina put by, neatly, upon her little table, the pair of plain gray serviceable hose. She arose. She looked up, for one heart-beat, at Elair the Song-Maker. She went quietly to a cupboard. She returned with a gold phial.

"Here, wicked Elair, is the Water of Airdra. Urc Tabaron procured it long and very long ago, as a proof of his art's perfection. But he was too wise to make any use of it, he said, after he had invoked three old wispy women, and had talked with them. 'The Norns, howsoever frequent may be their blunders, deserve our respect,' he said, 'because they control the fate of all men. I consent therefore to their unflattering opinion that this Fergail is better suited to be my granddaughter.' "

Then Oina gulped, saying: "I do not know what that meant. I know only that this bold-faced bad Fergail is yours for the asking."

After that, Oina wept quietly.

Elair waited, clenching his hands. He thought about the sea-green color of Fergail's eyes and about the red color in the curved lips of Fergail and about the black and yellow color of the flames which would burn Oina. He said then, —

"I shall not ask."

"But why not, Elair?"

"Because, Oina, in the first place, logic points out that I cannot settle any matter in which the Norns have a finger. In the second place"—his voice broke—"I cannot leave you, most dear and brave and most untruthful of children."

Thus speaking, he took Oina in his arms.

When her lips were free, she declared gravely, "Your will is my will, Elair."

Well, and that night, while Elair slept, Oina arose from her bed. She took up Elair's broad dagger, and she tiptoed out of the gray house to the clay pathway in frónt of the gray house. She cut from the pathway two of Elair's footprints; she painted them with cinnabar, the color of her heart's blood, speaking the Married Woman's rune; and in the oven she placed these two footprints, saying:

"Burn, O footsteps of Elair! Burn and bake firm, O footsteps of my beloved! Harden and become fixed for all time! Let there be no varying henceforward in the footsteps of Elair! So may the footsteps of Elair not ever depart from the clay of this pathway. So shall his dear folly be forevermore the happiness of my heart, and all his needs, even until this tall man dies, shall be tended faithfully by my busy hands."

*　　*

TWENTY-SEVEN

A WIZARD'S ONE OVERSIGHT

*

In this way did the weak conquer the strong; and so was Elair the Song-Maker led to abandon his wide adventurings and become a married man. In his heart was Fergail firmly enthroned, as the most beautiful and the wisest and the most worshipful of all women. And in his keeping stayed the gold phial with which his adored Fergail might be won at any moment, whensoever he chose to leave Oina.

Well, and that, he reflected, that might come about, by-and-by; but at this special instant, with a baby on the way, and with the clearing which Elair was now extending northerly from the gray house only half done, that must wait. Then their son was born; and no mortal could have deserted Oina just now, in her proud happiness, Elair reflected, as he set about his spring plowing.

For the champion whom kings had praised, and whom queens had not left unrewarded, had turned farmer now, since a man must needs fill in his time somehow in this ever-peaceful forest. His sword and his pistols and his suit of battle lay by unused; in his little home, in his tilled neat fields, and in his well-tended cattle, Elair's interest became deeper and yet more deep. Just temporarily, he had put by his harp of maple-wood and its too loud music, as being impractical with a baby in the house; and later, after his son Conan was not any longer a baby, Elair did not return straightway to his song-making, what with one thing and another.

For example, one of his first needs was to dispose of Urc Tabaron's thaumaturgies. When Elair went into the untidy huge room in which the wizard had conducted his studies, then Elair stood confounded by the profusion of magic-working materials heaped up at every side pellmell. His mother Airel of the Brown Hair had worked magic, it was true, in her own small way, so that in childhood Elair had picked up a fair smattering of the first principles of magic. But here were the materials amassed, during a century-long lifetime, by an untiring student and a supreme master of all abstruse arts; and Elair simply did not know what to do with such priceless and such highly dangerous implements.

So he experimented most warily; and although he made some disastrous mistakes, yet he got many pleased hours of diversion from the garnered wisdom of his father-in-law.

Now Elair conjured up, at one time or another, hundreds of white or black or gray spirits, with the various formulæ which he found recorded in Urc Tabaron's neat tremulous handwriting; and all these immortals came promptly to serve the desires of Elair. Even the supreme genii of the Sixth Hour obeyed the magic of Urc Tabaron.

These genii were eager to make Elair the ruler of all this world (just as Elair's sublime father had once been, Elair reflected), and to reveal to Elair the occult virtues of plants and of precious stones, of fire and air and earth and water, of milk and salt. Nay, they proffered yet more: for Tabris, the leader of these genii, said that all created nature would henceforward keep no secrets from Elair. The mysteries of form would be penetrated by him, and the illusive vestures of time and of space would be laid aside for his benefit, declared Haatan, the Lord of Concealed Treasures: and while Elair did not grasp precisely what Haatan might mean, the proposal sounded fair enough, and even generous.

In brief, these seven celestial spirits offered him omniscience, and omnipotence also, in regard to all earthly affairs, with a composure which Elair at first regarded as a thought strange, until he had recollected that to these great genii a planet must seem very little, if at all, more valuable than a pebble. In their keeping were many thousands and, it might be, millions of planets.

And in any case, Elair had no special need of a planet. He wanted Fergail. He explained therefore his more modest requirements, asking of the genii simply a plan by which he and his wife Oina and his love Fergail might all live together happily.

—Whereafter the seven genii replied, in abashment, that the mathematics of heaven had not ever mastered the problem of dividing one man between two women without an untidy and huge remainder of discord.

They vanished then, so that no trace remained of Susabo, the Lord of Voyages, or of Nitika, the Lord of Gems, or of Zaran, the Lord of Vengeance, or of any one of these seven supreme genii. And Elair, after shaking gravely his rowan-crowned head, set about charms of a more diabolical nature.

So was hell emptied of the seven spirits who had served Urc Tabaron in the lower branches of his art. So to Elair came Barbatos (that same fallen angel whose tongue was cut out by Michael) riding in a fiery chariot and carrying in his left hand a viper; Agares, Duke of the East, as yet defiantly bearing the forfeited sword of an archangel; Phobetor, in the shape of a dusky green cloud; Beleth, mounted on a pale horse, sounding harshly an iron trumpet; Focalor, who had three heads, like the head of a cat, of a Knight Templar, and of a peacock; Haop, who in most respects resembled a four-footed raven, except that he had also the tusks of a boar; and Gurson, who appeared to-day in the form of a pallidly beautiful boy, with scaly black wings, riding on the back of a camel.

"And what would you be doing here, gentlemen?" Elair demanded, with a vast politeness, of this most horrible assemblage.

They replied to him reverently; but not wholly in words. . .No; for beyond their speaking was a not quite heard music, Elair reflected. He seemed aware of a' great sea of malevolent, and fierce, and lascivious music, like a sea that followed with high-hearted lustiness after a leprous moon and all the dear poisons of the moon's cold corruption, a sea which agonized under perverse tides of moon-maddened ecstasies,— raising everywhere, beneath winds that had come out of worlds less innocent than ours, their proud waves of flashing and bitter and evil beauty. Through that frantic sea of music, hell spoke; hell called to Elair, rejoicingly and half wooingly; and the foul greatness of hell delighted him, even in the teeth of his sedate better judgment, by its horrifying magnificence. . . Well, and now it was as though across this immense insane sea of infernal music—as sprucely as trim little paper boats, Elair reflected—that the brisk answers of Elair's servants came to him.

"We desire, sir," said Beleth, "to instruct you in the languages of all mankind and of the even lower animals."

"Likewise," declared the three heads of Focalor, "in all abstract sciences; in moral philosophy; in soothsaying with judicious reservations; in every practical use of theology; and in the wax modeling of your adversaries so that, as the wax melts, they also will waste away with disease."

"We will show you," Haop croaked, genially, "how to control pestilences most fatally; and how to employ bankers and libels and stars of the fourth magnitude with equal destructiveness."

Phobetor said, "We will teach you the most generally popular methods of secret murder and of blighting crops and of souring the milk of a cow and of provoking small earthquakes."

"You may learn from us," put in Agares, brandishing terribly his huge sword, "how to release tempests from blue skies and any moderately sinful person from purgatory; and to induce among your unfriends boils or insanity or rheumatism, whichever you may elect."

"In addition," said Gurson, "we will reveal to you the ten best recipes for controlling the desires of women; and I assure you that some of these recipes have been known now and then to work."

"Come now," replied Elair, brightening, "but that sounds more promising; for we need only a plan by which my wife Oina and my heart's love Fergail and I too may all live together without inconvenience."

"Master," these fiends then entreated, piteously, "do you permit us to return to our own place! The simple arithmetic of hell has not ever managed to add one man to two women with real comfort for anybody concerned; and we, who have lived tolerably enough, for so many centuries, in eternal torment, dare not abide the result of your dreadful experiment in this middle class home."

Elair sighed; and dismissed them.

Well, and afterward, now that neither good nor evil seemed able to help him, he nevertheless continued to seek knowledge with the recipes and the odd paraphernalia of Urc Tabaron. In this way did Elair gather together many stray bits of miscellaneous information.

He learned, for example, how to draw up the dead from out of their graves, how to control good and bad luck, and how to make himself invisible with the aid of a stone found in the hoopoe's nest. He learned how to consult the Five Beryls of Baphomet, which answered all questions as to all happenings; and he learned how to compound the three ointments which enabled Elair, after a little practice, to fly about in the air as freely as a bird does. He learned how to control the Pythonic Word, the Mystery of the Salamanders, the Grotto of the Gnomes, and the ambiguous seraphim of the Heavens of Gad. Moreover, he learned how to cure epilepsy with three iron nails, how to win law suits with a bit of hematite, how to heal burns with currant jelly, and how to avert the dangers of travel with a turquoise.

The great trouble was that, out of so much diverse knowledge, Elair got no knowledge to his own purpose. No; for his late father-in-law (Elair decided) had been at bottom unpractical. Virtually omniscient, Urc Tabaron had been satisfied, in just one point, to fall short of omniscience. At no time had he devoted his undeniable talents to the sensible and the philanthropic task of finding out how to induce two women to share one man equally and amicably. That omission was disastrous. It vitiated all Elair's knowledge-seeking: for what Elair wanted was a way in which to win Fergail with the charmed Water of Airdra without deserting his wife and child; what he got were irrelevances about how to control lightnings, subdue kings, create gold, and induce palsies. There was no sense in an outcome so flatly inconsequent; and Elair saw that no one of Urc Tabaron's arts was of any real use to Elair.

It was then that, in his forthright way, Elair took action. He carried the paraphernalia of Urc Tabaron to a safe distance from the gray house, he piled up all in a great heap, and he set fire to the dead wizard's belongings.

*   *

TWENTY-EIGHT

THE GREAT BURNING

*

It is probable that no other person ever made such a bonfire as Elair kindled. For in the piled heap, which reached to Elair's shoulder, were talismans, philtres, fetishes, amulets, and divining rods; magic lamps, rings, caskets, carpets, spectacles, mirrors, and belts; wishing-caps, and caps of darkness; the black robes of a conjuror, and the white robes needed for necromancy; as well as two pairs of seven-league boots, and one pair of red tarask-skin gloves in which to hold thunder bolts.

Then Elair brought out of the gray house the skulls of eight parricides; and the dried head of a black cat which (according to Urc Tabaron's attached memorandum) had been fed upon human flesh for five days before being slaughtered; and a moonstone, about the size of an orange, which was surmounted by a cross and inscribed with the names of three seraphim; and a copper censer, containing a mixture of ambergris, storax, camphor and aloes, which mixture had been properly steeped for seven days in yet another mixture, of the blood of moles and of goats and of bats; and the little finger of St. James the Less; and a half-dozen candles made from the fat of ravished nuns, which candles were set in a pair of ebony candlesticks carved in the shape of a crescent; and a bit of the Holy Manger, duly autographed by the Three Magi; and a leaden cap adorned in bas-relief with the ill-omened sign of Saturn; and yet other strong and dangerous tools for the working of wizardry.

After that, Elair fetched out, and he placed upon the top of this strange scrap-heap, the books of magic, each one of which had been interleaved by Urc Tabaron with notes many times more valuable than were the books themselves. Here were the Great and the Little Albert, the Enchiridion, the Red Dragon, the Black Hen, the Grimoire of Pope Honorius, the Magical Venus, the Treasure of the Old Man of the Pyramids, and the Secrets of the Brown Druid, and dozens of yet other books. Far more important, though, here were the unique and the priceless three manuscript volumes in which Urc Tabaron had written down the invocations, and the magical recipes in general, which had made Urc Tabaron supreme among wizards.

Now to all these august matters Elair laid fire; and he began to burn everything painstakingly. While he was thus engaged, a grave voice spoke from behind Elair, saying,—

170

"Son of sublime SMIRT, you destroy such knowledge and such power as no other living man possesses."

Turning, Elair perceived the speaker to be that queer half-brother of his whom they called Volmar. And Elair replied:

"It is not about other men I am bothering. I burn rubbish of no worth to Elair the Song-Maker. For of what use are this knowledge and this power if they cannot give me my desire?"

"I will answer that question, it may be," said Volmar, "if you will first tell me just what is your desire."

"Why, but Fergail is my desire."

"And where, or what, or perhaps who, is this Fergail?"

"Truly, Volmar, but your ignorance is a matter to wonder over. Fergail is the Queen of Evain, and she is likewise the queen of this world's women. These are facts known to all well-informed persons."

"Ah, but now I can understand you, O married man who makes bonfires," declared Volmar, shrugging. "And I say to you it is better to marry than to burn."

"You have the advantage of me," Elair stated, stiffly, "because I cannot see that my bonfire or my marriage, or my desire either, is any of your concern."

"There is truth in your saying," agreed Volmar, "and so I must give you, in return for it, a saying which is equally true. I must tell you, poor married poet, that none makes an omelet without breaking eggs."

"Nobody knows more about omelets than does Oina," replied Elair, soberly. "I must ask her about that."

Volmar grinned, saying: "Moreover, I must tell you, O my brother, that, though necessity be a rude nurse, yet she raises strong children. And I add, for your consolation, my fellow unfortunate, that all cats remain quiet when their catnip is put out of reach."

"I do not see that cats have anything more to do with it than have omelets," said Elair. "We were not talking about cats; and certainly I was not thinking about cats. Instead, I was thinking that, after all, I can bear living without Fergail's love; but I could not bear to hurt Oina."

"Well, and indeed—or, at any rate, in strict theory —I could not willingly hurt my own wife," Volmar returned, "because the love which we once had for each other was of a nature so sublime that she gave up being a crowned Queen of Rorn, and having a husband worth twenty-seven of me, in order to become the wife of a blacksmith. Nor is it her fault, of course, that I once knew the flawless women of Auster."

"But what, Volmar, have the women of Auster, whoever they may be, to do with your wife and with cats and with nurses and with omelets?"

Volmar answered, with a perplexed and a strangely haggard face:

"Why, they come back to me, now and then, Elair,

do those most damnably fair sylphs. They condole with me, in a vein somewhere between wistfulness and derision. They whisper, with remote low voices, which are more sweet than Sonia's voice seems nowadays, when she is talking and talking and forever talking about that fine Feodor whom she might have married, that my wife is a person of whom I am rather tired, and in whom I find not very much good temper and no special sharp flavor of interest. Then I go to the tavern."

"In fact, Volmar, you are not often quite sober."

"It is not well for any married poet who remembers the women of Auster to be sober too long after breakfast," replied Volmar, gloomily.

"That is a bad aphorism."

"It is a most horrible aphorism," agreed Volmar, "because it is perfectly true. For indeed I suspect that, just as Mr. Smith says, all we who are poets, and who have the sublime SMIRT's blood in us, are doomed forever to desire that which we lack and to contemn always that which we have. So do I perceive nowadays that I somewhat rashly disregarded the call of perfection, just as you now, Elair, are disregarding the call of knowledge and of power, because each of us has happened to prefer a flesh-and-blood woman. Hah, and I won her! whereas you, my thrice-fortunate brother, you have lost your heart's desire! and in place of it have a woman who understands omelets! and yet you make bonfires!"

"Well, and what follows," asked Elair, "in a world wherein every gentleman is entitled to his own tastes? There is no hurt in a good omelet. I rather like omelets."

Volmar shrugged yet again. For a moment he was silent. Then he said:

"Why, it follows that, while you gobble down your good omelets, I go to the tavern. I take counsel with the white wines of Sauterne and of Champagne. I confer carefully with the wines of the Rheingau and Hochheim and Rheinhessen and the Palatine wines of the Rheinpfalz. All these help me for some while to forget the fair women of Auster."

"Yes, but—" said Elair, virtuously.

"I listen to many advisers," Volmar went on; and he spoke now a little light-headedly, as one speaks in a fever. "I seek them among the red wines of Burgundy —in particular do I consult the great Chambertin— and among the white wines of Burgundy also, which come to me consolingly all the long way between Branlon and the walled town of Chablis. I do not disdain the mild wines of Moselle. I regard affably the two wines of Oporto, both the ruby colored and the tawny colored."

"And these two, in their right place, are excellent. Yet you would be much better off, my poor Volmar, for some third sort of adviser—"

"Ah, but three cunning counsellors do bring advice to me. These three travel together, in the same hamper; they come out of Portugal; they are called Fino and Amontillado and Amoroso. Yes, and four likewise come to me from Médoc, even the revered clarets of Lafite, of Margaux, of Latour, and of Haut-Brion. You perceive that I do not lack for a bevy of noble advisers. And every one of these, Elair, helps me for some while to forget the fair women of Auster. Yes"—the man groaned,—"and they beget headaches which tell me that my wife is the better bargain, and a mate far too good for any drink-sodden beast who does not merit her occasional kindness."

"Then you have got splendid advice out of a bottle, Volmar: and I would beseech you to honor it, my dear brother. For a man's main concern ought to be with his own wife. He ought to remember always that it is she who keeps his house comfortable and who cooks for him his remarkably fine meals."

"Do you think so, O married man who makes bon-fires like this great burning, on account of your stupid bull-headed petulance?" asked Volmar; and even in the while that he spoke jeeringly, he wrung his hands. "Hah, and does your desire to talk this bland sort of reputable nonsense cause you—who were once a poet, my poor brother—to forget Fergail?"

"Well, but my case is quite different, Volmar. And of course I do not ever forget Fergail."

"It is the main trouble in this world, Elair, that to every man's belief his own case is quite different."

Then Volmar went away, grinning and twitching a

great deal, and reeling just perceptibly, in the general direction of the tavern. And Elair stirred up afresh his large, very terribly smelling bonfire.

"We are well rid of all cheating kickshaws," said Elair, that day, as he sat down beamingly to his dinner, "and I have done a good morning's work. I do not criticize your father, small mouse: yet his power and his wisdom got him only a wrung neck at the last. I take warning from him. And I mean to have no sorceries in my own home."

—Whereupon his fond wife, Oina the gray witch, replied, meekly:

"Your will is my will, Elair. Did you destroy also the Water of Airdra?"

"No," said Elair, flushing; and he continued: "But this bread and this pottage of lentils are delicious! It is a beautiful pottage and a strange pottage and a pottage that ought to be wondered at in sweet songs, by ten poets all singing together."

*   *

TWENTY-NINE

HOW A WHILE PASSED

*

Elair found his Oina a model housewife. So untiring, indeed, was her care for his every comfort that she conducted her gray magics very secretly, without his knowing about them as yet. Still he complained, at times, that she had borne him no more children after the advent of young Conan. Such children might have made Elair's home a rather more lively place: for Oina did not sparkle in conversation; and a solemn-eyed young Conan, there was no hiding it, regarded his father as a slow-witted and inefficient person: so that the gray house, howsoever comfortably managed, and howsoever soul-satisfying remained Oina's cookery, was—after all—a bit dull.

"Ah, Fergail," Elair would say, in his heart, "it is not thus you are living in the glory of your bright home and the pride of your youth. I concern myself with little labors and with little happenings while you fare splendidly among the great people of earth, as the queen of earth's women. My desire of you is undying. I shall not ever get out of my thoughts the sea-green color of your eyes or the red color of your curved lips or the gold of your hair. And it is very bitter to think that I, who succeeded in my quest for the Water of Airdra, should have won, not you, but this stupid little mouse of a woman."

Meanwhile he attended soberly to his farming; young Conan grew apace; and Oina tended her men folk tenderly, without any nonsense, putting upon them only such gray magics as she considered to be the best for their welfare, very secretly.

"For that which a person does not know," said Oina, "does not matter."

So was it that a while passed; and throughout that while there was no change in the life of Elair, inasmuch as into the forest of Branlon time was not permitted to enter. This was because the Lord of the Forest peculiarly disliked clocks.

He had reason: for throughout his long dream about being a master of gods he had been haunted, and indeed but for his never-failing urbanity he might have been annoyed seriously, by the never-failing platitudes of a black onyx clock. This mid-Victorian clock (as manufactured by the Ansonia Brass Company, in Connecticut, about 1850) had evinced the characteristic bad taste of its era by reminding the Master of the Gods, over and yet over again, that its ticking counted relentlessly every moment of his omnipotence. For no person had, at any time in his life, more than one instant of existence, said this tedious and taunting, too-talkative timepiece. It ticked tirelessly touching two topics. Every man's past, so this clock told you, even the past life of a master of gods, was fixed and was removed from his control: his future remained unfixed, perhaps, but it stayed equally uncontrollable, and equally non-existent, and equally not, in any real sense, his. You had only your one instant of existence, your one clock-tick. You had nothing else.

Now these platitudes were facts which, inasmuch as they were of a personally unpleasant nature, Mr. Smith did not find to be of considerable interest to a sound logician.

"So let us have no clocks in my forest," he had ordered, "and no calendar. Let us deport Time as an undesirable alien. For Time is a thief who steals youth and strength; an iconoclast who smashes all glory; a murderer who spares none. Time is a betrayer, as the gray dust of Thebes and of Troy and of Carthage well shows. Time is a demented wizard, who turns the fair-haired daughters of men into the wrinkled grandmothers of men; through the evil magic of Time are great-hearted and radiant boys converted into lawyers and merchants and school-teachers and convicts and clergymen and captains of industry. No, I will not make any terms with Time; and his crazed wickedness shall not enter into my bucolic kingdom. I will not honor the currency of Time. Against the nonsense of Time I decree a protective tariff, preferring to manufacture my own nonsense...In brief, since Time does not know the meaning of diplomacy, I will now sever all diplomatic relations with Time."

Thus spoke the Lord of the Forest; and in Branlon his speaking was law.

*   *

THIRTY

TROUBLE AT SUPPER TIME

*

So was it that a while passed, and yet another while passed; and Time's ruinous work was conducted faithfully in every place except Branlon. Then—toward dusk, in the uncertain hour when bats flicker and zigzag about fretfully in the last glowings of a dead sunset, and cannot yet find the acceptable darkness of the desired night season—then Elair sat down to supper with his quiet-spoken gray wife and his quiet, tall, rather snub-nosed son.

Then also Mr. Smith came smiling pensively. And besides Mr. Smith, a fat old woman came likewise into the gray house, crying out:

"What thing is this that I have been hearing from the mouths of my druids, in far-away Evain, O false Elair? For they say that you have forgotten your love of me, and are content to drowse here in a snug separating from any glorious doings."

Elair looked hard at her; his jaw dropped; and in his face awoke wonder, now that he knew this fat, blowsy, and weather-beaten creature. Yet he held fast, as Elair did at all seasons, to his strict sense of the proprieties.

"No person," observed Elair, with a vast politeness—in the while that he put aside his rich, red-colored, steaming pottage, and arose from the supper table—"no person of any sort, and most certainly no poet, who has beheld Fergail, can ever forget the queen of this world's women. Is it permitted, dear Lady of Evain, that I present to you my wife, as well as my son here?"

"These," said old Fergail, "these two are indeed fine proofs of your love's fidelity!"

"Ah, but a poet," Elair explained, "remains faithful in his heart, with a very sublime faithfulness, to which these incidents and these little by-products of his flesh's frailty are, when properly regarded, extraneous."

"I do not know about that," replied Fergail, "but I do know that my druids report to me you have found the Water of Airdra. And I have much need of it nowadays, Elair, joy of my heart."

"Why, but indeed, Queen Fergail," declared Oina, compassionately, "when one remembers that you will not ever again see fifty, no, nor fifty-five either, and when one thinks about the dissolute life which you have been leading all this while, one would almost call you not quite so bad looking as might be hoped for— although, to be sure, I have not ever seen you plainly by daylight,—and besides that, there are some men who do not very much mind their women's being as fat as a pig."

"Do you be silent, Oina!" Elair ordered her.

"—Or as without any shape," Oina continued, "as a feather bolster." She added, meekly:

"Your will is my will, Elair. Yet I did think it only kindly to comfort the poor creature."

But Elair looked dazedly about this familiar, neat and sober-colored room, which on a sudden seemed to him a pitiable and strange place.

"It is true," he said, "yes, it is true, that Fergail is ugly and old. It is true that, in our hearts at least, the three of us are old people nowadays. And I had not known it. The time that I have lived here concerned with useful and sensible small matters has passed very quietly; but as that time went by, it was taking away our youth and all the fond splendors of our youth from the three of us. For myself I do not greatly mind, or for Oina either; but it is not right that Fergail, who was a world's glory, should have fallen away into old age and much ugliness."

He went quickly to the cupboard; and he returned now toward Fergail, bringing a gold phial.

"Fergail, O my beloved Fergail, you who in every song which I made about you, were the delight of my eyes, the desire of my desire, my life's pulse, and a large number of other things which I have now forgotten, I alone of your champions have kept faith untarnished. It is Elair, the son of sublime SMIRT, who

183

now restores to you your youth so that it may be made steadfast."

After that, tall young Conan fetched a blue mug; Elair poured into it a part of the Water of Airdra; and the old Queen drank out of the mug which Conan, kneeling respectfully, had presented to her.

What happened then was beyond believing; and yet it did not seem strange to Elair. Strange and exceedingly strange it had seemed—and indeed, just as Charlemagne had phrased this affair, it had seemed libelous—to have a fat old gray-haired trollop wearing the dear name of Fergail. But to have Fergail back again, in the brave pride of that young beauty which had not its equal anywhere upon earth, did not seem strange at all, because this outcome was but the honorable keeping of a promise which spring-time and his high-hearted day-dreams had made, very long ago, to a young poet. The one puzzling part of the miracle, in fact, was that Fergail seemed a deal lovelier than Elair had remembered; and the reformed staid song-maker, in the while that he nodded approvingly, delighted to observe that throughout all these years he had loved with true discernment.

"Elair, joy of my heart," said the proud Queen, "do you now drink as I have drunk, and then take your reward, so that the two of us may reign gloriously over Evain in our not-ever-failing youth. And as for this little, dish-faced, snappish, and extremely ugly woman here, we will provide suitably for her needs, in a convent, or perhaps one of my dungeons would be better, now that all I have is yours for the asking."

"Ah, but, desire of my desire," replied Elair, smiling gravely, "I shall not ask."

"Hah!" said the Queen, angrily.

"No!" said Elair, with complete firmness.

Then the Queen said: "Elair, joy of my heart, do you stop talking any such foolishness! Do you remember that I have sworn by the most noble parts of the Red Stallion of Stairth to marry the champion who brought me a magic by which my youth would be made steadfast. You have done that thing for me. Yes, and you alone of all my champions have kept faith untarnished, as you said but a moment ago."

"Well, but, pulse of my life," said Elair, wriggling, "all poets do say things of that sort now and then. It is expected of them: and their remarks ought not to be taken too seriously."

"Elair, joy of my heart, and how can I help taking seriously the great oath I have sworn? I have sworn by the Red Stallion of Stairth to marry him who made my youth steadfast."

"Oh, but, but that is true!" said Elair, in his horror, now that he quite understood the frightful position of the dear love of his youth.

"There is no oath more binding or more terrible," the Queen continued. "Do you remember, Elair, that if I do not keep my oath then my druids will be compelled, howsoever unwillingly, to fulfill their clerical duties, though I am sure they are all honestly fond of me—especially Cathba and Carnac, even if he does have only one eye, the poor fellow. Not that it is really his fault. No, I do not mean to suggest that, no, not for one instant, Elair, because he could not well have expected the woman's husband to come home so un-expectedly. No: I mean only that they would have to have me torn into four pieces by four stallions; and I am sure I would not like it."

"I would not like it either, dear Lady of Evain," replied Elair; yet he added, stubbornly:

"But upon no terms will I be leaving my wife. And it is not right of you, you must let me tell you, delight of my eyes, to be talking about any such misconduct."

"Oh, but now indeed I hate you, Elair, joy of my heart, and a most depraved joy you are, to be planning to have me pulled about a big public field in such vulgar fractions, rather than for you to leave this stupid and dish-faced woman!"

Now the Lord of the Forest spoke, for the first time since Mr. Smith had entered the gray house.

"If you will permit me, my children, why, then— in exchange, let us say, for what is left of the Water of Airdra, which you do not need, Elair, and for which I shall probably find some use or another—why, then, it is just possible I might suggest a matter-of-fact way out of this most distressing situation."

"Take it, and welcome, Lord of the Forest," said Elair, "if only you can find an honorable way, or even a swindling way, to keep this bold-faced young woman from being quartered by wild stallions, and me from being eloped with."

"I suggest, then," said Mr. Smith, as he thriftily slipped the gold phial into his pocket, "a fact which was witnessed by the five of us, and observed only by me. All facts are of considerable interest to a sound logician."

At this statement Elair looked doubly forlorn; yet he said only, with large resignation,—

"That is true, no doubt, Lord of the Forest, but just what are you talking about, because I do not ever know just what you are talking about?"

"I am talking about the plain fact, Elair, that it was not you, but young Conan here, who knelt down upon this very rug, and who gave the blue mug to Queen Fergail."

"That is indeed a fact," cried out tall young Conan, in his delight. "It was I who gave her the Water of Airdra, and not you, my poor Father. So you must let me marry her, O my Father, rather than have her fine body broken into four pieces, and my heart into forty pieces, because my entire heart belongs to Fergail, my dear Father, and Fergail"—declared young Conan, his voice shaking with adoration—"Fergail is queen of this world's women."

"Hah!" said Elair.

Conan answered him, stoutly: "Were the world searched between the sunrise and the sunsetting there would not be found anywhere the twin of Fergail. For her eyes have the sea's color; the curving of her red lips is very wonderful."

"Yes, my dear son," replied Elair, smiling, "and the clear gold of her hair—as you were, no doubt, going on to observe—is like a flame. Yes; I remember."

Yet it is a fact that, as Elair looked at his tall son, the widened and fond eyes of Elair were blurred with something uncommonly like tears. Romance dies hard in the heart of a confirmed romanticist; and to be called on to grin over a parody of one's own lost idiotic splendors proves to such persons an awkward performance.

"Indeed, my son," Elair said, clearing his throat, "it is true that Fergail, in her looks, and in her light-headedness, and in all other possessions, is everything which a very young man could admire logically. And I had forgotten that, in addition to being my son, you are likewise the grandson of Urc Tabaron, whom the Norns ordered to regard Fergail as his grand-daughter."

After that, Elair spread out, a bit wearily, the toil-hardened hands of a ploughman, those hands which would draw no more music from a harp of fine maple-wood. He regarded yet again the familiar and neat and sober-colored home from which he would never be traveling away now except in his coffin. And he said:

"Well, then, let us honor piously the decree of the

omnipotent Norns, since, after all, it does not interfere with my way of living."

"Furthermore," the young Queen observed, with that pensive smile which Elair's heart had remembered always, "this handsome and well-spoken lad is very like you, my dear Elair, as you were in the days of your youthfulness. To be looking at him, after so many years, makes me feel like somebody in a delightful love poem, because I always did fancy you, rather. Anything which I may have said about hating you, Elair, joy of my heart, was just a manner of speaking, or perhaps I ought to say 'my dear father-in-law,' inasmuch as it really was he, and not you, who gave me the blue mug."

"You speak logic," Elair agreed, "so far as anybody can understand you: and it is wholly pleasing to find you, and the Norns also, in accord with logic, for at least this once. Do you marry Conan; and in that way fulfill honorably the terms of your oath."

*   *

THIRTY-ONE

THE ETERNAL HUSBAND

*

No, Elair, and it is not at all that I object to our son's being a king, exactly," said Oina—after the royal couple had driven away on their honeymoon, in the gold chariot of Queen Fergail, and after only Mr. Smith remained with Elair and Oina in the gray house, —"but still, at the same time, Elair, if you want me to be perfectly frank in saying just what I do think about that skinny scatter-brained young woman, with her bleached hair and her cat's eyes, it might be better for me not to."

"I am certain, Oina, that your opinion in everything befits a mother-in-law; and yet, upon the whole, I would prefer not to hear it."

"Your will is my will, Elair," she replied, meekly.

Then Elair regarded his sedate, plain-faced little wife with approval. He looked afterward at Mr. Smith, with a large complacency.

"Queens," said Elair, "are all very well in their way; and so, in their own way, are beauty, and applause, and power, and wealth, and poetry, and wisdom, and a great many other superb matters to which Oina and I have not any pretensions."

"No, my poor Elair," returned Mr. Smith; "and I fancy that, yet again, the dark magics of Urc Tabaron, which fetched you to Branlon, have something to answer for. They have got you contentment, that strong drug, that slow killer of noble-heartedness."

"None the less do I find it perturbing," Elair continued, "that Queen Fergail should have thought I would be leaving Oina, for any of these matters which are more superb than contentment. It does not seem to me a promising outlook, to have a daughter-in-law with such flighty notions."

Thus speaking, he had half put his arm about Oina, the gray witch who had reformed Elair the Song-Maker, before he withdrew his arm stiffly. He withdrew it because in the mind of Elair was moving a confusion of tenderness and of worship and of yet other large emotions such as, he felt, it was unbecoming for a husband of so many years' standing to cherish about his own wife.

Yet he thought happily about his own wisdom in declining to accept the wisdom of Urc Tabaron, and about his own shrewdness in escaping from so many wonderful fine ladies, such as Morgaine, and that dreadful feather-brained Fergail, and Eudocia, and Astrild, and a dozen or so other splendidly shaped and colored, bright beings, who would have made of Elair the Song-Maker a great lord, or even a demi-god perhaps, but for his shrewdness. Yes; he had bargained very thriftily with his one life upon earth, by getting out of it, not any power or wealth or large famousness, but just Oina. He had got, in brief, a contentment which rather frightened him, because it all depended on Oina entirely.

He knew that, always and very deeply, now, he had a need of this quiet-spoken, plain little creature; that, without her, his days would be comfortless; that he more or less adored her; and that, above all, if ever she discovered these facts, it would be extremely embarrassing. It was the sort of thing of which women took advantage.

So the reformed song-maker did not speak of these matters. Instead, he looked sidewise, with scowling disapproval at the disordered supper table; and he said, angrily:

"Come now, you dawdling slut! but I will not live in a pig-sty, as I have told you time and again. Do you make tidy this dreadful mess! And besides that, where are your manners, small mouse? Why do you not warm up a good supper for Mr. Smith and for me, now that this good-for-nothing Fergail has left all my red pottage stone-cold?"

PART FOUR

THE BOOK OF CLITANDRE

*   *

*

"Ecben is now governed, under a Constitution adopted April 13, 1929, by a two-chamber legislative body, consisting of a Senate (Czac) of 111 members, and a House (Hrohof) of 444 members, elected by universal suffrage, in a method which takes care of minorities through an efficient jail system. Freedom of speech, press, religion, companionate marriage, judicial bribery, birth control, etc., is guaranteed. The President (Träsc) is elected, upon a commercial basis, by the Parliament (Wonil) for as long as the public can be deluded by him."

*   *

THIRTY-TWO

HIGHWAY ROBBERY

*

Now the tale turns to the third magic of Urc Tabaron, which had been at work for some while before it caused a masked man to speak with exalted politeness.

"Your attendants, madame," remarked this masked man, "I have killed through a most unfortunate error. I can but apologize."

Gravely considering the two corpses at her feet, Marianne replied to this statement, with a courteous yet unmistakable air of reproof,—

"Murder, sir, is not thus lightly to be dismissed as a mere error in judgment."

And it was obvious that the propriety of her sentiments had impressed the highwayman favorably. He dismounted at once from his black mare; and removing his red-plumed hat, he declared, in frank contrition:

"I was not thinking about the decease of these lackeys with the seriousness which their fate merits. I admit my fault. These two have died bravely in defence of you, madame, in the while that their more intelligent comrade galloped away in search of the police. These two at this instant, no doubt, are being welcomed into paradise with a great deal more of enthusiasm than awaits him at the police station. So let us duly honor these undergraduate archangels."

"That, sir, is nobly spoken, with a ring of true poetry," Marianne conceded: "and yet, to a gentlewoman in my present distressed condition, fine words avail little."

Her situation, it was beyond dispute, seemed deplorable, and of a sort which in no feature befitted a maid of honor to the strait-laced Queen of Ecben. In broad daylight the coach in which Marianne was riding had been attacked by this masked horseman, as her party attempted to pass through an outlying spur of the forest of Branlon. Her coachman and one of her outriders, in the quick confusion of some spirited gunplay, had fallen victims to the marauder's superior marksmanship. The other outrider had at once vanished, in the direction of the near-by police station. And Marianne thus remained deserted, in a magic-infected forest, alone with two deceased persons and a desperado but too regrettably alive.

In such circumstances, the Queen's maid of honor produced her pocket handkerchief, and gave way to pardonable emotion, in the while she continued,—

"I assuredly am the most unfortunate of living creatures!"

"I deny that, madame," the masked man returned, with warmth.

She paused then in her weeping; and she put by her handkerchief. She upraised toward the young highwayman two enormous eyes, blue as cornflowers. This shrinking, tender, blonde girl, he perceived, was lovely beyond any poet's imagining; and great was the man's joy and delight for the well-remembered beauty of her appearance.

A large cloak of vair covered all save her dear face; yet this cloak was now open a little way, so that upon her breast showed a silver gleaming; and she gazed up at him forlornly, from out of a hood of vair, saying, in her frank terror:

"Let us be sensible, sir! Your orders to stand and deliver, combined with your dexterity in putting out of life my two attendants, have led me to regard your moral principles with suspicion. Is it not unavoidable that I should shudder to find myself thus left alone with you in the midst of a forest?"

"But I, madame——" he protested.

"For an indiscretion," she explained, "leads naturally to wrong-doing; and thence one slips, almost inevitably, into actual sin. You have indiscreetly killed two of my lackeys; with what I can but describe as foolhardiness, you have permitted Lelio (for such is the name of my third attendant) to ride hence in search of the police of Arleoth. You now contemplate, I cannot doubt, the wrong-doing of robbing me of those jewels which I was fetching back to wear at the court ball this evening."

"But I, madame—" he repeated.

"Oh, I do not dispute," Marianne admitted, broad-mindedly, "that, in so far as you are a highwayman, such wrong-doing is a part of your professional duties. I do not criticize the wrong-doing, in itself, but only the most dreadful carnal sin which you intend now that I am at your mercy. Well, then, to get over with the wrong-doing as quickly as may be possible, you will find my jewel-case is on the seat of the coach, to the left side."

She sobbed afresh, in the while that Marianne prepared to meet, without any extra discomforts, a doom worse than death, by unfastening her cloak of vair. When this cloak was put by, you saw that she was clothed wholly in black, with a dove embroidered above her young breasts in threads of silver. She resorted once more to her handkerchief, saying:

"I am helpless. So my conscience is clear. I shall only have to lament that a big and bold and impudent beast of a bandit has no conscience."

"But I, madame—" he cried out, removing his mask.

"Certainly I can see for myself that you are big. Your conduct has shown you to be bold. You have rather nice eyes, too"—she remarked, in a wanly smiling endeavor to be strictly fair about everything. "As for the impudence, well, but, after all, the amenities of court life have taught me that one young man is no pennyworth worse than another young man, when it comes to being alone with a defenceless and inexperienced girl, so that if, instead of being a bandit, you happened to be a leading banker or a baron—or for that matter, I regret to add, a bishop anywhere under forty—the terrors of my present state would be no less lively. For you men are all alike. Until, at any rate, you have passed fifty."

"But I, madame," he replied, "but I, I, I! Will you not ever permit me the poet's privilege of talking about myself? It is I who am the most unfortunate of living creatures, because I adore you. For an entire year, lacking but a month, I have adored you hopelessly."

"Why, but whatever can the monster of iniquity be talking about?" Marianne inquired, of nobody in particular.

Thus speaking, the fair young girl walked some little way apart from the relics of her former attendants, directing her progress toward a picturesque, grassy, and soft-looking ridge; she sat down among the violets which adorned this ridge; and she charitably turned back the flowing black sleeves which half hid her very lovely small hands.

Such affability emboldened the tall bandit to introduce himself as Clitandre, at present a protégé of Mr. Smith, the Lord of the Forest, who, by a strange magic, had released Clitandre from his prison in

Melphé, where the lad lay under sentence of death for house-breaking. Mr. Smith had completed this kindness by establishing the young man in the more wholesome out-of-door pursuits of brigandage. Yet Clitandre was not merely a highwayman but a general practitioner of theft in all branches.

His mother, Madame Arachne, he explained, had in some inexplicable fashion strayed out of Greek mythology into the dreams of a god, in which she had figured intimately. Clitandre had been the result of this intimacy. And Arachne, as Clitandre furthermore explained, had painstakingly perfected her son in the exercise of every acquisitive art, after the disappearance of his father, the sublime Master of Gods, and prior to her change of life when she again became a large spider, through a renewal of the old doom put upon Arachne very long ago by Pallas Athene.

Of his mother's charms and of her maternal devotion and of her never-tiring industry Clitandre spoke glowingly. He protested that only once had he found her equal among womankind.

"Aha!" returned Marianne, with a large-eyed and very lovable archness.

"Yes," said Clitandre, gravely,—"only once."

He looked full upon her; and that which she saw in his ardent dark young face both pleased and a little troubled her.

Thereafter, with a praiseworthy attention to practical affairs, such as befitted his mother's son, Clitandre fell to reloading his discharged pistols, and to speaking, with a refined fervor, about his first sight of Marianne in the market-place of Arleoth. He spoke then of the respectful passion which he, an ambitious and high-minded but as yet undistinguished member of the criminal classes, had cherished ever since that afternoon for the Queen of Ecben's maid of honor.

It was a pure worship, he assured Marianne, in the while that he carefully primed his big pistols, without any carnal taint. It was the immaculate star-towering love of the troubadours re-born in the heart of one who remained always, at heart, a poet, whatsoever might be the occasional, nay, the inevitable, prosaic passages in his professional career as a brigand. Clitandre desired merely to see his adored lady, now and then, if only at a distance, noting her numerous bright perfections; to worship these perfections; and thereafter to resume, with renewed ardor, the composition of his heroic love poem, "A Garland for Marianne," which would tell fittingly of his unexampled passion.

"Alas, sir," declared Marianne, "it is not well to speak of poetry, or of love either, to a maid of honor to the Queen of Ecben. The Queen's strictness in overseeing our moral principles is unbelievable; it swaddles us in ever-present maternal affection and a never quiet meddlesomeness; so that, only this very morning, it sent me on a depressing errand. For my dear friend Célie, I must tell you, was to-day confined in the Convent of the Magdalens, on account of three fervent sonnets and a half-dozen articles of male wearing apparel which were found in her reticule. I have but now returned from bidding my adored pet farewell at the gate of her consecrated prison. And I was going very sadly back to my court duties at Miradol when you interrupted my journey, which was already sufficiently heartbreaking, with assassination."

"Indeed, madame," returned the highwayman, mournfully, "I have committed great sacrilege. In the way of business I attacked your coach without knowing who occupied it. Judge then of my horror when I find that, of all creatures in the world, I have molested the one creature whom I worship!"

"But why," said Marianne, with grave innocence, "why should you worship me in particular?"

"Because, madame, I am a poet. Your perfections, as I have previously remarked, inspire me. They are even now inspiring me with a new stanza to my 'Garland for Marianne.'"

She regarded this tall and remarkably handsome malefactor with appreciation. She most certainly knew of no debauched young courtier who, when thus left alone with an innocent blonde girl, in this lonely forest, would have devoted the occasion to composing poetry.

"Your principles, Master Clitandre," said Marianne, "are above reproach. The dear Queen herself would approve of your principles, I am afraid. It follows that I shall look forward with intense interest to the receipt of your beautiful poem; and I shall devour every line of it with applause and unbounded pleasures. Especially if you can get it to me in the summer, when one has time for reading."

Clitandre answered: "If not with pleasure—O Lady, properly endowed with high station at a queen's court, and made peerless in pre-eminence by your bright virtues and by the gifts of the Graces in some hour of unusual prodigality—if not with pleasure, if not with your discerning applause, yet do you receive the inconsiderable verses of a still unpublished poet with charity! and do you glance through the spectacles of indulgence upon the slight results of prolonged labors! Not mine are the talents of blind Homer or of bald-headed Æschylus; and though the elephant affords to the huntsman ivory, and the civet-cat a sweet smelling perfume, yet may the hare give only his hide, and the calf cutlets."

Then Clitandre said: "Lady, the gods weigh the wills of men, not their offerings; therefore may you, who appear to me divine, well imitate your fellow divinities. Pallas Athene, although a thoughtful and serious-minded immortal, desired that web which was woven by my mother Arachne; therefore may you, it is possible, desire a tapestry into which the son of Arachne has interwoven fine words of diverse sounds with the shuttle of respectful adoration. If I have not labored with the good will of the Muses and a discreet

placing of my cæsuræ—if my tropes ring unhand-
somely—then let it be from you that the offspring of
my foiled striving receives its doom. If otherwise, then
let it be the well-shaped and the silk-soft hand of
Marianne, more white than is the pallid paper which
conveys to her my love very timidly, yea, let it be the
worshipful hand of Marianne which, in exchange for
her 'Garland,' places upon my brow a wreath of laurel,
the poet's customary reward."

And Clitandre said also: "It is permitted you, Lady,
to convict me of all sins except only the crime of care-
lessness. So far as I was able, I have always paid an
untiring homage to my Muse wheresoever I might
happen to be, even in a prison cell. But the talons of
the law have often molested my wooing of chaste
Erato; wigged judges and rude jailers have instructed
me more deeply in penal codes than in scansion; and
the police also have refused to honor the license of a
poet. Over and yet over again, and under many aliases,
have I fled from all sorts of fetters save only those of
Apollo which constrain the inspired bard; and in the
shadow of the scaffold I have written, it may be, with
some little unevenness."

To this simple but sincere speech Marianne had
listened with unconcealed emotion. She was touched
by the frank fervors of the young highwayman's passion. But other matters now engaged her attention and
proclaimed its interruption to be inevitable; so that
Marianne sighed regretfully, and observed:

"I am moved, sir, by the single-heartedness of your devotion. A maiden's modesty must check me from saying more at this particular instant. For it now occurs to me that the police, as you suggest, are immune from many emotions of a superior nature. And I notice that Lelio approaches us attended by an entire squadron of constables from Arleoth."

Clitandre arose, loosening his long sword in its brown leather scabbard; and then, drawing two of the big silver-mounted pistols from the half-dozen which adorned his wide crimson belt, he declared:

"I deduce death. I infer that it becomes my duty to rebuke with carnage the incivility of these policemen, who have thus interrupted a conversation of grave importance."

"It would be far more dignified, Master Clitandre," Marianne pointed out, "as well as very much more scathing, to express your displeasure by withdrawing in silent contempt. It would also—in view of their numerousness, apart from the circumstance that each constable carries a large blunderbuss—be a great deal more prudent."

The young man perceived the justice of this advice, and replied:

"Moreover, if I remain here, madame, I must necessarily despatch a number of them before I have the chance to express my contempt at full length. The slain persons would thus miss the point of my discourse. Yes, you are right. It will be more adequate to direct against the chief of police a satiric poem denouncing his department and all members of it in such terms as will blight the remainder of his existence and consign everybody of his profession to eternal shame."

Thus speaking, Clitandre the poet highwayman mounted his black mare, and resuming his black mask, he bowed ceremoniously. He then rode away, in a local hailstorm of hurtless bullets, leaving Marianne, unharmed and unrobbed, to be rescued by the complacent constabulary.

*   *

MR. SMITH PLAYS CHESS

*

When Clitandre had returned to Volmar's home, upon the southern borders of Branlon, he found Mr. Smith was spending the evening there. They all supped together, except Mr. Smith, who ate nothing. After that, when the King of Osnia's daughter was about her dish-washing, and when well-fuddled Volmar had gone to sleep upon a couch under a robe of sables, then Mr. Smith took from out of a bag that was woven of gold threads a chess-board, made of gold and of rubies, and the chess men carved in onyx and moulded in bright orichalc. Thus handsomely did he play at chess with Clitandre in the while that the young highwayman talked about the day's doings.

Nor was it a great while before the Lord of the Forest had heard his tall thieving son's fine rhapsodies about Marianne indulgently.

"Child of a dream," replied Mr. Smith, "when I released you from a deep dungeon it was in order that you might follow after your own dreams unhindered. So do you continue by all means to adore this blonde dream-woman. And do you count on my aid whenso-ever it may be needed. Check."

"Sir," said Clitandre, in a warm glow of enthusiasm, which promptly cost him a bishop, "you remain the most splendid of patrons. I regret only that you do not empower me to steal something in your behalf, because, as I shall always remember, I would have been hanged last spring, on account of the Duke of Melphé's best pair of candlesticks, but for your staunch friend-ship for my parents."

"Let us distinguish, Clitandre!" replied Mr. Smith, modestly. "I was not ever your father's true friend, even though I did know sublime SMIRT, I flatter my-self, better than did most people. I very often thank fortune for this fact, upon at least two grounds. Check again, I believe. As for your mother Arachne, well, but as I always said, there was something about the way in which her head was set on her neck that I found specially charming; and her predilection for eating her husbands, after she had once used them, was after all but the combining of a certain fastidiousness with the virtue of thrift. So it follows, my dear boy, yes, it follows that I delight to see the son of Arachne mak-ing a young idiot of himself thus wholesomely."

"Ah, sir, but Madame Marianne is perfection!" said Clitandre, as he castled.

"She customarily is," returned Mr. Smith, "at your age. Check. And that she thinks well of you I do not doubt, for you have much the look of your father."

"It is good hearing, sir," replied Clitandre, reverently, and with the loss of a knight, "that I should in any manner resemble that divine hero whose great fame had no equal either upon earth or in heaven."

"Well, in a way, Clitandre—check—that is true, just as that is true about the Borgias and Mary's little lamb and Judas Iscariot. Still, one does distinguish. Check."

"Yet one does not split hairs, sir—except at the grave cost of tonsorial blasphemy—in according reverence to sublime SMIRT. Yes; the game is yours, Lord of the Forest. Nor can I play now another chess game," said Clitandre, rising, "because I have an engagement which summons me forth."

It was an announcing which Mr. Smith received with urbane disapproval, in the while that he leaned back, and lighted a cigarette, and remarked:

"You work too hard, Clitandre. Yes, you inherit your mother's untiring industry. That is a fault on the right side, of course: still, it is not well, after giving all day to highway robbery, for you to devote the night season to burglary. No mortal constitution can stand a strain so incessant."

"Sir, it is not larceny but love which to-night requires my attention."

Now was Mr. Smith abeam with divine complacency; and he said:

"Why, but can it be that, impressed by the *bel air* and the fine eyes which you got from your father, this Marianne has granted you an assignation?"

Clitandre was horrified; and he showed as much, in declaring:

"Such an event, sir, is as far beyond my merits as it exceeds the imaginable limits of my revered lady's condescension. I can think of nothing more dreadful, or more sacrilegious, than is this notion of my approaching Madame Marianne as one normally does approach lesser creatures."

"Truly," replied Mr. Smith, "but it takes a long while of blundering to convince any young poet that every woman is made out of flesh and blood. Only at the cost of many sleepless nights, and of much toil and digging in dark places, does he grant that which the more stolid accept as a plain axiom in the first dawn of puberty. But let us discuss matters of less universal interest."

"In fact, sir, I think it would be a great deal better not to think about any such enormities in connection with her whom I worship whole-heartedly, and to whom my eternal faithfulness is pledged for all time. No, Lord of the Forest, I propose to pass this night with a young woman named Nicole, whom I met in Arleoth this morning; and whose elderly husband, by good luck, is now absent from home."

"Come now," said Mr. Smith, "but to console the bereaved, even the temporarily bereaved, and to comfort the lonely, and perhaps also to labor in place of the impotent, is, from every point of view, a fine employment for charitably inclined young men."

"In that case, Lord of the Forest, I shall ask you to excuse me until breakfast—"

In reply, Mr. Smith exhaled philosophically a smoke wreath, which if not in all a paternal blessing was at any rate a consent of unflawed urbanity.

"Moreover," Mr. Smith resumed, "it is praiseworthy that you should intend to remain faithful to your adored Marianne in your thoughts and in your verse-making rather than in your body. It shows a quite proper respect for the operations of the mind, as opposed to one's merely animal faculties. So must both charity and ethics counsel you, Clitandre, to go forward at once to the consummation of your unhallowed desires."

"Why, then, Lord of the Forest, I shall say good-night to you—"

"And besides that, in its every aspect," Mr. Smith continued, affably, "love is a most interesting passion. As has been well remarked, love is a divine rage and enthusiasm, which seizes on man, and works a revolution in his entire being: it unites him to his race; it carries him with new sympathy into nature; it enhances the power of his senses; it opens his imagination; and it adds to his character heroic and sacred attributes."

"Very well, then," said Clitandre, taking up his plumed hat: "then, with your permission, I shall attempt at once to develop my character; and to open my imagination, I believe you said it was, sir; and to enter with sympathy into the workings of nature; and to unite myself with my race, or in any event with one charming member of it."

"By all means, my dear boy," Mr. Smith urged him. "For somewhat unreasonably has a carping lawyer protested that it is wrong for man, who was made for the contemplation of heaven and of all noble objects, to kneel before any lesser idol in the shape of a fair woman,—and thus make of himself a slave to his own servant, the eye, which was given him for more serious purposes. Yet the eye is a faithful and far-reaching servant; we do well to reward it with the edifying spectacle of beauty in a hot sweat. Moreover, now I think of it, neither Bacon nor Emerson has as yet said these superb things. But they will say them by-and-by: and the truth of sage sayings is not a matter of chronology. So do you go at once to your Nicole."

"I shall obey you with pleasure, sir, the moment that you have ended speaking thus learnedly."

"For why indeed should anybody be speaking at any such length about love?" Mr. Smith assented. "To do that is time-wasting. What only matters is that it is in vain we resist the passion of love. So let the wise person yield to it silently, without any prolonged and useless talking. As yet another philosopher is going to declare, I do not know just how many hundred years from this evening, it is far wiser to contend with bulls, lions, bears, and ferocious giants, than with love. Love domineers over every living creature, and can make mighty, or lunatic, or sorrowful, whomsoever love touches. It follows that the man is no better than a fool, or an idiot, or at utmost a school-teacher, who does not acknowledge, through a tribute of awe-stricken dumbness, that this same love is an exceedingly great go'd. For all these reasons, Clitandre, you ought, in my opinion, to make haste to serve this great god, instead of dawdling here and talking about love thus endlessly."

"I intend to do that, sir, as soon as I may. Only, it is you, Lord of the Forest, who are detaining me here with your eloquent advice to go away at once."

This was a statement which self-evidently grieved Mr. Smith, by its large unreason. So he said:

"Now you are talking long-winded nonsense, Clitandre, because it is well known that no young person was ever yet checked in the pursuit of his amours by any advice, no matter how good that advice might be. Yes, and you talk a great deal of nonsense, Clitandre."

"Why, but only about facts, sir," Clitandre answered; "and all facts are of considerable interest to a sound logician."

"Ah, ah!" said Mr. Smith.

"And when I say 'considerable,'" Clitandre explained, "I mean worthy of being considered."

"Do you get along with you to your Nicole!" replied a well-pleased Mr. Smith, "inasmuch as the impudence of this younger generation proclaims them to be beyond saving morally."

*   *

THIRTY-FOUR

IN NICOLE'S ROOM

*

Clitandre came to the little frame-and-plaster house in the Street of St. Silenus at about ten o'clock; and huge was his surprise to discover the second floor of this house brilliantly illuminated. He most certainly had not expected this; it seemed unaccountable; yet, finding the garden gate unlocked, as Nicole had promised him it would be, he went in, and he passed to the rear of the place. Here also, just as had been arranged, the side door proved to be ajar.

He tapped discreetly; but nobody answered him. By-and-by Clitandre entered the dark passageway, and he crept gently upstairs. He came to a flaringly lighted room, and thus peeped through the doorway, upon an interior which he adjudged to be startling, for immediately before him, upon a broad table in the centre of the room, lay two naked bodies.

Of these, one was the corpse of a young man whom Clitandre did not remember to have seen earlier. But the other stripped corpse, beyond any doubt, was that of plump, merry, black-haired Nicole—yes, very ob-

viously, of black-haired Nicole—whom Clitandre had
hoped to admire—it was an ironic reflection—in precisely this state of undress. For another odd thing, at
the big fireplace beyond this so dreadfully burdened
table, three of the constables of Arleoth, in their dark
green-and-silver uniforms, were burning the straw
mattresses of a bed. Clitandre inferred that these men
must have been destroying the clothing of the dead
also, for the air smelt unpleasantly of burned cloth.
From over the mantel a neatly painted Virgin and
Child smiled down upon everything benignantly.

"But then, Valère, what can you expect of a known
rascal like that?" one policeman was saying.

"Indeed, Ariste, I remember him ten years ago,"
said the second policeman, coughing. "Fit to strangle
you, this smoke is. No, but nearer twelve it must have
been, because that was in my first wife's time."

"A superb woman, that, Valère! A sad loss to a great
many of your male friends!"

"You may well say that, Ariste. We are here to-day
and gone to-morrow. Yes, and he was just the same
then, if not more so, on account of his being younger
in those times. No butter would ever melt in his
mouth, bless you! Oh, no! not at any price. But the
lawyer found out different, you remember."

They all three laughed heartily at that.

"Ah, but indeed we do remember, Valère. Him,

with his bald head and his fine alibi!" said the third policeman, as he stirred up the close packed straw, with a long curtain rod. "Like an egg!"

"And she was not the first of them, either," pointed out Ariste, virtuously. "My, but how it all comes back!"

"No, and not by a good armful, if you mean the fat widow woman. Careful there, Geronte, or you will have that there chimney on fire! What did you mean, Ariste, by 'a great many of my male friends?' "

"You were not talking about your male friends, Valère, but about the fat widow woman. You will doubtless recollect that she married the grocer, after all, she did, just the same, Lord help him!"

"Yes," agreed the red-haired third policeman, "and there was a baby in rather less than no time, I seem to remember. So he got out of that too."

"They do, mostly," Valère remarked, despondently, "until it makes an honest man fair fit to question Providence. But I still do not see what you meant by 'a great many of my male friends.' "

"Why, but I meant, of course, that all policemen admire virtue, Valère, because they necessarily see so little of it."

So was it that the three constables of Arleoth discoursed lazily, as they burned up a pair of large straw mattresses under the supervision of a smiling Virgin

in blue and white and of a Child who blessed them
with two eternally lifted fingers; and as Clitandre tiptoed, with a softness begotten by experience, away
from Nicole's room.

"The fact appears obvious," Clitandre reflected, in
the back garden, "that the affairs of my charming
Nicole have taken a bad turn. Let us keep out of them.
She seems, at all events, to have died without pain.

"Well, and I pardon her," he decided, as he walked
safely down the Street of St. Silenus, "although I cannot doubt she betrayed my love. Her companion, on
the table, could not possibly have been the husband
whose advanced age and physical deficiencies she
lamented. No; that sturdy and quite handsome young
man was far more directly my rival, in the rôle of her
lover. With him she deceived me; and for their
perfidy they have both been punished."

He sighed, to think of how strange life was! how
rough-handed in its jests! and in its justice how in-
scrutable! Then Clitandre resumed his meditations,
saying:

"It is true I do not know how, or for what reason,
or by whom, they were punished. The entire affair
is mysterious; and the remarks of the police, as usual,
are not enlightening."

With that, the young highwayman sighed yet again;
he approached the huge dark cathedral of St. Lucy the
Martyr, a most holy place; and so his thoughts passed
naturally to the pureness and the modesty and the

blonde beauty of Marianne, beside which such sordid matters as evil-minded policemen and stray, hole-and-corner illicit love-affairs showed in their true ugliness. He resolved not any longer to think about these ubiquitous nuisances which, night-in, night-out, laid claim to so many young poets.

"Moreover, I can inquire into this tragedy to-morrow morning, at complete leisure. I shall then find in it, perhaps, the material for a most handsome elegy, an outcome which would be gratifying, even in the light of Nicole's probable unfaith. I would not let any woman's unworthiness stand between me and the composition of a really first-class elegy lamenting the world's loss of her unparalleled virtues. Nor would any other true poet, I imagine, be guilty of such unthrift."

Thereafter Clitandre heaved a third sigh, because he knew that, in the long run, he would not ever get any real pleasure out of Nicole's death, no matter what might turn out to have been its cause and its circumstances.

"Yes, I foresee that any possible explanation of this dear, dark-haired young minx's murder cannot but turn out to be a disappointment, when it is compared with any one of the nine very beautiful and horrific explanations now in my mind. Life does not ever live up to the intelligent demands of a poet; life has no conscience, in this respect; and to coerce that which has already happened is a matter of some difficulty.

One can but shrug; and then set for life a yet finer, brand-new example. —Which reminds me that, in the mean while, I have no moral right to let Nicole's double-dealing avert my poetic abilities, such as they may or may not be, from continuing their refined labors upon 'A Garland for Marianne.' "

So he turned now toward Miradol.

*   *

THIRTY-FIVE

MAIDS OF HONOR

*

All that evening Marianne had remembered the incident of the young highwayman. The court ball was magnificent; her partners in the dance were ardent; and yet the polished phrases in which they expressed their dishonorable desires rang hollow, somehow. They lacked the dear naïveté of her poet lover, who at that instant was pursuing his arduous profession among goodness only knew what dangers, and yet always remembering the maiden hallowed with his affections.

Heigho, but it was strangely sweet to be loved thus boyishly by a young poet! And that she might meet him again was an aspiration which Marianne must very certainly introduce into her prayers every evening before retiring.

Well, and something of the romantic interest which had been aroused by her meeting with Clitandre was conveyed by Marianne to her friend Angélique that

night, as the two maids of honor, clothed now in
dressing-gowns, and with their hair down, sat cosily
chatting in Marianne's bedroom on the third floor
of the castle of Miradol. Marianne at this time was
putting away her jewels.

"He might have taken all these bright pebbles,
Angélique. All these I had with me in the coach, as
I told him. But he took nothing."

"Nothing whatever, darling?"

"No," Marianne replied, blushing ever so prettily.

"Such misplaced continence," remarked Angélique,
"appears to me foolish. In fact, I consider it discour-
teous, inasmuch as you two were alone in the forest."

"Your mind," returned Marianne, "remains in-
curably corrupt. So noble was his manner that I did
not think about the great jewel of my honor, except
just in passing, of course, as girls have to do now and
then. But it touched me, it did touch me sincerely,
Angélique darling, the unbusinesslike way in which
he did not make off with these lesser jewels."

"Given his chances, my sweetest, I at least would
not have been so bucolicly honest." And Angélique
gazed with frank envy at the gem-littered dressing-
table. "No other girl at court has such jewels as you
have. And it is so affecting, my pet, that each one of
these bright lovely things should have its sentimental
association."

"It is that which I value chiefly," Marianne admitted, with a fond sigh. "This emerald bracelet, for

example, whensoever I see it, recalls to me the dear Marquis, in the gay days before he married. This brooch is an ever-present reminder of the dear Baron —before he married. In point of fact, I believe it was the dear Chevalier, but the principle is the same. And these pearl earrings revive always the most delightful memories of the dear Bishop. I do not mean, of course, the Bishop of Sorram: he was a pendant, and only turquoise at that. No, I mean the dear Bishop of Arleoth."

"And was that in the days of his celibacy also, darling?"

"But of course, Angélique. Such holy persons cannot marry. Besides, you well know my scruples. I do not accept the friendship of a married man. I think it immoral."

"Ah, but the necklace, dearest!" cried Angélique, raising a stout rivulet of large diamonds. "Now for such a necklace even a maid of honor might almost wink at immorality, for it is a king's ransom."

"No, darling," Marianne corrected her, smilingly, "it is only the ransom of a duke. You see, poor Charles was compelled by his rank and that uncle of his to marry. And he had written me a great number of indiscreet letters, even about her, my sweetest, that was the most delightful part of it all. And he wanted them back, of course."

"I see," said Angélique, "perfectly. And so, what happened?"

"Why, nothing whatever. I showed him a copy of one or two of the worst ones. Then he gave me this necklace at once. And I gave him his letters. And we parted quite pleasantly."

"My pet," said Angélique, admiringly, "but you do manage affairs so well! With such correctness of principle! And with never the least breath of scandal! But whatever can that be?" Angélique asked, with a change of tone, now that a sudden uproar of musketry fire began in the courtyard just beneath Marianne's windows.

"It is only the palace guard firing at somebody and missing him," Marianne answered, with a slight yawn. "No doubt, some reprobate was trying to get in at the window of one or another maid of honor; and against such impropriety the dear Queen has issued the most strict if somewhat old-fashioned orders. They have never hit anybody, though, since that time, you remember, when the dear King had to sit on cushions, and we all pretended not to notice anything, for weeks."

Brown, rather fat, and good-hearted Angélique was by nature prudent. She therefore counseled:

"Yet do you lock up these pretty jewels at once, my dearest. It may just as easily be a thief, because, in the polite circles which we adorn, stealing is almost as frequent as seduction."

"Well, and even if your cynical aphorism be true," Marianne replied merrily, "I do not know but one practising professional thief. And I am tolerably certain the guards' target cannot be my tall and high-hearted Clitandre."

"Alas, madame," said the young man who now entered with haste from the balcony—in the instant that he removed his red-plumed hat and bowed gallantly to the two ladies,—"it is none other."

*   *

THIRTY-SIX

REGARDING A WINDOW

*

Clitandre, as he explained forthwith, had been con-templating the window of his elect lady with emotions which had flowered superbly in three brand-new stanzas to "A Garland for Marianne" before the med-dlesomeness of the palace guard, on their midnight round, had compelled him to climb the waterspout and seek refuge on her balcony.

"I praise Heaven," Marianne returned, hastily tucking up her bright hair, and re-arranging her blue dressing-gown with decorum, "that my poet has so happily eluded their malice."

"Thus far," Angélique emended. She had returned from the balcony, with her plump face uncommonly grave; and she said now:

"They are seeking for you below, Master Clitandre —for such I assume to be your name—with lanterns and newly reloaded muskets. Even to the brusque mind of the professional military man it is apparent that, barring the unlikely event of your being a cherub equipped with wings, you must have entered one or

another of the windows in this part of the palace.
A search has been ordered. It follows that all is lost.
For how may you now hope to escape from the but
too well guarded apartments of a maid of honor?"

"He must descend," said Marianne, "by the outer
window, which opens upon the park outside the
castle. There one encounters no guardsmen."

Angélique regarded her with compassion. "And for
an excellent reason, my pet. The outer side of the
fortress of Miradol is a bare bleak wall which, as the
dear Queen well knows, defies climbing. No; it is possible that an insect could descend the sheer hundred
feet of smooth stone beneath your window; but it is
out of reason to imagine that Master Clitandre or
any other mortal person could manage it without
either a scaling ladder or a ruinous tumble."

"That is true," Marianne answered, unhappily.

"There remains the door," Clitandre suggested.

At that, both the ladies cried out; and they told him
of the six eunuchs waiting in the corridor outside, in
black armor with their faces painted black and white
and red, with black plumes on their heads. Thus terribly garbed were the incomplete but hard-hearted
men-at-arms who guarded the Queen's maids of honor
every night, on account of the strictness of her
majesty's moral principles.

"I can but ask, then," Clitandre said, after a moment of reflection, "that the one or the other of you
should scream for assistance. These sentinels will

enter. Do you then denounce me as the house-breaker that, in point of fact, I occasionally am. They will arrest me. And all will end happily."

"Your plan appears excellent," Marianne admitted, "but for the drawback that it involves your being hanged."

"Death, my adored one, is the fixed end of every man's life. I do not, it is true, desire any such immediate ending. I would prefer to finish my 'Garland for Marianne' without being hurried. But it appears not possible for me to escape unseen from this room. It is most certainly not possible for me to be found here in circumstances"—Clitandre blushed, and he looked modestly away from the two maids of honor—"in circumstances through which your reputation would suffer."

"Oh, but come now!" said Angélique.

"People misconstrue such matters," Clitandre explained. "From the circumstance of a young man's being found in Madame Marianne's bedroom they would draw very shocking conclusions."

"It is true," said Angélique, in a sad twitter, "that for Master Clitandre to be caught here as a thief is permissible. A thief is not compromising. A thief might happen to anybody. Otherwise, do what we may, darling, Master Clitandre will be found here in the morning. Our reputations will be ruined. The dear Queen will behave, as she always does, like an infuriated turkey gobbler with overtones of the tigress.

She will rend both of us to-morrow, just as she did poor Célie yesterday. We too shall be locked up in convents. And our talents would be wasted in a convent, simply wasted, my precious, among nuns and very old clergymen and penitent persons. Besides, Master Clitandre would be hanged just the same, after having compromised both of us."

"You speak sagely, madame," said Clitandre; "so now do you scream with equal wisdom. In this way will the affair be settled to everyone's satisfaction."

Angélique opened her mouth experimentally; and then this brown-haired, stoutish, kind-hearted young woman shrugged in despair.

"I cannot do it," she confessed, with a half-sob. "Logic prompts me to such a shriek as was never heard in any one of the dear Queen's torture chambers. And yet, the nobility of your devotion, my fine young man, to my darling here—well, it chokes me, because I too adore Marianne. No: I simply cannot bring myself to be the cause of your destruction. Instead, I shall go back to my own rooms. And then only Marianne will be compromised and turkey-gobbled at."

"I am foiled," declared Clitandre, "by that mania for self-sacrifice which is habitual to all good women. The guardsmen at this instant are searching for me. At any moment they may forcibly enter this room. My detection is inevitable. And both of you elect to risk eternal dishonor by tacitly emulating clams. It is compassionate, it is seraphic, it is heroic; but it is likewise injudicious."

In his desperation, the young poet knelt humbly at the feet of Marianne. "For an entire year, lacking but the month of May, during which I stole boys for the King of Tarob, I have adored you. Reward my devotion, beloved, with one single yell which will save your honor."

"Clitandre," she answered, "I cannot yell. It would not be dignified."

"Oh, and at such an instant, my heart's dearest, do you intend to stand upon dignity!"

"To the contrary," she replied, sombrely, "I intend now to reward your devotion at some risk of killing it."

"You speak of impossibilities," Clitandre said, with a fond smile, "because so long as life lasts, I shall love the most pure and fair and noble lady whom I have known."

"We must see to it, then, Clitandre, that your life is preserved at least long enough"—the girl returned, touching half maternally his dark hair as he yet knelt before her—"for you, O my dear, foolish, very handsome poet, to finish your great poem."

Marianne went to the window opening upon the public park; and, stooping, she unclosed the compartment beneath this window. She drew forth from the compartment a stoutly made rope-ladder, well-weighted, and she lowered this over the window-sill.

The upper end of this ladder, you now saw, was permanently fastened beneath the window-sill.

"In fact," thought Angélique, admiringly, "it is a splendid, an always handy, and a stable contrivance, such as not even the fat Bishop of Arleoth would hesitate to climb up and down, with his pearl earrings. Nor, I infer, did he. Oh, but yes, one can now well understand how, even in this well-guarded third-story apartment, my sweet Marianne's friends have managed to cultivate her friendship, the minx!"

"You perceive, Master Clitandre," said Marianne, in her sweet, always gentle voice, "that it is simple enough to descend from this room into the park of Miradol."

He had risen. He now lifted a haggard gaze from this permanently installed rope-ladder which, in the same instant, had established the continuance of his safety and the unworthiness of his love. For there was really, he reflected, not any mistaking the implications of a ladder which connected his Marianne's apartments with a public park.

No; the moral standards of court life were not the moral standards which he had learned to revere at his mother's knee when, at all available moments between the indigestion of her last widowhood and the fever of her next marriage, she had lovingly taught him how to distinguish between evil and good. This most beautiful, blonde and saintlike maid of honor was, from an ethical standpoint, no better than the

plump, charming bourgeoise Nicole. In the same evening poor Clitandre had thus found himself to be
betrayed by the only women to whom, within the last
month, he had sworn undying affection: and he began
to doubt if true constancy could be a virtue at all
known to any female person.

"I perceive, indeed," Clitandre remarked, with his
voice breaking, "that to enter and to leave this bedchamber is a simple matter. I perceive the real nature
of you fine court ladies. I perceive the great depths
of my folly; and fiends grin there."

Marianne returned, with sincere compassion: "My
adored child, I did not seek your somewhat exigent
love. I did not merit it, either, perhaps. But I prized
it. And I had only my choice between the risk
of killing your love and the certainty of killing
you, Clitandre. And I really do think you are being
rather ungrateful, to resent not being hanged."

He answered, "It would have been more kindly,
madame, to let me die in my ignorance; for I must die
now, when my time comes, without faith in anything
in this world."

He turned then to the jewel-littered dressing-table,
pointing toward its heaped brilliancies. He spoke
sharply.

"And are these also paste, madame, like your beauty
and your purring innocence, your modesty and your
coy virtues?"

She replied frankly, moved to an unaccustomed

humility by the young highwayman's grief. "They are
the gifts, Clitandre, of those yet other men who have
descended this ladder."

Ceremoniously the proud freebooter took from his
finger a sapphire ring; and he dropped it among the
many-colored gems, saying:

"I must pay my toll, then with the sole trinket I
have about me. I leave also yet other gifts. For I leave,
in this dreadful, gilded and brightly cushioned and
sweet-smelling room, my youth and a poem not ever
finished. Oh, but I know very well that with the aid
of time I shall forget you and the dear anguishes of
my boyhood likewise. But I shall not ever forget that
poem which, had you been worthier—or if you had
but shown the grace to continue deluding me—would
have become one of the world's most great and ever-
living love songs."

For an instant Clitandre was silent. He spoke by-
and-by, with restrained grief, saying:

"You and I must quite perish now, Marianne. Yet
it might well have been that my adoration and your
bright cheating loveliness would have survived us
for a brave long while, could I but have retained my
ignorance for a month more, or even for a week or
two. We would have lived on forever—with Launce-
lot and Queen Guenevere, with Romeo and his Juliet,
with King Solomon and his Shulamite (whose deserv-
edly famous name, I believe, no Biblical commentator
has as yet unearthed), and with yet other of the stand-

ard major saints in Love's calendar. In far-off centuries, in unimaginable cities as yet unbuilded, and
in undreamed-of remote lands which at this present
speaking have not fallen under the spell of polite letters, young hearts would have thrilled with my passion,
and young eyes would have turned you-ward en-
kindled with a poet's ecstasy, forever and forever, my
sweet, if only I could have remained a blind owl, a
dolt, an enamored loud-braying jackass, long enough
to complete 'A Garland for Marianne.' Indeed, I have
no real doubt that in due season—and with, perhaps,
some of the more lively passages omitted—my poem
would have been adorned with editorial notes and
used as a textbook in many colleges."

Clitandre spread outward both hands in despair.
He said, drearily:

"Yes, we have lost our immortality by, at utmost,
a fortnight. The reflection is bitter. I could have finished my masterwork quite cosily in the city jail while
I was waiting to be hanged. But alas! your misguided
kindness, Madame Marianne, has brought into my life
an element of sophistication; you have contaminated
my mind with cynicism; and no great poem was ever
completed except from vast stores of naïveté. So I shall
not be a supreme poet now. I shall sink back into the
drab, jogtrot, humdrum life of a general practitioner
of larceny, until my time comes to be turned off, on
some prosaic scaffold or another. Many ages yet un-
born will not honor the centenary of my birth."

Marianne, standing beside the dressing-table, replied only:

"You will forget me. Yes, only this very moment, Clitandre, you said you would forget me. But, then, it is not as if you men, yes, every one of you, were not exactly alike. You have not the constancy and the more tactful reticence of women."

Clitandre regarded her piteously for an instant. He sighed: and he inclined his head in forlorn assent. Afterward he moved sadly toward the rope-ladder, when Angélique caught at his arm.

"My infants," said plump, practical-minded Angélique, "even in the presence of a great tragedy, it is needful to keep one's head."

Thus speaking, she turned out the three lamps. "So now, now at least, my dear lad, the public at large will not see you climbing out from a brilliantly illuminated window. For the rest, a thing done has an end. It is quite understood that literature is impoverished; that your vocabulary is unequal to the occasion; and that your heart is broken. Yet for the sake of your neck's integrity, Master Clitandre, do you now get out of this window quietly, without any more rhetoric."

Instead, the infatuated young man had stepped toward Marianne. His arms clasped her, and his lips met her lips, in the darkness.

"You have slain a great poet, my sweet," said Clitandre, "not knowing that which you did. None the

234

less do I beseech of posterity that mankind may forgive you as utterly as I now forgive."

Then he left the two maids of honor, by way of
the same ladder which had helped, with polite discretion, so many other fine gentlemen to effect their
departure from happiness.

* *

THIRTY-SEVEN

THE COMPASSION OF WOMEN

*

At the window the two girls watched the young poet's descent; they half saw, in the starlight, his politely raised hat after he had reached earth; and they divined too his prompt disappearance into a grove of laurel-trees. They breathed the sweet scents of the spring night, as the good odors of growing plants arose from the park of Miradol. With extreme caution they drew up the rope-ladder; and they put it back into its hiding place.

Kissing each other happily, they then cried out, the one to the other:

"My pet, our reputations are saved!"

"My darling, our good names remain spotless!"

After that, Angélique rekindled the three lamps, heaving a vast sigh of relief.

"And so," replied Marianne, with a more gentle sigh of true sorrow, "so ends my too brief romance. I really do believe in prudence, and in circumspection, and in appearances, and in all maidenly virtues, Angélique, as heartily as does anybody; and yet, somehow, it is sad to reflect that a poet has died in this room to-night, killed by these virtues."

But Angélique was now looking at the dressing-table, with well-widened brown eyes.

"It would seem undeniable," she replied, "that your fine-talking young thief did not depart altogether in the unpractical rôle of a poet. Here is his twopenny ring, for you to remember him by. But your dear, beautiful diamond necklace, I perceive, is not here. You will be put to the pleasure of replacing it."

"Come now," said Marianne, in warm admiration, "but that was a superb gesture; and at last Clitandre has done something except talk! In the same instant that he embraced me here in the dark, Clitandre was acquiring with his left hand my best piece of jewelry. For I, Angélique, I am now no more to him than is any other woman. He has expressed the fact, with a fine sense of symbolism, to an accompaniment of brisk action. Yes, I admire Clitandre. I begin to think that, after all, he will get on in this world."

And yet, after Angélique had left her for the night, Marianne fell to thinking somewhat wistfully about her lost poet lover. She had shaken, if she had not wholly wrecked, his faith in womankind; and that of course would be to him a great aid in his career. Well, and she hoped that professionally Clitandre would prosper. None the less, there were so very many competent men of business, and so few fine poets, the girl reflected forlornly.

Heigho, but upon this night she had killed a poet in order to confirm a beginning thief in the pursuit of his rather sordid, commonplace vocation! And that Clitandre, the poor, young, ruined, very dear romantic, did not mean ever to pardon this poet's murder, was well shown by the ruthlessness with which he had adopted toward his repudiated love an attitude coldly professional. In thus ending all possible private relations between Marianne and himself, he had behaved sensibly, and with a plain monetary profit: yet for a young poet to behave sensibly in his love-affairs entails always an anguish, and in fact a sort of temporary *felo-de-se*, such as Marianne could not but pity from her heart's bottom.

Fond and ever-tender is the sympathy of a well-reared young woman; though it be extended to all living beings, and even to the most liberal-handed of her decrepit lovers, yet toward a good-looking young man it fares gladliest: and for that reason, at this same instant, Angélique also, in her own rooms, was thinking, with a lively compassion, about Clitandre. He had lost Marianne forever; and that was a great pity, men being what they were in their silly notions about prim-mouthed blondes. Still, the necklace was of a tidy value, apart from the fact that it could so easily be broken up and then reset unrecognizably. It would make, for example, a pair of magnificent bracelets.

Yes, beyond doubt, Angélique reflected broad-mindedly, the chance to acquire in the darkness all those beautiful diamonds, with complete safety, had been too tempting for flesh and blood to resist. She did not really blame Clitandre. Instead, Angélique took out the necklace, from the pocket of her pink dressing-gown, and she put it in her jewel-case, with a charitably condoning smile.

PART FIVE

THE BOOK OF LITTLE SMIRT

* *

*

"In Chang-Chu. . .in 1933-34 there were 25,606 elementary schools, with 9,680,734 pupils, and 1,292 kindergartens, with 107,236 pupils. There were also 546 secondary schools for boys, 733 girls' high schools, 104 normal schools of wizardry, 31 other high schools, 911 technical schools, and 50 special technical schools for the higher branches of magic. Through the influence of American customs, English, as the language of commerce, has become a required study in the elementary schools, but not in print."

*   *

THIRTY-EIGHT

MARRIAGE OF BEL-IMPERIA

*

Now the tale speaks of the fourth magic of Urc Tabaron, telling how it upset the economy of Madam Tana's household in far-away Chang-Chu. Madam Tana was a wise-woman with a tidy practice in abstruse arts. She lived in retirement, seeing few persons except her clients; her one servant, Klinck, who was supposed to be a familiar spirit; and her son, Little Smirt,—as she had named the boy in honor of his father, that sublime Master of the Gods, whom Madam Tana had met in a cave during the days of her now remote youthfulness.

This Little Smirt was a well-thought-of young scholar, whom his mother's watchfulness had made remarkable throughout all Chang-Chu for the sobriety of his conduct. In the dissipations common to young men he took no part: he remained chaste and pious. His elders with one voice applauded Little Smirt; and they cited him to their own sons as a fine example of what these sons ought to be, and, most regrettably, were not.

Well, and one day, when Madam Tana was abroad in the discharge of her profession, great was Little Smirt's surprise to find himself visited by Bel-Imperia, the famous singing-girl, with whom Little Smirt had before to-day exchanged a few repartees but no familiarity.

Madam Tana's misshapen and remarkably tinted servant brought to them a tray containing wine and bread and cakes and apples. Then Little Smirt entreated Bel-Imperia to favor him with a song.

—Whereupon the young lady began a funeral dirge; and Little Smirt pulled an uncommonly long face.

"These mortuary sentiments," he remarked, "while judicious and improving to the mind, and for all that they are expressed with a suitable amount of gloom, cannot reasonably accord with the quite other sentiments of any fortunate male person to whom it has been granted to gaze upon the unparalleled charms of Bel-Imperia."

She replied, modestly, "The elephant of your approval, Little Smirt, has seated itself, with misguided condescension, upon the tadpole of my merit."

"I would not deny," Little Smirt continued, "that from virtually prehistoric times the elegy has been a familiar and generally popular form of art. Indeed, two very fine examples of the elegy may be encountered as early as in the nineteenth and the twenty-fourth books of the *Iliad*. I allude, of course, to the lament of

Briseis for Patroclus and of Andromache for Hector. But evening draws on, with Mama apt to return at any moment; and so, without going into the possibly non-Homeric origin of this poem, I remark merely that an elegy is not exhilarating."

Bel-Imperia smiled sadly; and she began a love song. Little Smirt applauded that liberally.

"For it is thus that I love you, Bel-Imperia," said Little Smirt, "with the large difference that your song does not express one tenth—or, indeed, any fraction, or jot, or gleam, or even a light shadow—of my unrestrained adoration, which will outlive all time."

"Time passes at a variety of paces; but always he approaches a grave-yard," declared the singing-girl. "On this day, which is set for my funeral, it appears unbecoming for the inconsiderable brain of Bel-Imperia to extend any hospitality to thoughts of love."

"Bluntness," replied Little Smirt, "was ever the herald of sincere passion. You speak nonsense, Bel-Imperia. This is not the day of your funeral but of your wedding: for here at hand are all matters demanded by the local custom of Chang-Chu for our immediate marriage."

"Well," said the singing-girl, "but an accomplished tall scholar like you, Little Smirt, must go his own willful way though the dead bar it."

Thereafter they exchanged the two apples of peace, they tasted the sons-and-grandsons cakes, they shared the nuptial cup of rice wine, they ate together the

bread of long life: and Little Smirt (who had inherited from his divine father a fine talent for instruct-
ing his hearers) spoke captivatingly, for about five
minutes, as to the wedding customs of various lands.
When these ceremonies had been performed, Bel-Imperia arose; and she began to sing a tender and
gracious melody, which was called, so the girl said,
"The Dark Road to Branlon."

"My wife," said Little Smirt, "that is a strange sweet
song, and a new song, too, I am thinking, for the words
of it are not known to me."

She replied: "My husband, many words are the
frailty of women. So let us now dismiss my ignoble song, as of no least practical importance to anybody, because the fact has been justly noted by philosophers that music cannot even cure a toothache."

"Well, I would not pretend," Little Smirt said, "to
have made any really thorough study of music, inasmuch as my mastery of several instruments, including
the dulcimer, the trombone, the shawm, and the piccolo, remains as yet theoretic—"

"I am sure, my husband," she again interrupted
him, respectfully, "that, since you are a master of all
noteworthy arts, the contemptible instruments which
you name cannot rationally have deserved your valuable attention. And I never did like the piccolo,
either."

"My wife," he exhorted her, "let us not indulge
in unscholarly overstatement! Three or four things

are unknown to me with absolute certainty, and perhaps a full dozen."

"Now you are being over-modest, my husband; and I cannot believe the garnered fruit of your studies to be thus speckled."

"In fact, now that we discuss music, it does occur to me," Little Smirt admitted, "that horns and trumpets were invented by the Etrurians. I consider it remarkable that the first organ is said to have been made by a barber. I believe that the earliest flutes of which we have record were manufactured, variously, from the wood of the lotus-tree and the leg-bone of a kid. To the other side, I do not just at present recall the origin of the lyre, of the triangle, of the harp, or even of the barbitos, which is mentioned favorably by both Anacreon and Sappho."

"My husband, I accept with due gratitude all these savory crumbs from the high table of your omniscience, where eloquence feasts uninterruptedly with learning."

"But," Little Smirt continued, "as a practising poet, I do, quite naturally, know by heart all the world's better-thought-of songs, from its earlier epics, bucolics and idyls, down to the current madrigals, sestinas and epithalamiums. Yet your fine song, my wife, I do not know at all. And I deduce it must be a brand-new song."

"My husband," replied Bel-Imperia, "it is an old song, as ancient as human grief, and as far out of fashion nowadays as are the naïve magics of April or the neat turn of an epigram. For that reason I will write out the words of this song, here upon the august walls of your revered and infernally accomplished mother; so that at leisure your acute mind may trifle with such debased futilities as the offensive Bel-Imperia has but lately rendered with the voice of a rain-crow."

Then, using a red crayon, beautiful Bel-Imperia wrote upon the wall the words which she had just sung. Little Smirt read them slowly and perplexedly, for these words seemed now without any meaning. He turned, to say as much, as well as to protest against the unjust simile of a rain-crow; and he perceived that his wife had vanished.

"That is a fine trick to be playing upon an impatient bridegroom," said Little Smirt, merrily, as he looked first behind all the screens and then under the divans.

*   *

THIRTY-NINE

CONCLUSIONS OF MADAM TANA

*

For what reason, O my son and most undignified of all fools," demanded Madam Tana, who entered at this moment—attended by her servant Klinck, who came hopping ponderously behind her, carrying a market basket,—"for what reason, O heavenly afflicted creature, are you lying down upon my rugs peeping under my divans? and what do you mean by this silly talk about the impatience of a bridegroom?"

"All men, Mama," Little Smirt replied to her, dusting his knees, "are bidden to seek heaven: but, as goes your second question, I shall spare your blushes by not answering it."

"You need not," declared Madam Tana; "inasmuch as my senses have well served me, both in my high-hearted youth and in my austere old age. Yet when, O my son and most unhappily misguided of idiots, did you become a bridegroom?"

"It was but a moment since, Mama, or it might have been five minutes ago, that I married Bel-Imperia, the fair singing-girl."

The old wise-woman looked at him very gravely. Her shrivelled underlip quivered; yet when she spoke, it was with her usual harshness.

"Bel-Imperia died the day before yesterday," said Madam Tana. "Her burial tablets have been erected; her not in the least remarkable body has been put under ground; and all probable needs of this hussy beyond the tomb have been duly provided for and burned, in the form of a paper coach, six paper chairs, a box of cosmetics and of rubber goods, a paper bed large enough to accommodate two persons, and a neat fortune in counterfeit paper money. I know this, because I have but newly returned from her funeral. So do you explain to me, O my son, just what has happened."

Little Smirt, in a state of some natural confusion, told of how Bel-Imperia had visited him; and Madam Tana's scarlet-colored servant—for red was the hue of Klinck everywhere—croaked out an assent as to this having been no dream but a true happening.

"That the girl was not mortal seemed plain to anybody," said Klinck, "inasmuch as at her finger-tips she had bright shining claws, and her body cast no shadow. I noted these facts, but considered them none of my business. And besides, Madam Tana has had many such improbable visitors since she deserted sublime SMIRT to follow after the white rabbit that lives in the moon. I have learned to serve all such visitors without comment."

"Then do you continue to do so," said Madam Tana, striking him: but to Little Smirt she said, gently,—

"O my unfortunate son, do you likewise continue."

Little Smirt obeyed her, giving a complete account of his wedding; and the old woman listened, nodding her wise gray head.

"You appear honorably to have married a dead person," she said, at last. "This is serious, O my son; and from all points of view you would have done far better to have indulged illegally that disgraceful appetite for immodest young females which I have so constantly caught you attempting to satisfy."

"Oh, but, Mama," Little Smirt protested, "a sound knowledge of anatomy is needful to all scholars."

"—For whether this dead trollop," Madam Tana went on, "will be re-born as a bird or an animal or a human being, and whether male or female, depends upon the meritorious actions of her last life. I imagine that most singing-girls evolve into some lower order of vermin. But in any case, the spirit of Bel-Imperia will keep its power over your spirit."

"I desire that, Mama, for my hand and my heart likewise have been given to Bel-Imperia, and I cannot live without her."

"I spoke in very much this way, my son, in the days of my youthfulness, when a white rabbit ended the love between me and that good-for-nothing father of yours. But time cured me."

After that, Madam Tana stood for a while with her gray head tilted backward, peering as if in perplexed disapproval at the strange red writing upon her wall, of which Little Smirt could make nothing; and her withered lips moved silently. She was puzzling out, you perceived, some meaning, after all; and she sighed over it.

Then the wise-woman burned incense in a brass tray until the tray was filled with ashes. She smoothed flat these ashes. She held up the still-smoking brass tray above her head, with both hands, and she cried out the Thief Charm, saying:

"Aragoni Parandamo Eptalicon Lambouréd! Be it shown what power has stolen the soul of my son!"

Afterward Madam Tana lowered the tray; and Little Smirt saw that upon the ashes was now an imprint.

"It is like the hoof of a goat," said Little Smirt.

"Yes," said Madam Tana, "for this is Urc Tabaron's signature. This involves the Lord of the Forest. So it seems you have married yourself into the entourage of a sort of god, or, at any rate, of a local deity. You might have done worse, when one considers matters calmly—and allows for your hard-headed imbecility, —inasmuch as that worthless father of yours was a very great god, and you cannot well help taking after him. In any event, everything is plain now; and you must seek for your Bel-Imperia in Branlon."

"By what road, Mama, shall I come to Branlon?"

"I will find you a guide," said the old woman.

*   *

FORTY

THE DEAD HAND

*

Madam Tana returned by-and-by, bearing in her right hand her left hand, which, as Little Smirt saw with astonishment, had been chopped off her wrist. Now it was a peculiarity of the hands of Madam Tana that she had been born without any little finger upon either hand.

She spoke sullenly to Little Smirt, saying: "This hand will be your guide. Do you lay it in your breast. Then when my hand presses upon your right side, do you turn to the left; but when the cold fingers of my hand clutch at your shallow and worthless heart, do you turn to the right; and so will you come to Branlon across this world and across half the lands beyond common-sense."

Little Smirt said, "But why have you thus mutilated yourself, Mama, in order to serve my desire?"

She replied, with venom: "In order, O tall blockhead and most addlepated of all fine-looking imbeciles, that your desire might be served. There was not any other way."

Well, and at that, Little Smirt embraced her, weeping copiously.

"There is no love," he remarked, "in any way comparable in its unreason to the love which a mother cherishes for her son."

She pushed him away from her, saying, "Nonsense, you great clodhopper!"

"Yet every mother," Little Smirt continued, "first encounters her son in childbed as the direct provoker of sufferings which are reputed to be considerable; she needs perform for the brat throughout his childhood all those uncaptivating if sanitary tasks which are necessitated by the unreticence of the young; and her reward is that, should she by-and-by make of him a mammal at all suited to polite circles, it is in the home of some other woman that the jackanapes will be displaying the sparse virtues so painfully and so laboriously taught him by his dear mother. He is for her, in short, a source of anguish, of hard work, of dirt, of anxiety, and of ingratitude; and she requites him with love. It is a phenomenon I do not at all understand."

"There are many things which you do not understand, you gross long-legged dunce," declared Madam Tana, "and among these I would include your own incessant talking."

"Yes, Mama," replied Little Smirt, meekly, "even though, with care, I do now and then catch the general drift of it. Anyhow, I was going on to remark

that, just as of all sons I am perhaps the most unworthy, so among mothers are you beyond doubt the
best."

"Well—" she said, speaking almost gently.

"Nor do I exclude," Little Smirt continued, "the
most pre-eminent of the world's mothers. Indeed, when
I consider Niobe, and Nature, and Eve, and Rachel,
and Necessity, and Cornelia (who was the mother of
the Gracchi, Mama) , and the old woman who lived in
a shoe, and that very famous she-wolf who suckled
Romulus and Remus—why, then, Mama, I feel
wholly certain that by rights you belong somewhere
in this noble category."

Madam Tana then struck him with her remaining
hand, saying,—

"It is in fact the curse of a she-wolf that she bears
cubs."

"Oh, but, Mama, but you have quite misunderstood
a refined classical allusion," Little Smirt protested,
rubbing his cheek.

"That is possible, you young windbag, even though
your saying so does not make it any whit the more
probable. At all events, do you now stop your eternal
chattering, which reminds me but too unpleasantly of
your divine father; and do you be off to your hussy
in Branlon."

"I owe to you at all times obedience," replied Little
Smirt, fondly.

He wondered, in his touched heart, why they must

at every minute be squabbling, in defiance of the
deep love between them; and he suspected that, if he
got from his father a certain loquaciousness, it must
have been from his unspeakably more dear Mama that
Little Smirt had inherited a reliable talent for making himself disagreeable. Well, but heredity, he reflected, was a vast problem; and the present instant
seemed rather ill-chosen for its complete solution.

After that, he kissed his dear but intolerable mother;
he put on his purple cap adorned with a jaunty peacock feather; and he took up his spear, which had two
tassels on it, to denote a hero and a scholar.

He then mounted his gray horse, turning westward.
So was it that Little Smirt set forth in search of a dead
woman, with the lopped-off charmed hand of another
woman to guide him.

*   *

FORTY-ONE

CHASTITY OF A SCHOLAR

*

Now the hand of his mother was to Little Smirt an unfailing aid. It lay in his bosom like a cold frog. But at every forking of the road, the hand would indeed move sluggishly, he found; and it would thus show to Little Smirt which fork led toward Branlon. It guided him in this way across nine kingdoms, six duchies, and four principalities, without at any time leaving him doubtful as to what was the right road and the right course of prudence also.

For example, when he had ridden but a short distance, across a barren and hillocky plain, broken here and there by large white stones and by tall clumps of coarse whip-like grass, he came to seven palm-trees. Among these trees stood a gold-colored pavilion, about which lay scattered the bones of dead men. Above the entrance to this tent hung an empty birdcage; and at the entrance to this tent, near a table-top of jacinth placed on two stools of ivory, sat a woman clothed in scarlet who was wholly beautiful.

"Health and fair days!" said Little Smirt.

She replied, "Health and fair days, and delectable nights also!"

"Aha," said Little Smirt, "but that is a timely wish, for already the evening draws on."

She came near to his stirrup, stately in her gait as the peacock under whose plume Little Smirt travelled, and graceful in her every movement as is the swaying bough. This much Little Smirt observed: for his mind was now seeking similes; so he marveled at the glorious hair of this woman, which had the color of midnight, and at her skin white as lime, and at her gleaming eyes like the large stars in a time of frost.

"Truly the evening draws on," said this most lovely lady; "and the wise birds are already going to bed in the tree-tops above us. They are at liberty to keep one another awake there, even until dawn. But for me this is a more desolate evening, tall youth: for my husband has gone upon a long journey, from which he will not return until to-morrow afternoon; and he has left me here, quite alone, to guard his treasures as I best may."

Little Smirt said: "So you have treasures here, most beautiful of ladies, at your own free disposal, inasmuch as your husband will not be returning until to-morrow afternoon? Of what nature are these treasures?"

"Can you not guess, O gently speaking, sweet troubler of my heart?"

"Well, in most Oriental countries," replied Little

Smirt, soberly, "such treasures would, in all likelihood, consist of fine carpets of raw silk and fringed mats of scented goats' leather; and cups of carnelian studded with rubies, and gay satins and figured brocades; and large camel bladders filled with ambergris and with musk and with camphor; and perhaps you have likewise a number of knicknacks made out of ebony and of ivory and of Andalusian copper."

"You have not hit it as yet, O fair scholar more comely than the moon. I guard thirty treasures: but no one of them have you mentioned, nor have they maddened you with delight in them, as yet."

"Oh! ah!" said Little Smirt, whose profound studies had, of course, included Spanish and a great host of old Spanish customs. "Can it be, O my life, that, of these thirty treasures, three are white and three are black and three are red? Is it possible, O woman of beauty, that, of these treasures, three are long and three are short and three are wide?"

"Indeed, that is the exact way of it, dear scholar more ruddy than the sun," she returned, smiling: "and so great is my joy in your handsomeness, so boundless is my desire to increase your knowledge, that if you will but come into this tent, then I will show you every one of those treasures which are the peculiar delight of my husband."

"Well, inasmuch as Gregory the Great tells us seeing is believing, that appears to me a fair test," Little Smirt answered, "if only because it is not righteous for any scholar, whatsoever may be the funds of his secular information, to dispute the word of a pope."

And then, just as he made ready to dismount from his horse, the cold hand in his bosom pinched him with a vigorousness which caused Little Smirt to gasp.

"Nevertheless, madame," Little Smirt continued, gravely, after one instant's pausing, "those treasures which belong by law to your husband ought not to be looked at and handled, and variously enjoyed, by any other person. No, I commend your warm hospitality; but upon second thought, I shall not accept it."

Then he rode on, without taking very much pleasure in the high-mindedness of his own conduct, because hospitality is a virtue, he felt, which ought to be encouraged rather than snubbed. Indeed, for all that Little Smirt could tell, he might have acted with extreme rudeness toward the lady's husband also; and that possibility rather troubled the conscience of Little Smirt.

He did not, of course, know the nationality of this beautiful and well-shaped young woman's husband: but as a scholar, whose studies had included ethnology, Little Smirt did know that the peoples of various lands expressed their hospitality in various ways. Well, and this so tactfully absent husband, quite conceivably (it now occurred to Little Smirt), might be a native of some one of those lands in which hospitality was made tangible, and every sort of good luck was favored—and a woman's liking for variety was indulged also—by the loan of the host's wife overnight.

For, as Little Smirt reflected, this friendly practice obtained everywhere among the Eskimos, the Himalayans, the Guarani, and the Dyaks of Sidin in West Borneo. It had long been customary among the Arabs and the heroic races of Ireland. Moreover, the people of Caindu in Eastern Tibet considered the loan of one's wife to a stranger to provoke the immediate favor of the local gods and a prompt increase of the lender's prosperity. Throughout all New South Wales any such loan was known to be an infallible method of averting every threatened misfortune. . . Oh, but, yes, the situation in which Little Smirt now found himself was quite deplorable: for, conceding the lady's husband to be a member of any one of these races, then Little Smirt would not merely have snubbed this gentleman's benevolence. He would actively have provoked for the poor man out-and-out bad luck, through an uncharitable display of morose continence.

"But then," Little Smirt decided, "it is not as if Mama had any regard for ethnology or were ever the least bit broad-minded as to the welfare of other people. And it follows, from her old-fashioned selfishness, that I am not permitted to satisfy my interest—natural to a scholar—in the quaint local custom through which the tent of this lady is kept surrounded by gnawed skeletons."

And another time Little Smirt came—across a broad shallow river, in which naked shepherds floundered about, waist-deep, shouting and laughing, and swearing too, now and then, as they dipped their sheep—to a broad plain dotted with cypress-trees and with white houses and with church towers. He thus approached a sacred hill, about which male persons of all ages were assembling to honor the creator of every mortal being in that special neighborhood, the great god Phallus.

This hill was overgrown with cypress and pomegranate and myrtle; in this grove were twelve hundred priestesses, each one of whom waited alone in a small two-roomed residence, that had a peculiarly shaped knocker on its door of teak-wood; every one of these priestesses, whensoever any man knocked, was ready to assist him in the prescribed ritual, except only during the four days' holiday which each priestess enjoyed every month; and this sacred hill was enclosed by a high fence, made out of copper spears, adorned with big love-knots of green copper, and broken here and there with tall gates of figured brass.

"I would do well to honor this great god Phallus," reflected Little Smirt, because the range of his studies had, of course, included comparative religion.

But no sooner had he approached the bridge, handsomely builded out of copper and spread with bright scarlet cloths, by which you crossed the deep moat surrounding this sacred hill, than once more the hand of Little Smirt's mother pinched him.

And again Little Smirt rode on, shaking his head; for, inasmuch as he himself was of divine descent, he did not like ever to see any person neglecting his religious duties; and the god to whom Little Smirt had perforce denied exaltation, was a most famous and ancient deity. Him by-and-by Little Smirt addressed in the following terms.

"O father of all living creatures!" said Little Smirt; "the provider of life's most ardent pleasures! the animated, the ever-resurgent hope of our immortality, through whose genial labors the youth of each mortal generation is renewed unimpaired in the generation which succeeds it! I cannot guess through what gloomy error my race condemns you to live swaddled in many concealments, and to seek out a hiding place in small dark dens of cotton or of silk or of balbriggan."

Then Little Smirt said: "In regard to this vital point we behave without any decency. For we walk about with unblushingly unveiled faces, upon which are inscribed plainly our stupidities, our pettiness, our misdeeds; and in brief, we flaunt before Heaven every possible argument for mankind's immediate extermination. But we hide away, like an infamy, the creative power of all men; even in its infancy do we wrap up in a napkin that talent which may yet enable us to make a new race superior to ourselves. Yea, we avert, even in sermons, from the ever-lively promise of mankind's future. Our folly is heart-breaking; our indecency is beyond description."

And Little Smirt said also: "Oh, but very great is our folly! For we foster despair and pessimism, and misanthropy also, by displaying everywhere in public the faces of our fellow creatures. But we do not ever encourage any optimism by causing—through one or another slight change in our national costume—every adult male to make manifest at all moments his creative gifts. We do not keep visible these powers at every street corner, to be for us a glad covenant with the future; and to lighten even the drab terrors of democracy with an ever-present reminder that the land which we infest is by-and-by to be repopulated throughout. We ignore the sole hope of posterity."

He looked back now, for the last time, at the sacred gardens into which so many piously excited persons were thronging to discharge their religious duties. And again Little Smirt cried out, with unfeigned regret, to the great god Phallus.

Yet Little Smirt still spoke with that fine affability which the son of a master of gods ought to exhibit to all his father's underlings. And Little Smirt said:

"Alas, O divine one, whereas both the spirit and the flesh are wholly willing to carry out your appointed ritual, the attentiveness of my dear Mama is far too unwinking for me to contend against it. I lament my apparent incivility; and I apologize. Do you remember that the affection of my mother constrains me! Do you think indulgently about how many mothers have constrained you, O divine one, in those happy night seasons when they opposed your utmost endeavors and quite wore them out. And in brief do you, who serve most women delightedly, now pardon me, who have no choice except to obey, even in the gnashed teeth of my religious convictions, the most dear of all womankind."

*   *

FORTY-TWO

THE INGLORIOUS JOURNEY

*

So was it that Little Smirt journeyed toward Branlon without ever carrying the hooves of his gray horse or the gleam of his gay peacock feather out of the set way unprofitably. And he found that a young champion, in travelling through the lands beyond commonsense thus partially chaperoned by his mother, got on with almost distasteful celerity. His success everywhere was unfailing—as yet,—whatsoever might be the deficiencies in his self-indulgence.

He stayed, nevertheless, intelligent, in addition to being, more or less, a physical coward. He thus recognized that the point of view of an aged wise-woman, whom many decades of professional practice had familiarized with all sorts of enormities, must necessarily differ from the point of view of a young man in whom inexperience was tempered only by the thin pleasures of profound scholarship.

"Mama is right," he decided, "just as she always is right in every question of logic. I lament that rightness, at least now and then. I could wish, now and then, that my mother had not applied for so many years to all branches of human wickedness the homeopathic arts of a wise-woman. I could desire, now and then, but particularly during these long lonely evenings, that Mama were not such an expert in iniquity, or so old a hand at directing, in exchange for a moderate fee, all carnal temptations, as to foreknow but too clearly the results of my dallying with either."

And Little Smirt said also: "If only my dear Mama were not what the blunt-spoken world describes as a lady of doubtful repute, then I might hope to allure her, once and a while, into permitting me the diversions which no sane abbess, no anchorite, no haloed seraph, would refuse thus implacably to the leisure hours of a young champion on his travels in the lands beyond common-sense. But against the prudishness of an aged gentlewoman who is by profession a pastmistress in the homeopathy of evil there is no possible arguing. She knows a great deal more about every practicable kind of misdemeanor than I know; and she intends to retain her superiority in knowledge, I perceive, by keeping me chaste and temperate."

Then Little Smirt said: "To be kept always chaste and temperate, by a dead hand, is a sad affliction for a hale young gentleman on his travels in the lands beyond common-sense. Yet upon the whole it seems wiser for me to put up with this affliction rather than to run any risk of irritating my revered and short-tempered and regrettably gifted mother. Since I regard Mama, in brief, with affection, with distrust, with unbounded reverence, and with a lively amount of fear, it follows that I had best go on looking for my wife, as I best may, under this very dreadful burden of prudence and of reason and of more than cenobitic continence."

After that, Little Smirt permitted the dead hand to guide him without much further resistance. And it did guide him, for some while, through a speedy and inglorious journey such as no other recorded champion had ever made in the lands beyond common-sense.

Quite in vain did the splendors and the allurements of all superb magics such as by ordinary bedazzle a man's judgment make their flashy appeal to Little Smirt, whom the hand of an old, cold wise-woman constrained into a saint's innocence...Well, and that, as he granted, was unavoidable. To the long experience of Madam Tana all the marvels and the thaumaturgies of romance, and all the seductions of evil, which moved glowingly about the lands beyond common-sense, must appear to be no more remarkable than do keys to a locksmith or steaks to a butcher. Such matters were her own métier.

She, as an expert, could consider, not any notion of delay on account of the beguiling solicitations of these lands' endless wonder, but simply the points in which she herself would have made this wonder more wonderful and far more beguiling. In brief, if Madam Tana might conceivably applaud, now and then, as a connoisseur, yet as a mother, she must remain stonily disapproving: and of this obstinacy Little Smirt must, in turn, accept the ignoble benefit, whether he wanted it or not.

Since he approached Branlon from the east, he visited no country which Elair had traversed. But in yet other respects did the journeying of Little Smirt differ from the unchaperoned journeying of Elair very notably.

For example, if Little Smirt approached an enchanted castle, such as Elair would have swaggered into through mere curiosity, or the hut of a Baba Yaga or a dragon's den, such as Elair would have left occupied by death only—or even did Little Smirt so much as come near to an armed champion ready to fight any and all comers in the high cause of his lady's honor,—then the cold hand of Madam Tana would compel a détour imperiously. Her implacable hand would at once lead Little Smirt out of the public highway, into bushes, and across ditches, and about muddy barn yards, until it had fetched him skulkingly beyond danger.

But above all, if any woman whatever approached Little Smirt with a combining of good looks and of good will, why, then the hand of Little Smirt's mother would assault the bosom of Little Smirt as viciously as if he were wholly to blame, and as if he had acted with unheard-of outrageousness, in provoking a young woman's philanthropic regard.

So did the dark magic of Madam Tana guide her beloved son through the lands beyond common-sense, without any hurt or delay, as yet, and without any least carnal indiscretion to look back on affectionately; and with his chest pinched black and blue.

* *

FORTY-THREE

ON A LOST GARMENT

*

Thus all went well for a while, until by-and-by Little Smirt came to a large wood; and when he had gone but a short way among the trees of this place, he heard a divine melody. Inferring that immortals were present, but not knowing their mythology, he dismounted from his gray horse; and he prostrated himself, upon his face, behind a thick holly-bush.

He heard next a chattering of two girls' voices, toward which he did not venture to raise his eyes. But when this pair of goddesses had gone by, Little Smirt arose; and in the path before him lay an essential female garment.

"Hah," Little Smirt remarked, "but this sight inspires me. It is true that the inspiration is of a flimsy and hand-trimmed nature; but the well-gifted poet learns how to convert every sort of emotion into loveliness."

Thereafter he took out writing materials, and he spread the essential garment flat on the ground. But as he picked up his pen, made from a swan quill, the dead hand of Madam Tana came out of his bosom, walking clumsily upon its four fingers, like a hurt insect, and took the pen away from Little Smirt. Very hastily the left hand of Madam Tana then wrote out upon the white surface of the essential garment a sublime and austere ode, twenty-eight lines long, in praise of the beauties and the chaste charms of Bel-Imperia.

"Now, but that is odd," said Little Smirt. "Here are fine verses, not wholly unworthy of me. Yet I had meant these verses to express, in a rather more roguish manner, quite other sentiments, with which nobody's wife anywhere ought to have any improper concern."

"Do you happen," replied a girl's voice, "to have seen a garment which was dropped hereabouts?"

Little Smirt raised his eyes; and thus travelling over a pair of gold-sandaled feet, up two very well shaped, naked legs to a short red silk skirt, across a flat small belly, and between two virginal breasts, his eyes came, in a glow of complete contentment with these travels, to the beautiful face of a wood nymph, about which shone an aureole of gold-colored hair.

"I have indeed found such a garment," Little Smirt answered, arising tumultuously, "to the great joy of my heart; for by the approved laws of the lands beyond common-sense, that careless immortal who misplaced this garment must consent to become my love."

He stepped forward, smiling. Then the hand of Madam Tana pinched his breast with such viciousness that Little Smirt uttered a squeal, which he shaded off, more or less plausibly, into a sigh of heroic melancholy.

"But, alas, my heart is given elsewhere," Little Smirt continued, "and for that reason, O woman with most promising legs, I respectfully waive all claims to your person."

Thus speaking, he restored to the wood nymph the garment in question. And she inspected it with dismay, saying,—

"Chaste but unfortunate champion displaying the fine peacock's plume, you have defiled the royal underwear of my divine mistress with your scribblings, and there is simply no telling what will become of you."

"Do you conduct me to her," said Little Smirt, his teeth chattering slightly, "and I will present my apologies for the misplacing of a poetic outburst."

"Well," said the wood nymph, "it may be that, as a scholar and a man of refinement, and as a person of such lofty continence as to despise my poor charms, you can make your peace with her. It is certain that if you attempt to escape from this wood without having placated my mistress, who is Queen of the Kogaras, then the wrath of at least nine immortals will combine to destroy you in a fashion no less humorous than excruciating. So you had best come with me."

She then led Little Smirt into a cleared space in which stood a red summer-house; and she bade him wait there, among the seventeen figures of wrought gold, shaped like tigers and ducks and dogs and lions and deer and apes, which stood inside this summer-house.

The wood nymph returned by-and-by, saying, "There must be a magic in your writing, for my mistress has considered it with a cooing noise and the smiles of a life-long imbecile."

"Aha," said Little Smirt, "so your mistress is a good judge of poetry."

"I do not know about that, O most continent and ill-advised scholar. I know only that, for some reason or another reason, she appears so pleased by your sentiments as to wish to condone, in so far as that may be possible, their improper location. So do you kneel now, for my mistress approaches."

Little Smirt at once prostrated himself; and when the divine lady had entered the summer-house he knocked his head upon the yellow and red stone pavement of the place, crying out:

"This unworthy stranger is from a far-off and imperfectly civilized country. Condone therefore his barbarities and overlook his existence."

The lady answered him: "Jestingly, but not otherwise, may the phœnix beg from the wren the loan of a feather. For what indeed, O too generous Little Smirt, is there upon this unworthy garment for me to pardon, unless it be the resplendent excess of your chaste devotion?"

He arose swiftly; and in his arms he took his beloved Bel-Imperia.

* *

FORTY-FOUR

PROSPERITY OF A FRAUD

*

So was it Little Smirt discovered, in one breath: (*a*) that, without knowing it, he had reached Branlon; (*b*) that, without knowing it, he had married the Queen of the Kogaras; and (*c*) that, without knowing it, he had yet again behaved with surprising prudence for a young man of his age and heredity.

Now the Kogaras (whom Mr. Smith had taken over from Oriental mythology) had the appearance of somewhat small, beautiful, blonde young women. They possessed tiny golden claws in place of fingernails; and it was their doom to become mortal every five hundred years, just as Bel-Imperia had become mortal, until death charitably restored them to Branlon and to their woodland pleasures in Branlon.

Well, and since the next incarnation of Bel-Imperia was an affair comfortably remote, now began for Little Smirt a new and unclouded existence. He lived very happily with his wife, in a modest hunting lodge builded out of copper and some sort of shining bright red stone, between the forest and the ocean: unblemished were the lawful joys of their honeymoon; grief seemed to have cut their acquaintance; no troubles visited their snug home.

Here they fared simply. They did not live so stolidly as lived their nearest human neighbors, Elair and Oina, who reaped with untiring industry the neat fields of their own meadows so as to feed their own matter-of-fact cattle in their own prosaic farm, surrounded by the charmed forest of Branlon. Instead, day after day Little Smirt and his Bel-Imperia would go a-hunting together, or it might be a-fishing or a-birdnesting, like well-bred vagabonds: and they would fetch back, for their bronze cooking pots, red deer from Strathgor, and squirrels from Tarba, and salmon and woodcock from out of Darvan; and eggs of nine sorts from the oak-groves of Pen Loegyr; and at Clioth they speared salmon and eels, and otters also. Nor did they lack for sweet blackberries and mushrooms and tender bramble sprouts and wholesome watercress. Day after day they thus lacked for nothing which any sensible person could desire; and the nights likewise of this young couple were happy, all through their honeymoon.

Moreover, Little Smirt had famousness. The fidelity and the strength of Little Smirt's love, and the fine phrasing of his sublime and austere ode, had been duly reported, by his fond wife, to her fellow nymphs and associate demi-gods: they applauded such constancy; and his high-minded legend was now added to the other strange legends of Branlon. Everywhere the Wild Huntsman and the Metsik and the Gübich recited with enthusiasm that superb ode which Little Smirt, under the stress of carnal temptation, had written, in a lofty defiance of any such temptation, upon the underwear of his own wife. Among the tree-tops the Nïagrusiar repeated the tale of his heroism and his chastity. The Norg and the Vargamor praised Little Smirt as a paragon of all lovers. When the Tutosel hooted at him, the tone of her voice was admiring.

Little Smirt now and then would recall that, but for the intervening hand of his Mama, he would have written upon the famous garment such verses, and would have made, to his wife's attendant nymph, such advances, as would have given to his fortunes a disastrously different turn, and would have won for him tributes not wholly applausive from the gold claws of the Kogaras. And at such times he would think with a sort of remorse about the old lady's fond care of his well-being.

Meanwhile he kept the cold hand in his breast; and the hand continued to guide and to serve him. It showed him always the most profitable road to follow; it pinched him if he was about to make a blunder; and when Little Smirt wrote any verses nowadays, then the instant they were finished, the hand would unbutton his blouse, and would climb out of his bosom, like an unwieldy, rather unpleasant looking insect; and it would edit his verses so as to make them conform, in every detail, to the pure-minded and pastoral tastes of Branlon.

Did his verse show any least trace of the morbid or the licentious or the pessimistic, the hand would correct all that in, so to speak, no time. It thus caused the writings of Little Smirt to remain pure and wholesome and uplifting, to the never-failing delight of the local immortals. There was nobody, said the woodland people, in any way comparable to this most praiseworthy of poets, who made you feel (as the Tutosel phrased it, from her legitimately romantic point of view, as a technical spinster) that the world was a pretty good sort of place.

"Nevertheless," said Little Smirt, to his wife, "I have not yet seen your august protector, that Mr. Smith who is Lord of the Forest."

"That will happen in due time, my husband; for time, as a wise person has remarked, cures a great many more maladies than does any properly licensed doctor."

"Yes, but when will it happen that the Lord of the Forest will see fit to applaud my verses?"

"It will happen," replied Bel-Imperia, "just as everything else happens in Branlon. And by that, I mean it will happen when Mr. Smith so desires; but not earlier."

*   *

FORTY-FIVE

THE FROG THAT TALKED

*

Little Smirt prospered in this way until one morning
when he and his wife Bel-Imperia went together to
look for mushrooms, of which Little Smirt was peculiarly fond. Fair Bel-Imperia had about her a beautiful
cloak of two colors, of purple and of bright green;
she wore a gown of yellow silk tied up with a knot
between her thighs; she went buskined; and in one
hand she, who remained always a huntress, carried
two spears of ash-wood tipped with bright steel.

Well, and as they walked through the forest they
came to a large tree which they recognized to be the
product of some art alien to the magic of Branlon,
because the trunk and the branches and the leaves
also of this tree were white, like clouded glass. For
another odd thing, which they both noticed, upon
the lowest branch of this tree sat a scarlet frog, about
as large as a three-year-old child, a frog which wore
only a black breech clout and a huge, elaborately
curled, black periwig. Moreover, this frog was speaking about Madam Tana.

"Her abstruse arts have not served Madam Tana," the frog sang, "now that she pursues them single-handed. Oho, cries the malevolent White Rabbit, peering out from the moon, oho, and am I to be fobbed off with the doings of one hand, while its fellow serves the pastoral romanticism of Branlon? Oho, but my old servant has fallen away into secretive well-doing; and for this breach of faith I must be requited and righted, O benighted lost Tana, poor Tana! Oho, Tana, Tana!"

"But what batrachian abuse is this," said Bel-Imperia, "which enters into the realm of my revered protector, the Lord of the Forest, and yet is not a part of his venerable magic?"

"It is an evil magic," Little Smirt returned. And then, to the scarlet frog, which he knew to be the ambiguous servant of Madam Tana, he cried out,—

"Klinck, Klinck, and how do affairs prosper with my Mama?"

"Oh, very excellently, and in accord with the desires of all reputable persons, Little Smirt," replied Klinck. "Nobody can work the magic of a wise-woman except with the left hand."

"That is true," said Little Smirt. "All Mama's magic is of the left hand, so that her loss of this left hand, now I think of it, must be rather inconvenient. Mama cannot preside properly, as Queen of the Synagogue, over the impressive ceremonies of the Lesser Sabbat, now that she has not any left hand to be kissed, in addition to other portions of her dear self, by the neophytes."

"That is but a small part of her present worries, Little Smirt."

"With her left hand," continued Little Smirt—and he also was now the prey of some worriment—"must be mixed the philtre of powdered earthworms and of periwinkle which awakes amorous desires,—as well as the philtres which inspire, severally, courage, and feminine confidence, and high-hearted delusions, and kindly insanity. Why, but those strong philtres were the main sources of my dear Mama's livelihood!"

"Well, and nowadays she can brew none of them," said Klinck, in the abrupt and unfeeling tones which disfigure now and then the deportment of most demons.

"When Mama has been retained to defend a client against this or the other troublesome enemy," said Little Smirt, in an increasingly uneasy frame of mind, "it is with her left hand that the black-handled knife must be dipped into the blood of a gander during the moon's increase."

"Nobody knows that better than I do, Little Smirt. Would you teach a familiar spirit his own business?"

"Moreover, Klinck, it is with her poor dear left hand that the wax image of this enemy must be so disposed of as to make firm her client's peace of mind even until Judgment Day."

"That is true, Little Smirt, though I do not see

why you should thus continue to instruct me, after my five thousand years of steady practice as a familiar spirit."

But by this time Little Smirt was fairly aghast; and he cried out:

"With her left hand must be tied that chaste knot which prevents a marriage from resulting in any erotic behavior; and with the left hand must be kindled the inspiring fires of St. John if a wise-woman hopes to get out of them any real encouragement of a client's praiseworthy desire for virility. Why, Klinck, Klinck, a wise-woman who has been bereft of her left hand is no longer fitted to succeed in her philanthropic profession!"

"That is undeniable, Little Smirt, even though you might have thought about it a bit sooner. Nowadays it would wring your heart, Little Smirt—and mine too, if I had any—to see Madam Tana toiling away, quite in vain, with her right hand."

"Ruin is my just portion," remarked Little Smirt, "for I have treated my dear Mama with out-and-out inconsideration!"

Then Klinck said, chuckling unpleasantly in the shadow of his enormous black periwig:

"No; the right hand cannot work the special magic of a wise-woman, as we both know. The right hand has so often failed Madam Tana, even in compounding the most simple sedative mixtures, that her once liberal income from the heirs of deceased wealthy persons has dwindled away into virtually nothing. In brief, the old lady has quite lost her most dreadful reputation, and she is no more honored nowadays than as if she had been virtuous from her cradle upwards."

"And it was her great-spirited desire to serve my desire," said Little Smirt, very miserably, "which has led my dear Mama into this terrible pickle!"

"Yes, Little Smirt; and moreover, the old woman's cheated clients are all in a rage against her."

"Alas," said Little Smirt, groaning like a bellows, "but this is indeed horrible hearing, because all the most prominent people employed my Mama!"

"Well, and now her lunar masters have forsaken her, Little Smirt, on account of her pure-minded doings here in Branlon; her arts fail, on account of her left hand's loss: and at this instant she is locked up in the city jail of Chang-Chu, on account of nine civil suits brought by the vestrymen and the clergy whose affairs she has misconducted."

"But, oh, dear me!" said Little Smirt; and he began now to tear at his black hair in anguish.

"Nevertheless, let me add for your comfort, Little Smirt," said Klinck—and his scarlet froglike face had become sympathetic—"that your mother is not to be burned alive in the market-place immediately. This awkward delay, I must tell you, has been caused by the late illness of the public torturer, who is not yet well enough to conduct the preliminaries of Madam

Tana's burning, in a fine mustard-yellow robe painted with nine black devils."

Little Smirt sobbed, "Klinck, you are breaking my heart!"

"Aha, but do not give way to despair, Little Smirt, for the doctors report he is doing quite nicely."

"But I did not mean that at all, you infernal infernal spirit! I meant that, even as I said in my folly, there is no love in any way comparable in its unreason to the love which a mother cherishes for her son. I meant that I still do not understand this phenomenon; to the trained mind of a scholar it appears quaint and irrational. And I meant also that I must go to her at once, because this persecuted, very wonderful, dear woman is more noble than any virtuous person alive anywhere; and all that I have, I owe to her love and to her self-sacrifice and to the untiring ways of her cunning."

"Then the more fool you," replied Klinck, "to be going back into any such great disrepute and great danger! But in any event, I have discharged my errand."

With that, Klinck vanished. And he took with him —as Little Smirt at once noticed, with a scholar's interest in all quaint and irrational-seeming phenomena—the large and strange, ghost-like, gaunt white tree from which red-colored Klinck had been talking.

*   *

FORTY-SIX

RELATIVE TO TWO WOMEN

*

At this instant, the cold hand in Little Smirt's bosom moved clutchingly; and of a sudden, the hand was no longer there.

Then Bel-Imperia wept, saying: "Now the partridge of peace departs for the dark marshes of misfortune; now the lemon of lamentation curdles the cream of companionship: for the way of the immortal Kogaras is not the way of mankind. To return to your human world is forbidden me until my next incarnation, when I shall again assume mortal flesh, yes, and feathers likewise, in the form of a starling, which is what made me think about partridges."

"We can but be patient, my wife," Little Smirt submitted. "So, when may your next incarnation be looked for?"

"Alas, my husband, I shall be hatched out in Scotland about four hundred and ninety-nine years hence, as mortal beings compute their almanacs outside the charmed forest of Branlon."

"Truly I shall need a great deal of patience," said

Little Smirt, "and I fear lest my patience, after all, when I am that old, may result in no extreme ecstasies."

"Indeed, my dear husband, if you leave Branlon, then our life together is at an end for all time. Nor is there any least moral need to unloose the black dog of your duty against the bland cat of contentment. My husband, I, who am the twenty-third daughter of a banyan-tree, think highly of filial piety. Yet the known virtues of your revered mother are chiefly remarkable for their non-existence; if you return to her, you can but hope to share her poverty and her disgrace, along with, it well may be, her yellow robe and her faggots: whereas here our happiness is untroubled."

Thus speaking, as clearly as tears permitted, Bel-Imperia clung fondly to her beloved Little Smirt; and he embraced her with equal fondness, replying, in heart-broken accents:

"O fairest and most graceful of womankind! O most soft and bright and sweet-smelling! O my dear wife, more elegant than the gazelle, more pure than the snows of winter! Truly, my heart is taken in the snare of love; and of my own will I can deny you nothing, for in your transcendent body lives my delight, and by your amiable disposition my contentment has been fed nourishingly. In all the wide world no happiness like the happiness of your husband has been seen or told."

Then he gently put aside his Bel-Imperia; and wiping his tear-dimmed eyes, with a fine handkerchief made out of lawn ornamented with drawn threadwork, Little Smirt continued:

"Yet all my happiness, and all my local fame as a well-inspired poet, and you too, my adored wife, I owe to the ingenuity of my dear Mama. Who am I that, from my shrewd choice of a womb in which to start life, I should expect benefits which would prove eternal? She has bought for me such felicity as no other man has known, my wife, in bringing me to enjoy your tender and refined affection, which I in no way deserved, through the exercise of abstruse arts over which I had no mastery."

"She is an abominable creature," declared Bel-Imperia. And for this once the small and beautiful blonde wife of Little Smirt spoke, in the rôle of a daughter-in-law, without any polite Oriental flavor of metaphor or of periphrasis, as well as with unmistakable ill-temper.

Yet Little Smirt answered her in the calm tones of a scholar.

"You assert that Mama is an abominable creature; and from the standpoint of a strict moralist, your statement is perhaps true. But then I am not a strict moralist. My moral tone is consolingly low, a mere whisper. It follows that if ever I begrudge any sacrifice to my dear Mama, I beseech that Heaven's justice may take hold of me by the hair, and the anger of hell may grasp both my ankles, so that Little Smirt may be torn asunder for this world's welfare. No, my adored wife; no, I must leave you instantly, in order to serve, if I indeed may yet serve, that great-spirited and unmoral being whose flesh is my flesh, and whose ways are my ways, and to whom my heart also, as I now find, belongs in its entirety."

"Oh, but a mountain of rhetoric," sobbed Bel-Imperia, "has given birth to the mouse of malignity; the fair moon of our marriage is obscured by a mist of much pig-headed nonsense; and the man does not love me any longer!"

—To which, Little Smirt replied, as he thoughtfully took out of her hand the two spears of ash-wood tipped with bright steel:

"My wife, let us not indulge in unscholarly over-statement! Let us be rational! Not ever until this moment has the man loved you; for not ever until this moment has Little Smirt been, if but partly, a man."

Thereafter, all grief, but all firmness too, he quitted his beloved Bel-Imperia, whose tiny claws at this instant glinted everywhither in the throes of hysteria and of hatred. It was really a most fortunate thing for both these unhappy lovers that Little Smirt had shown his consideration for his wife's better nature by removing both those sharp-pointed spears from her keeping, Little Smirt reflected.

Meanwhile he trudged onward, a lost vagabond

now, to get Madam Tana out of prison, and away from the unwholesome influence of the public tor-turer, as Little Smirt best might. But he felt doubly lost now that he was not any longer guided, nor aided to escape from his wife's shrieks for vengeance, by the dead hand of Little Smirt's all-intimidating and all-knowing Mama.

* *

FORTY-SEVEN

THE JUDGMENT OF MR. SMITH

*

Now, when Little Smirt had gone but a short way, still carrying the two spears, he found seated on a log a tall gentleman of majestic and agreeable demeanor. Beside him lay a silver staff tipped with a fir-cone.

Toward Little Smirt this personage raised a pair of remarkably bright and steadfast eyes; and after one final meditative puff he put aside, with a most graceful gesture, his cigarette. Then the sublime stranger spoke affably, saying:

"A victory and a blessing go with you, Little Smirt! Yet for what reason do you desert my protégée, the Queen of the Kogaras, with such limited ceremony that she is demanding I either change your opinions or else blast you with lightnings?"

Little Smirt trembled, now that at long last he beheld the all-powerful Mr. Smith. But Little Smirt, in his despair, as he laid down the two hunting spears, replied boldly enough:

"I will tell you all, Lord of the Forest. And if, after hearing my misadventures, you desire to punish me with lightnings, or with an earthquake, or with any other symptom of divine irritation, for the deceits which I and my dear Mama have put upon my beloved wife and upon the pure-minded immortals of Branlon, then I shall not cry out. For between us, we have well earned it."

Thereafter Little Smirt told his story, relating everything just as it had happened. And Mr. Smith—after an uncharacteristic season of taciturnity, during which he had listened with close attention to Little Smirt—began by-and-by to smile, with a most reassuring benevolence.

"Come now," he remarked, "but after all, you are not, at heart, the depressingly virtuous young gentleman about whom Bel-Imperia, and in fact entire Branlon, has been telling me."

"Alas, Lord of the Forest, it is true that I have behaved with uncompromising rectitude from my youth up; and I have painstakingly preserved my fidelity as a married man: yet I was bullied into the practice of all these virtues by my resistless mother. It follows that the moral credit is hers, whereas I have got only the inconvenience."

Now the bright eyes of Mr. Smith kept on looking reflectively at this tall, badly frightened, half-blubbering, and yet resolute Little Smirt; and in the pleased heart of Mr. Smith moved some compassion and a grave envy, because of the quaint ways of young people.

"You have loyalty," Mr. Smith pointed out. "You have given up, of your own will, your wife, whom you love, and the delights of your life here in this most magnificently designed forest—which I cannot doubt you appreciate,—in order to serve Madam Tana's welfare in the uninviting atmosphere of a jail. Now, as a sound logician, my dear boy, I have not ever been able to convince myself, upon the ignoble low grounds of reason, that any man or woman was a creature sufficiently admirable to merit the sacrifice of another person's comfort: yet, in spite of logic, I do now and then give way to my loyal memories of your all-wonderful mother. Moreover, Little Smirt, you have a sense of the *mot juste*, for you describe your mother as 'resistless.' Yes, that is a pair of superb virtues: and I rejoice we should share them in common."

"Why, but, Lord of the Forest, can it be you were once acquainted with my dear Mama?"

"I was not ever acquainted with anybody, Little Smirt. I move in a mist of dreams which shuts out the truth about other persons. So let us phrase it, Little Smirt, that I dreamed about Madam Tana somewhat ardently during the year preceding your birth."

"In that event, sir, you may well have been privileged to know also my father, the sublime SMIRT, because it was at this exact time that they used to misconduct themselves in a cave."

"As to the immense value of that privilege, Little Smirt, it does not become me to speak," Mr. Smith answered, with his accustomed modesty. "You can but ask your mother about it: and I would advise you to believe in the truthfulness of her reply just as far as you may consider that course advisable."

"My mother, sir," Little Smirt reminded the Lord of the Forest, "has the blunt candors of any man's wife when it comes to discussing her spouse, my sublime father: and besides that, she is a great distance away, in addition to being in prison."

"To the contrary, Little Smirt," replied Mr. Smith, quite as placidly as if he were talking good sense, "I have made use of the fifth magic which I got through Urc Tabaron's rather foolish superstition that there is luck in odd numbers, as well as of the Water of Airdra which I got through Elair's pig-headed devotion to his ugly gray little wife. It is a familiar fact, my dear boy, that superstition and pig-headedness may very often result in prosperity, for other people; and in this case, you and I would appear to be the beneficiaries."

"Why, but, yes, of course, Lord of the Forest," said Little Smirt, who was all bewilderment, "I know beyond any doubt you are right; only I do not know, sir, just what you are talking about."

"I am talking about the delightful circumstance, Little Smirt," replied Mr. Smith, with a continuing exhibition of divine urbanity, "that behind you now stands your mother, precisely as she was when you and I first knew her."

*   *

FORTY-EIGHT

IN BLACK AND SILVER

*

Turning about sharply, Little Smirt thus faced a tall dark girl who was dressed in long robes of black and silver; he found her the most beautiful and the most dear of women whom he had ever seen: and his heart leapt with fond pride. He was actually taking credit to himself, he reflected confusedly, for having such a superb and all-wonderful mother. This was his sole thought in the moment that he embraced his adorable, brand-new Mama; and he began to blubber like a whipped baby.

The young prig had loved her very much—or, at all events, to an appreciably less selfish degree than he was capable of loving anybody else—when his Mama was unlovely and old, and when she had been involved undesirably in her homeopathic treatment of human wickedness: but to have his mother thus youthful, and so highly agreeable to look at, and restored to the at least relative innocence of a girl of twenty, appeared to Little Smirt a large deal more satisfactory. So, for no reason at all, Little Smirt began to cry; and he continued to cry copiously, as he embraced the young Tana who had borne him.

"Ah, but what a mama you are, Mama, for a scholar of my age, of my discretion and my gravity!" he remarked, dancing happily about her, in circles. "How nice it is that your hands are all right again! And what lovely clothes you are wearing, Mama!" Little Smirt added, looking down at the long silvery-colored robes, which were embroidered everywhere with black stars and black suns and black comets.

Then he hugged her again, saying, with a huge sob, "Yellow would have been so unbecoming to you, Mama!"

She replied: "Get along with you! and where is your handkerchief, and your self-control too, you abominable young windbag!"

But Tana did not speak at all harshly. Tana was quite happy, because, being his mother, she was no more reasonable about Little Smirt than he was about her.

"Well, and I too believe," declared Mr. Smith, "that I have wisely invested the fifth magic of Urc Tabaron. For I also, I am moved by emotions of the most exalted kind. I am conscious of an insane elation: I feel in me an irrational proud stirring of the blood. Yes"—Mr. Smith continued, with a surprising condescension, which displayed all the warm graces of affability without cooling in any way the respect due to his dignity,—"yes, it is quite as though I were

indeed hearing that fanfare of trumpets such as ordi-
narily greets the return of a queen to her loyal kingdom."

Young Tana regarded this smiling and urbane Mr.
Smith levelly, without any least smiling.

"What does this nonsense about trumpets mean,
you who are nowadays called Lord of the Forest? Yes,
and what other windy nonsense, SMIRT, have you
been talking to the poor boy who takes after you only
too well in his own weakness for talking nonsense?"

"Ah! oh! aha!" cried out Little Smirt, when he had
heard this astonishing speech; "but do you imply,
Mama, that Mr. Smith here is the sublime SMIRT
whom you met in a cave in the days of your first
youthfulness? and that the Lord of the Forest is my
own revered father? Well, but this is indeed a most
remarkable and delightful coincidence. It dismisses
from our consideration lightnings and earthquakes
and all similar cataclysms, as repartees unsuited to a
quiet family gathering. My sentiments are appropriate to the occasion; and I entreat your paternal blessing, sir," he added, kneeling.

"You have it, my son," replied Mr. Smith—with a
becoming blending of majesty, of emotion, and of his
not-ever-failing modesty,—"for whatever my blessing
may be worth."

"—And between ourselves, sir," Little Smirt continued, resurgent, "is it not noteworthy how everything which Mama does should invariably turn out to

have been for the best? For you will observe that even her immoral conduct in succumbing to your improper advances—in that cave—has resulted, at long last, in true happiness for everybody concerned. Had she behaved properly, we three must necessarily have missed this ecstatic moment. I, for that matter, would not ever have existed, to be a fond comfort to your declining years. These are facts which in the mind of a scholar must give rise to a number of not uninteresting speculations —"

"Yes," said Mr. Smith; "yes, to be sure. Your mother and I quite agree with you, Little Smirt, that your mother is in every respect a remarkable woman. Well, and inasmuch as we quite agree with you, there is not any need to develop your thesis. Instead, my dear boy, you had best be off to your as yet heartbroken wife, who, I am certain, must be missing you a great deal at this very instant. But your mother and I, at this precise instant, would not miss you the least bit, Little Smirt—now that all ends happily, to everybody's contentment, in accord with the old laws of faëry, which are so much more venerable, and which are more lovely also, than are any human laws."

Little Smirt took the hint; and he took likewise the two spears which belonged to Bel-Imperia. He then ran through Branlon, in order to give back to his wife her sharp-pointed spears intrepidly.

PART SIX

THE BOOK OF TANA

* *

*

"American investments in these countries Dec. 31, 1934, aggregated over $404,000,000, according to the Department of Commerce, of which direct business investments (in about 100 firms largely in Garian and Arleoth) were $62,000,000; investments in Rorn corporations, $139,000,000; in Ecben Government securities, $161,000,000; in personal property (mare's-nests, borrowed plumes, Spanish castles, fiddlesticks, Hibernian bulls, ingannations, etc.), $1.37; and in municipal securities (Sorram, Achren, Druim, etc.), $42,000,000."

FORTY-NINE

* *

DEALS WITH CONTENTMENT——

*

I may now live in contentment," said Mr. Smith. "The desired work is done, the more thanks to Urc Tabaron's magic. To the south of Branlon, Volmar is getting on well enough as a blacksmith, at all seasons when he is sober enough to distinguish between his anvil and his bellows. Northward, Elair's farming prospers at every season. Clitandre is building up a conservative but sound trade in peculation to the west of Branlon. As for Little Smirt, I suppose that, in his red and yellow hunting lodge between the east part of the forest and the ocean, he had best stick to writing—with your assistance, my darling—his most edifying poetry, inasmuch as the lad seems to be fit for nothing better than authorship."

"But—" Tana at once replied, very properly, to the implied and the uncalled-for and the over-presumptuous criticism of that son whom she had never permitted anybody else than herself to criticize.

In consequence, she now spoke with a chilled indignation which at the same time managed to be a com-

301

plete summary of Mr. Smith's failings, and to regret his envy of his superiors, and to dismiss his judgment as being not worth bothering about, all in the one monosyllable.

"Nevertheless, my dove," Mr. Smith answered, benignantly, "let us not argue the matter. For I am, in point of fact, very well content, now that the sons of an old dream have returned to me. They have come severally as a drunkard and as a fool, as a thief and as a fraud. I can find among them no Roland, no great-hearted paladin. There is no son of Smirt who at all resembles the son of Charlemagne. Yet do my sons content me: and so—with an heroic resignation to circumstances and with a fortitude upon which it would perhaps be immodest to dwell—I do not complain."

"But my Little Smirt," Tana pointed out, very patiently, as one who explains matters to the more feeble-minded, "is neither a drunkard nor a fool nor a thief."

"Nor has anyone, my pet, ever imagined, I am certain, any such canard about that most admirably conducted young scholar," replied Mr. Smith. "And for that reason did I make bold to hint at a fourth sort of foible."

"But—" said Tana.

"Oh, beyond question," said Mr. Smith; "yes, to be sure, I was wrong. Yes, you are quite right; and I agree with you thoroughly, my love. I have always found it most safe to agree with that tone of voice when it was feminine."

"Nevertheless, SMIRT, if I have taught my son, and in fact if I have forced my son, to restrain his paternal instincts, yet it was for the boy's own good, let me tell you, as well as for the improvement of his character in general."

"There spoke the devoted wife and the fond mother, with the same recriminatory voice," observed Mr. Smith. "But I am not SMIRT any longer. That dream has vanished. There remain of it only the four children of my dream; and although no one of them appears to me immaculate, yet the artist well knows that the children of no dream are ever quite that which he had hoped for."

She regarded him sombrely, and even with an odd sort of compassion, saying,—

"And so these three long-legged ruffians and my bright, properly behaved, well-educated Little Smirt are to be the lean recompense of your dreaming—of your not as yet ended dreaming, poor Lord of the Forest?"

"You misinterpret me, Tana: and it is always a mistake to interrupt an artist when he is artistically leading up to a climax. No: I was about to say that, through the ever-blessed fifth magic of Urc Tabaron, you also remain."

"Well, and what follows?" asked Tana.

She had mingled, provisionally, the voice of a

pleased woman with the voice of a mother who remembered the way in which a mere demi-god had been talking about her son.

"It follows," he replied, smiling, "that you expose my weakness, body and bone. I have weaknesses: let it be admitted. I have also some skill—for that too let us grant, in the high cause of veracity—at the marshalling of well recruited words. So upon holiday occasions these words troop willingly enough at my bidding, to express the ironic or the learned or the derisory. By turns they become glamorous or carping or gaily frivolous. They shift from the tinselled into the naïve or the nostalgic, as I command. They are well-bred, or they are resignedly pessimistic, or perhaps they advance with some rather ugly allusive sniggerings, or it may be they sparkle with engagingly phrased outbursts of beauty, just as the whim takes me. In brief, they express all those qualities which adorn the familiar word-play of Mr. Smith. The affair is harmless, a mere dress parade. Ah, but, my dearest, but when I would lead my fine words into a grapple with sincerity, then they waver. They retreat with a zeal unexampled in the annals of warfare. They abandon me; and I am left without support, upon an uncongenial field of battle, fidgeting before the unamused face of sincerity. I am left gulping and wordless.

"For this reason," Mr. Smith continued, "I cannot speak now, at this marvelous instant. For you have been restored to me. The great love of my life—and indeed the one profound passion of my existence—has been cleansed miraculously from all stains of time and, if you will permit the suggestion, of evil also. A lost dream returns very gloriously at this glad instant, bringing back to me its peace and its innocence and its beauty, in a fashion which I find to be more or less incredible. Before any such deep happiness I prefer not to voice the inadequate. No; for I am frightened by my own happiness. From its too piercing loveliness I must seek refuge in silence and —as I have admitted—in disbelief likewise. My heart rings with joy; there is a proud music in my heart: but in my mind there is doubt; and in my mouth silence.

"That is a large pity: for if I were not wholly tongue-tied," Mr. Smith resumed, "I would hymn worthily my delight in Tana. It is about the dearness of Tana that I would be talking very handsomely, at full length, with all that perfectness of diction which has been commended by so many excellent critics when I have touched upon lesser themes. I forbear to cite their remarks; it would embarrass me. Moreover, my innate modesty forbids any disputing that when these erudite persons declared my genius to be a most notable genius, they were talking good sense. So I protest only that not even my unparalleled genius in handling words is able to do any real justice to my delight in Tana. For this reason, above all other reasons, do I remain silent, without trying to put my present joy into frail words. I dare not display *hubris* by attempting the impossible."

All this he said at a time when Mr. Smith sat alone with Tana, in Mr. Smith's home, at the deep midst of the charmed forest of Branlon, whither no one of his sons had ever penetrated. And Mr. Smith, through the long while that he talked about why he was keeping silent, regarded his Tana with smiling approval.

Well, and it was a facial expression which he now altered into a look of shocked surprise.

"Why, but can it be," said Mr. Smith, "that, without noticing it, I have been betrayed, yet again, into *hubris?*"

*   *

FIFTY

——WHICH A CLOCK QUALIFIES

*

M r. Smith stared sharply about him; and he thus noted a wonder which was no part of the magic of Branlon, for behind him, on the mantel-piece of his own home, a black onyx clock now ticked indomitably and defied Branlon's embargo upon all clocks. So for one instant did this small time-server materialize out of Mr. Smith's dream about his being a master of all gods; and yet, in another instant, there was no sign of any clock to be seen anywhere. But the perturbed Lord of the Forest could still hear its ticking; and he knew, only too well, the meaning of this horrible, small, ever-busy noise.

It assured him, he knew, that for the demi-god, no less than for the supreme god, time waited, and time made ready the dim enmities of time, and time planned a discrowning. Not even a mere modest Mr. Smith could evade time. For it was this same clock, as he now recollected, which had haunted him throughout his high-hearted dream of being supreme over everybody, by counting relentlessly every moment of his omnipotence; and by telling him that there was one instant, then another instant, and then yet another, but only one instant at a time; and by telling him that, for no living being, could any one of these instants ever return.

These truths, of course, were mere truisms. Yet the clock's re-appearance in Branlon, as a tangible and defiant intruder, aroused grave suspicions.

"In that dream I believed I was SMIRT. I was then conscious only of my thoughts, my interests, and my beliefs as a master of all gods, and unconscious of my present individuality as Lord of the Forest. I awoke from that dream; and it seemed to me I was myself again. Still, I cannot be certain. Still, I do not know whether at that time Smith was dreaming he was SMIRT? or whether at this time sublime SMIRT may condescend to dream he is Smith? or whether some third person, as Urc Tabaron believed, has dreamed about both of them? I can but accept the knowledge that the chances are two to one against my being Mr. Smith; and two to one in favor of the possibility that I still move in the affairs of a dream. All Branlon and my tall, dear, rather foolish sons may very well be but the creations of my never-idle wit and fancy and erudition. And yet Tana, I somehow know, is quite real."

He regarded her for an instant. And in this instant he knew that, no matter who he might happen to be, nothing else mattered except that Tana was real.

"But the clock also is real. And in my dreams, as I can now see, any least suspicion of *hubris* will evoke always this tiny and sombre reminder, this ever-busy *memento temporis*—and, in brief, this same clock—to assure me that time labors to take away my current dream also, in due course; and to bring me, it may be, yet more dreams; but to bring even to me at last, whoever I may turn out to be, as time brings to all living creatures, death."

And yet too, he reflected, in all his dreams—now—would be Tana. There had been a great many other women, it was true; and there might be still more of these incidental women. But they passed; as Rani, and as Oriana, and as Airel, and as Arachne, and as yet many other very comely and most adorable creatures, had passed quite casually in his dreams, so they all passed; and that was an end of them. Well, and Tana likewise passed, it might be; but by-and-by Tana would always return. He knew that—now—with a deep and a somewhat terrified joy.

"There is no power," he said, aloud, "which can ever any more divide us. Or not, at least, until that ubiquitous black clock—with which you are somehow allied, I do not know how—has triumphed over my vigor and my erudition and my wit and my fancy, and until my life is quite ended."

"No," replied Tana: "for I am served at all times by the powers of the moon, and by all else which is unstable and false and fickle. And so, until time ends for you, and no matter where your light heart may scamper—like a dead dry leaf,—still, Lord of the Forest, your thinking will be my kingdom."

At that, he took both her hands in his hands; and he looked at her with a sort of resigned fondness.

"I do not complain," he said, sturdily; "for your dear, deformed hands alone have brought peace to my thinking. In these strange, in these rather horrible hands, which are not like the hands of any other woman, rest my happiness—and, it may be, my misery and my destruction also. I do not understand this. It is not necessary I should understand. It is enough that when I am with you I touch contentment."

"Yet not utterly, poor Lord of the Forest; because in your thinking a clock ticks relentlessly, as it counts the passing away of your dream and of all your dreams."

His eyes remained fond; his look was unwontedly grave, his voice quiet, as Mr. Smith said:

"I still move in a dream, dear Tana, perceiving very dimly those large truths which I know to be fixed and terrible and righteous, and which I may not understand because of my littleness. Where love is, there must be death also. This thing my dream tells me...And you"—he said, his voice rising—"you are both!"

"That is as it may be, Lord of the Forest: but does it make good sense to a sound logician?"

"No, Tana: it does not make any sense at all to my

brain. But my heart knows it is true. You content me because you are both love and death."

He shrugged then, saying: "Well, but that same Charlemagne who sent me a-hunting for my four sons, that forlorn great Emperor who might not win back to his Gilles as I to my Tana, he none the less had the root of this matter. Yes, he spoke wisely. It is far better for me—who, in spite of my wit and my fancy and my erudition, must always be the shared toy of two commonplaces—not ever to think over-gravely about this pair of supreme commonplaces which we term love and death. Yet that they are indivisible, my heart tells me; they overrule all that fine life which we foreplan in our youth, and which we do not live in our maturity; and a wise Mr. Smith—if indeed I still be Lord of the Forest—will make shift to accept the bitter along with the sweet."

"Then do you sit down beside me, at my feet, like a pacified child who has talked quite enough foolishness," said Tana.

And the Lord of the Forest obeyed her, meekly.

She spoke then, without any haste, stroking the dark curls of his hair with formal gestures. Now the words of Tana resembled the humming of bees, they were like the sedate noise of a top turning round and round and round, ceaselessly. And they must have been magic words made powerful with a wonder unknown to the fancy and the wit and the erudition of the Lord of the Forest, because it seemed to him that their sound was the sound of a spinning-wheel upon which all the thread of his life was spun. It seemed to him that much doubting, and some discontent, and every possible ill chance, went away from him forever, in the drone of this peace-giving noise and under the fond touch of those peace-giving, deformed hands.

Yet all the while he could hear likewise an unseen clock, a clock which was hidden somewhere, and which ticked faintly, without ever ceasing.

"It speaks of new dreams, it may be," the Lord of the Forest thought, drowsily, "into which I shall wander by-and-by, forgetting this special dream. And perhaps I must wander on and on, and still onward, without ever finding any assured faith or any certainty, until all dreams have ended. But, as yet, this dream endures; and I, like Faust, I reach now the moment to which I would cry out, 'Tarry, thou art so fair!' "

He looked upward at Tana's dear face; and he smiled at her, sleepily, without firm belief, but with entire adoration.

"That my dream lies, I have no grave doubt. But it is a good dream, a most charitable dream. It tells me that, through the kindly magics of Urc Tabaron, my tall sons have been drawn back to me, and that Tana also has been brought back to me, from out of very many long-perished, fond imaginings. It tells me, in brief, that the desired work of my life is done;

and that I may now live in eternal contentment. Yes, all these things my dream tells me, at this fine moment, at this special and wholly splendid clock-tick. So this moment contents me; and whether my illogical dreaming reports true things or untrue things, I esteem it the part of a sound logician not to inquire."

EXPLICIT